I0719839

# ELEMENTS IV
# TIME TO RISE
# WILLIAM RICHARDS
# STALKING P ART

This book is dedicated to my Aunt Lynne. She passed away right before I released my first book, never getting the chance to read any of my work. We know that you're watching over us all, and we all miss you dearly.

Thank you for everything.

# CHAPTER 1
## PASSING THE TORCH

OVER DECADES, ELEMENTALISTS HAVE BECOME an increasingly prevalent part of society. It started with children, who found themselves blessed with strange abilities to generate and control different elements from within their bodies. And over time, as those first discovering these new powers grew older and started families of their own, the population of Elementalists continued to rise until the superhuman race, comprised of both young and old, roamed the earth. They remained small in numbers, but now almost all cities in the world boast a sizeable population of the group.

Through years of debate, testing, and various forms of research, eventually it became universally accepted that all who were part of this emerging race could generate one of eight elements from their body and wield it in ways they saw fit. Those elements were light, shadow, wind, earth, ice, fire, water, and electricity. Every Elementalist born to date is able to generate and command one of those elements.

That said, many mysteries still surrounded Elementalists, with perhaps the most pressing question, and the one that's eluded researchers the longest, being the limits of possible expansion of one's power. What heights could a single Elementalists reach, and at what cost would such strength come?

For the first time in nearly a year, the city of Toronto finally saw a moment of peace. Since driving away Luminosa and forcing their horrid group into hiding four months ago, there were far fewer disturbances around the city. Things were gradually calming down.

Without that lingering threat hanging over the city as a collective, the citizens of Toronto resumed their everyday lives. For most, that meant returning to work, going back to school, and, overall, moving forward.

But Luminosa's loss wasn't a complete win for the city. They'd achieved the first — and possibly most important — step in their goals before fleeing. They forced the city's greatest champion, The Hero of Light, into an official retirement.

After the Heroes' battle against the former Luminosa member Ignis (who now resided in Penatang Jail), he was left no choice but to accept that his world-saving strength was no more. The full impact of such a loss wouldn't be felt until a hero was called upon again, but, for now at least, the world would be on its own. Or so it assumed.

It remained unaware, but another hero, one who played a vital role in defeating Ignis, still remained. And with the guidance of his father — the original hero — he'd work to uphold the peace he longed for, and protect his late mother's dreams of a united world between Humans and Elementalists.


"Why isn't this working?" Minisc Premier groaned as he fell on his butt. He sat on the dry grass a few hundred feet from his house, in a wide, open field. Along the horizon was a forest's worth of small tree buds that would soon grow into a flourishing jungle. But that would take decades to happen.

Since his former training arena suffered the scorching flames of Ignis' rampage, as did the forest that had been behind Minisc's house, he and his father were forced to train in the open field instead.

Minisc made no effort to get to his feet, instead sprawling on his back and looking up at the cloudy, sullen skies. He pushed his wavy blond hair out of his eyes, taking in a deep breath before exhaling slowly. The smell of fresh grass briefly seeped into his nostrils, allowing his frustrations to subside. A voice suddenly interrupted his reflective thoughts.

"You need to stop thinking so hard. Let the energy flow through your body, it needs to take control. Shut your mind off and just feel the nuances of your element."

The man speaking to Minisc was none other than the earth's saviour, known as The Hero of Light, Don Premier. He was better known to Minisc, however, as "father." The man stood tall and proud as the sun glistened off of his bulging muscles—though for those who saw him most often, the decline of his famous military physique was obvious.

The Hero wore a track suit that fit his still sculpted body so well that it looked painted on, unlike his son who was adorned in a sweaty T-shirt and tattered shorts.

Minisc sat up, wrapping his arms around his legs. The mounting aches eating away at his body were unrelenting, and his stamina dwindled with each sudden jolt through his chest.

He looked up at his imposing figure of a father. "That's easy for you to say—you've been using this skill for twenty-five years. I've been trying to use it for what…a week?"

The skill Minisc was referring to was the hidden secret that first created The Hero of Light—the technique known as Celestial Light. Only a select few knew of the technique and its incredible effects on those who were able use it. But most could only dream of attaining such power. Awakening and tapping into Celestial Light increased both the speed and power of an Elementalist while also boosting their senses, such as hearing and even vision.

Of course, this sharpened state brought about a host of negatives as well. The toll on the user's body was extensive, and even the slightest bit of damage increased bodily pain.

For Don, after years of training, the skill became second nature, but anyone else who dared to attempt the feat was met with far more painful results.

Only one other being in recorded Elementalists history managed to master such an otherworldly state: Don's nemesis, and the former leader of the nefarious group Luminosa — Dusk. The evil overlord had mastered the skill and called it Eternal Shadow to align with his shadow element.

But even with the tyrant now behind bars, Don knew that threats were always looming. And with his mystic power all but a lingering memory, the desire to pass on such a skill fell to Minisc. After all, Brooklyn, Dusk's apprentice, was alive and remained ready to seek revenge.

Don glanced down at his son. "I know it can be tricky, but you need to empty your mind. Any form of doubt is going to cause you to lose control."

The ground started to shake, and any birds sitting on the house's perch flew off in fear. Golden vein-like lines ran up and down the Hero's muscles as he reached full power. The fierce wind blew back Minisc's hair as he watched his father stand in full glory.

After a few seconds, the wind died down and the majestic light around Don faded. Unfortunately, those brief moments would be the extent of his once limitless power.

Standing up, Minisc scrunched his nose and tightened his

fists. Intense concentration commanded his face, and the wind around his feet started to build. A faint glow enveloped his body, and he could feel a strange sensation as his extremities suddenly became warm, like being curled up in a thick blanket. The heat filled him from head to toe. After a moment, he started breathing faster and harder.

"Slow your breathing and relax your body," Don instructed, but the light from Minisc vanished before he could follow his father's guidance.

Minisc dropped his hands on his knees, bent over and started gasping for air. "I…don't think…this is working…" He fell back on his butt again, so exhausted that he couldn't stand for a second longer. "Are you sure I have the power to do this? I mean, it took the strongest Elementalist in history to learn Celestial Light, right? So what're the chances that *I* can actually do this too?"

Don scratched his chin. "Honestly, for a long time I've wondered that myself, and admittedly I've had my doubts. You've always shown great ability—ever since you were a child—but it takes exceptional strength paired with a ready mind to achieve such a state. That being said, when we fought Dusk, just for a glimpse I saw you release that potential. Though it only flickered for a short moment, it was more than enough to confirm my belief in you. Then it happened again when you defeated Ignis. That day, I saw the true power stored inside of you on full display. We *all* did. You proved to me that if anyone could master Celestial Light, it was you." Don folded his arms. "When you were fighting them, what were you thinking about?"

"Thinking about?" Minisc paused, but just for a moment. "I was thinking, 'Please don't let this be the day that I die.' That's about it. And if that's what it's gonna take to get back to even just a fraction of your strength, then no thanks—I'd rather not."

Don furrowed his brow. "Hmm, yes—I'd prefer it if that

weren't the case either. I guess for now maybe we should call it a session. You've been working on this all afternoon. At some point, you'll do nothing but exhaust your body right into the ground."

Minisc frowned. He could hear the disappointment in his father's voice. Nothing hurt Minisc more than letting his father down, and with the Hero so thoroughly convinced his son could learn such a sacred skill, each day that passed when he struggled felt like a failure. On top of that, it seemed like he was getting further from unlocking the power rather than getting closer.

But he knew what was at stake and how critical the skill was. If he was to defeat Brooklyn and Luminosa once and for all, it would come from mastering Celestial Light. It was now his duty.

Since the defeat of Ignis and the fleeing of Luminosa, crime rates in the city had seen a steady decline. That freed up the Elemental Council to take on a number of the smaller syndicates in the city. But everyone knew it was only a matter of time until Luminosa would return. The three Elementalists—Brooklyn, Bronx, and Bex—would come seeking vengeance, and when they did, Minisc needed to be ready. Especially with his father no longer able to protect them.

Only moments after returning to their home, Minisc passed out on his bed. Three hours of sleep later, and with most of the day now gone, he forced himself into the backyard again. This time, his father wouldn't be around.

He stood with his feet firmly planted on the ground and tried to clear his mind as best he could. Giving up so easily was not in the boy's DNA, and as long as a threat remained over the peace between Humans and Elementalists, he knew what needed to be done.

Whether Minisc wanted to truly admit it or not, he was well

aware of his new role. It was more than just learning Celestial Light. He was meant to be the saviour of the world, the one to stop Luminosa. Nothing could get in his way of that. Unfortunately, every time those thoughts ran through his mind, they produced more doubt than motivation.

A slight breeze whistled through the air, and Minisc rubbed the sweat off his forehead. He closed his eyes, trying to shut away all his negative thoughts. First he listened to the wind, then to the chirping of the birds, and relaxed his muscles. *Concentrate. Feel your element flowing through you. Let it build up inside and spread all throughout your body. You can do this. You need to do this.*

He cocked his fist, ready to unleash some form of attack — a blast into the sky that would be capable of ripping the moon in two if need be. A beam of light that would cement his ability to learn Celestial Light.

Thrusting his hand high into the sky, his fingers began to sparkle with bright light, seemingly ready to explode. But before he could unleash his incredible attack, the warm tingle in his body morphed into white-hot, searing pain. He let out an agonizing cry, dropping to his knees and doubling over. He fought back tears, wincing, but his anger was another battle entirely. *Damn it — why can't I get this right? What am I doing wrong?* He slammed his fist into the ground, which only caused him more pain, before pushing himself up. No amount of agony would force him to concede.

Through the window of their kitchen, Don stared at his son, observing the boy continue his attempts at Celestial Light. Stroking his chin thoughtfully, he witnessed Minisc dropping to his knees again. When he heard his son crying out in frustration, his heart sank. He could feel his arm starting to tremble. He hated seeing his son being put through such excruciating discomfort, all because he himself could no longer be the protector he once was. He wanted to tell his son to stop, but he fought his parental instincts. Not only because he knew that speed bumps were a necessary part of learning, but also because he knew that once Minisc set his mind to something, there was no stopping him.

As Don admired his son's determination with each failed attempt, he was reminded of his own youth, the days where he also struggled with mastering the technique. Of course, his own teacher had been far tougher on him than he was being with Minisc.

A thought entered his mind, and he shuddered as a chill crawled up his spine. He looked at his son, and then to his left where his phone sat on the countertop. He closed his eyes as he weighed the pros and cons of his newfound idea. Now in retirement, he attempted to take a more mentoring role with his son's training, but perhaps he was still too close to the boy.

When it came to learning Celestial Light, he could vividly recall the pain that he'd endured. Such a level of bodily strain could put anyone in their grave, and, admittedly, forcing his son into that same situation was a hard pill to swallow. He couldn't help but take things easy for his son's sake.

But maybe there was someone else who could bring out the best in him, someone far more callous and distanced.

Don glanced up at his son again, seeing the boy back on his knees and struggling for air. Minisc's muscle spasms were evident even from the house.

*I know that he could teach him...but Minisc would kill me if I did that. But it might be the only way to get him to reach his maximum potential.* Don grimaced at the idea. Horrifying memories flooded back, forcing his heart to beat rapidly. He took a deep breath and reached for his phone.

After another half hour of repeated attempts, Minisc finally dropped onto his back again. His body screamed; it was like he was sitting in a volcano, and the only thing keeping him from melting into his grave was the cool breeze of the evening air. Through heavy breaths he gasped, "This…is…impossible." He dug his fingers into the dirt and made a weak attempt to push himself up, but his body refused. Minisc's mind might have been ready, but his body felt different entirely. It was ready to take the rest of the night off.

Pinned to the ground, he gazed up at the moon, which cast a beautiful pale blue glow across his body—until a shadow suddenly loomed over him like an eclipse. He slowly looked up at his father.

"I think you've trained hard enough for now. Maybe it's time to call it a night. You don't want to miss your first day back at school because you beat your body to a pulp."

Minisc tried to mask his frustration with a faint laugh. "I think we're well past that. But it's fine—I'll just sleep here tonight. It's quite comfy, actually." He let out a yawn, and his father laughed.

The Hero bent down and picked Minisc up, just as he drifted off into a light sleep. He carried him into the house like he'd done when he was a child and then placed him on the couch. Finally, his son looked at rest, instead of his face gripped with palpable pain. It was a wholesome sight, but it only made Don feel even more guilty than before.

"Hopefully the old man will go easier on him than he did on me."

# CHAPTER 2
## RETURNING TO NORMAL

LIKE MANY KEY SPOTS IN TORONTO, ELEMENTAL Academy suffered devastating damage from the recent Luminosa attacks. Left in shambles, the school underwent a large reconstruction project in hopes of having it ready for the new school year. It was a massive undertaking, and many of the resources that the city offered were dedicated to the rebuild, similar to what they'd done with the Elemental Council building. And thanks to an incredible effort, what had laid in ruin through the summer was rebuilt by October of the same year. Although it left the students a month behind in their learning, nobody could complain at the grand accomplishment.

Besides, the students of EA managed to gain plenty of experience in their time away from the classroom. Thanks to the city repair initiative, all the students took part in various sectors across the EC. It gave them real world experience, and it also quickened the pace of recovery for their city.

In addition, the extra month of construction helped give the school a fresh polish, including some key upgrades that had been sorely lacking since its creation.

Despite the circumstances surrounding how the changes came about, the school had long been overdue for some enhancements—especially with the population of Elementalists still climbing. Enrollment for the coming year was at an all-time high.

Anticipation for EA's reopening brought a palpable excitement. Students were spread all over the large rectangular lawns on each side of the main path, while others sat around the many picnic tables outside. Everyone wanted to catch up with their friends and share their experiences from the last four months. Smiles were all around.

Except for one boy.

"There's no way I'm ready for three more years of this," Jules groaned, running his hand through his ruffled, maroon hair. When he first arrived at EA, his excitement was unmatched, and he jumped at the chance to learn from the best that the EC had to offer. But now that he'd experienced the thrill of working with his brother—something that had been a lifelong dream—returning to his old life was of no interest.

He walked side by side with one of his two best friends, the ever cheerful and school-loving Lily. Her chestnut brown hair, bound in a ponytail, bounced as they walked.

"Come on, you must've missed it. Even just a little?" Lily said. "And besides, there're still plenty of things we can learn while we're here. Our teachers have years of experience over us, and we should be trying to absorb as much of it as we can. You know, we'll never get a chance like this again in our lives."

"Yeah, yeah, I know—but it's nothing that Yuri couldn't teach me. Plus, aren't you the one who's always saying that experience is our best teacher? What better experience could I ask for than working with him?"

Lily sighed, knowing that any argument would be pointless.

The two stopped on the sidewalk just outside of the school's tall, steel gates as they waited for Minisc to arrive.

Luckily, it didn't take long until the pokey boy eventually strolled up the street. In classic Minisc fashion, he let out a yawn with his eyes half shut as he sluggishly made his way over to his friends. He had a small bandage on his nose and another under his eye, along with a few more wrappings on his wrists that reached up to his forearms.

Jules laughed. "Jeez Minisc, we haven't even started school yet. How could you be that bandaged up already?"

Before Minisc could answer, Lily stepped closer to him and examined every inch of his bandages. Minisc did his best to ease the girls' concerns.

"Lily—relax, I'm fine. I've just been doing a lot of extra training with my father. That's all."

Lily frowned. "Still trying to learn Celestial Light?" She was one of the few who understood just how much of a struggle the skill was proving to be.

"Any luck?" Jules asked.

Minisc shook his head, sighing. "Does it look like it? I can't believe the strain it puts on my body. Every time I make an attempt, it feels like I'm gonna die."

"Don't worry, I'm sure you'll figure it out sooner or later. You always do," Lily consoled.

"Yeah, you're your father's son—*of course* you can learn it," Jules added.

Minisc knew that his friends were right, but dejection still hung over him like a curse. He nodded with a fake grin before the three headed off to class.

"They really gave this place a makeover, huh?" Lily noted as they stood at the front entrance of their newly rebuilt school. From the outside alone, the golden letters hanging off the awning had a renewed shine, and the building's fresh, red bricks and paint job made it feel particularly striking.

When Luminosa had attacked, the exterior of the school suffered far less damage than the inside, but in the interest of safety the EC decided that it was best to give the school a total overhaul.

"They really did. Minisc, do you have any inheritance left after this?" Jules joked.

Minisc rolled his eyes. "President Osiris and the EC funded the majority of the rebuilds...even The Hero of Light doesn't have this kind of money."

As they made their way through the familiar halls to their new classroom, they admired the welcoming decorations, as well as the vibrant red and white banners that brightened up the walls. And everywhere they turned, on every floor they climbed, there was a consistently positive, infectious vibe amongst the students. They were all excited to return.

For Minisc, walking through the school brought about a strange feeling. Despite knowing that he'd return to school, his focus had remained squarely on learning Celestial Light, and so the thought of being in a classroom and enduring lectures from a teacher on the basics of his skills now felt foreign. On the other hand, school represented a sense of normalcy in his life. A sense of peace amongst Humans and Elementalists — something he hoped would last for another few decades.

They planned to cut through the cafeteria to reach their classroom faster, but when they stepped into the largest area of the school, the chatter was deafening.

Jules scanned their jampacked surroundings. "Is it just me, or does this place seem more crowded than before?"

"Didn't I tell you guys? When my father proposed to redo the building, he asked for a few new programs to be created as well. EA added more science programs this year, plus other administrative and business programs for students to enroll in. I guess President Osiris saw the value in giving Elementalists more options than just joining the EC to fight crime."

"That's so great," Lily said through her flawless smile. "It's almost like they're creating a full-fledged school for Elementalists now. Before you know it, more schools like this'll be popping up and every Elementalist will have this opportunity."

"Yeah, Father said that this is much closer to what my mother had envisioned when she developed EA. I'm glad that President Osiris accepted the proposal."

"I guess after everything that's happened in the last year, they saw all the different ways we can be helpful, even when it's not kicking Luminosa's butt," Jules added.

The three hurried up the stairs and through the crowded halls toward their classroom. Despite it being a new year and a rebuilt school, their familiar classroom stayed in the same location.

When they walked in, Minisc couldn't help but smile. Everything looked exactly as he remembered it—from the two person desks and the board filled with scribbles at the front, all the way down to the stale white walls that he used to regard as a prison. He was never a huge fan of school by any stretch, but after being away for so long, he realized that he appreciated the return. It was a welcomed sense of familiarity. It felt normal and good.

The classroom was full of familiar faces too, but the one who they anticipated and hoped to see most remained absent.

"Where's Coro?" Lily asked, "Did he decide not to return to EA?" She and Jules looked toward the only boy Coro had ever opened up to.

"Actually, last I heard, President Osiris made a special exception for him to take partial research and development courses alongside our regular classes. He said that he wants to do what his father never did, which is put his scientific mind to work for the benefit of society and *not* its downfall."

Jules shrugged, pulling out his chair and tossing his backpack to the side of the desk. "Guess that makes you the undisputed strongest in the class then…but don't worry—I'll catch you this year. Just you wait!"

Minisc simply shook his head, knowing that Jules was always in a competition to be the best. But Minisc? He just wanted to focus on learning Celestial Light.

Minisc and Jules took their usual seats in the back row of the class, while Lily sat one spot in front of them. Unlike the boys, she had her books out with a pen and paper, ready and eager to learn.

In contrast, Jules fished through his bag for any scraps of paper he could find.

Minisc leaned back in his seat and gazed out the window. A good portion of the time he spent in school was used admiring the changing leaves on the trees lining the horizon. It was a pleasant way to let his mind wander freely.

He might have beat Dusk, and there was no doubt that his strength had grown leaps and bounds over the past year alone, but the thought of some basic school training with no pressure or life-threatening circumstances would do him some good.

The clock struck nine, and from down the hall, the sounds of sharp, clacking heels sent instant chills up Minisc and Jules' backs. They remembered that sound. Suddenly they sat up straight, sharing an expression of fear before shuddering in unison as the door slid open.

"What happened to new year, new teacher?" Jules whispered through clenched teeth.

Minisc dropped his head to the desk and groaned. "We just can *not* catch a break…"

Storming through the doorway and taking her place at the front of the room with unrivalled authority was their teacher— rather, their dictator posing as one. Her curly, copper hair and business-suit attire could be associated with many people, but the deadpan stare she fired at her class upon her entrance was one of a kind.

Ms. Wright, their first-year instructor, stood at the front of the class and glared at all her students. She scanned through the many faces until she locked eyes with Minisc and Jules. Her lips curled into a sly, intimidating smirk. Her evil grin spoke volumes to the two boys. It said, "You two thought you could escape, didn't you?"

They each offered sheepish smiles in return, trying to avert their eyes by staring at their desks.

Ms. Wright was one of the few people who knew the full extent of what Lily, Minisc, and Jules had experienced in the previous few months. As requested by Minisc and his friends, those battles remained a secret to the outside world; not only had a number of laws and regulations technically been broken, but it was also in a bid for the kids to keep some privacy.

However, with Ms. Wright being aware of their improvements, Minisc knew that she'd only push them harder. A scary thought seeing as she was already a strict disciplinarian.

Luckily for the boys, Lily saved them from the killer glare of their teacher. She threw up her hand and waved to the woman with a cheerful smile. Amongst the rest of the class that refused to breathe around their teacher, Lily showed her excitement in spades.

In a rare display of kindness, Ms. Wright twitched her boney hand in a small, reciprocal wave toward her student, and a simple but genuine smile broke away from her hardened glare.

Nobody could deny the woman's soft spot for Lily as a student. At first, she couldn't believe that a student as meager and inept at using her element would survive in EA, but after seeing the relentless work Lily put in both during class and after, plus the mental growth she displayed, those doubts were quickly washed away. Also, in a world often trying to beat the positivity out of people, the constant bright and cheerful personality made Lily hard to dislike, even for a teacher who rarely showed emotion.

Not that she'd ever admit it publicly, but Ms. Wright cared about all her students, and she only pushed them as hard as she did to get the best out of them. If anyone dared to try and harm any of her students — even slightly — they'd be in for a world of hurt.

Light greetings now finished, Ms. Wright wasted no time reverting back to the crusty and harsh demeanor she was infamous for.

"I understand that these last few months have been strange, but I hope all of you made good use of your time while working with the Elemental Council." Then, with a raised eyebrow, "Now I hope that as aspiring graduates of EA, you continued training and honing your skills even without me around to push you. We are well aware that due to events far outside of anyone's control, you students have been dealt a disadvantage by being behind almost two months, and to amend that, the school board would like us to cut out two months' worth of education to make up the difference this year." When the class heard this, they knew what was coming around the pike. "I, of course, think that is a ridiculous proposition. Every student who walks through these doors with dreams to join the EC will undoubtedly be faced with numerous challenges that are far from fair in life. This is the choice you've decided for yourselves in striving for your goals, which means that I see no reason to treat this class any differently than the perils of the real world. You are now second-year students, and there's no more taking things easy. We've got a lot of work to do, and now that you've all seen just how dangerous the outside world can be, it's my job to ensure that you're best equipped to face those dangers."

Any other class would've been left stunned by their teacher's blunt assessment of the future, killing any excitement of their return in the process, but for Minisc and the others it was par for the course. After a year of experiencing their teacher's no-nonsense and crass demeanor, they were well prepared for an even harder year this time around. Not that it mattered for Minisc, Lily, or Jules after what they'd just endured — they were ready for anything their teacher could throw at them.

Ms. Wright continued addressing her class, but with a little less bite. "I realize that this is our first day back, but in a normal semester as second years, you'd be starting our school's apprenticeship program by now."

"Apprenticeship program?" Lily asked.

"Correct." Ms. Wright walked to her desk and picked up a stack of papers before handing them to each student at the front of the class, who passed them toward the back of the room until everyone was staring at a long permission slip. "As I'm sure all of you've learned by now, the best teacher you can have is experience. That said, unlike your participation in the EC's city rebuild project, these apprenticeships will grant you a more prominent role that'll be in line with your true futures at the EC. Each of you will pick a department within the EC and contact the superior there, asking to join them for two weeks. Normally, we'd only allow you to join those that work specifically on the front lines of the EC, but due to the continual growth of both the school and the EC itself, students may select any department they desire this year." Her bite returned with her next sentence. "Let me be clear, however — this is no vacation. When your two weeks are over, you'll be required to fill out a report explaining what you've learned, along with having your superiors do the same. You'll have a week to decide, so make sure you choose wisely. This could be a big step in your development as top-flight Elementalists."

For most, the EC was known as the over seers of Elemental affairs, and that often meant enforcing the laws imposed on Elementalists. Working on the streets or fighting other Elementalists was seen as the biggest job, and definitely the one most students attending EA were aiming towards. But in recent years, the EC expanded their roles past just handling elemental crimes—now they were trying to learn more about the race as a whole. They introduced research departments, where studies on Elementalists took place in hopes of unlocking more secrets about their powers, and even newer departments on the administrative side. That branch was responsible for things like communications to the public, registration of newly born Elementalists, and debating laws or bills being implemented. It opened up many more avenues for Elementalists who weren't as gifted when it came to battle or using their element in those capacities.

The morning continued on as usual, but the news of the students' apprenticeships brought about a definite buzz.

Though they'd all worked in the EC previously, they weren't granted the same privileges and rights as others in that position, like full members.

For example, the free use of one's element that came with being an EC member hadn't been extended to the students. They were still required to adhere to junior Elementalists' laws, which meant that elemental use needed to be under supervision. Also, most of the work didn't involve patrolling the streets or handling crimes. Instead, they were placed in roles where they'd be helping those affected by the attacks and taking care to ensure society stayed afloat.

This time as apprentices, they'd be recognized as full-fledged members of the EC. All laws and privileges would apply.

When classes ended, Minisc, Lily, and Jules took to the outside picnic tables for lunch. The weather was perfect, and the sun beamed down with a calm warmth that would likely only last a few more weeks.

While enjoying their meals under the sunshine, the trio knew that they needed to iron out the all the important details of where they'd be heading. Of course, the decision was a rather simple one to make.

For Jules, his dreams started and ended at working alongside his older brother Yuri.

Although relegated to more investigative work thanks to the loss of his element from Luminosa's element-erasing virus, Yuri remained a prominent figure in the EC, and Jules would jump at any chance to work with his sibling. Also, Lily and Minisc knew the older Embroider brother well, and they always enjoyed his company and wisdom, so for all three of them it made logical sense.

While Lily and Jules continued to discuss the apprenticeship and started filling out their paperwork, Minisc stared blankly at his food.

"Thoughts, Minisc?" Lily asked, trying to bring him out of his trance. It was obvious that he was on another planet at the moment.

"Huh?" He turned to see his beloved friend staring back at him with concern. "Sorry…honestly, I still haven't fully wrapped my head around being back in school again. And now we're doing apprenticeships in just a few weeks, and…I guess I was just hoping that we'd ease back into more of a regular routine."

"Oh, come on—you know Ms. Wright better than that," Jules laughed. "Given any chance to ratchet up her teachings, she's gonna jump at it."

Lily pressed further. "So do you have any objections about doing the apprenticeship under Yuri?"

Minisc shook his head slowly and said, "No, that's fine…"

After his second lackadaisical answer, Lily picked up on her friend's usual trend.

"Okay Minisc, spill it. You're not eating, you were barely focused in class, and now you're not even thinking about where we should do our apprenticeship. Something else is on your mind, and I want to know what it is."

"Lily's right," Jules chimed in. "You've been even more spaced out than normal, so what's rattling around in that brain of yours? Is it still Celestial Light?"

Minisc sighed, resting his head in his hands. "Pretty much. I just can't stop thinking about it. Every night I've been training for hours, trying to grasp this 'state,' as Father calls it. But it's no use. Every time I think I'm getting closer, my body shuts down from overwhelming pain. I can't even reach the level I did when facing Ignis. And with Luminosa still out there and Father retired, I know I need to learn it." Minisc paused thoughtfully, sitting up straight. "But I guess these constant failures have been starting to bother me a bit." He hadn't noticed previously, but his fists were clenched and his face gave off more frustration than the softness his voice suggested.

"Come on, you can't be too hard on yourself," Jules said in an attempt to comfort his friend. "After all, there's a reason your father and Dusk were the only Elementalists to ever truly master such a power. It's bound to be difficult."

Jules and Lily could both feel the pressure Minisc was putting on himself to master the sacred skill. However, they completely understood why. It was important, and maybe even critical to their futures. But he was still just a teenager. They all were. They had a lot of growing left to do, both physically, and, even more importantly, mentally.

Lily added, "We both know that you can learn it. But there's no need to put so much pressure on yourself. You're not alone in this. Remember that."

"Yeah, we'll be right by your side the entire way. And if Luminosa does come back, we'll all be ready to stop them with you!" Jules grinned, snapping his fingers. "Hey, I've got an idea. You said that you were having trouble bringing out that power you used against Ignis, right? Maybe you just need someone who can push you in battle the way he did. I know your father doesn't have his old strength to challenge you, but I bet that *I* can. Why don't I come over after school and we can do some classic sparring? And that way your father can teach me Celestial Light, too." Jules laughed, realizing that he let his true intentions slip.

But before Minisc could rebut, Lily jumped in. "Hold on, you two aren't leaving me out of this! If Jules gets to learn Celestial Light, then so do I. But I'm calling it Celestial Water instead!"

They both stared at Minisc with eager grins. He sighed in defeat.

"You guys are insane, you know that? You have no idea how hard this has been for me, and now you want to treat it like studying for a test. I promise, this is far more difficult than anything you've ever done."

As the words left his mouth, he realized that he'd made a crucial mistake.

"Oh, really?" Lily goaded as she stared at Minisc, almost nose to nose. "Are you saying that we can't do it because we're not as strong as you?"

Minisc held up his hands, waving them in defense. "No, I didn't mean it like that at all. I just meant that it's really taxing on the body and…"

Finally Minisc exhaled, looking up at the sky, his words fading into defeat. There was no arguing when his friends took it as a challenge. "Fine—we can go after class and see what Father has to say about it."

Lily and Jules cheered with high fives to celebrate their victory.

Just like he'd promised, once the school day ended, Minisc and his friends returned to his home in hopes of undergoing some intense training. Only Minisc knew what they were truly in for, but he was happy to have his friends by his side.

The three stood in the middle of his familiar open field, dressed in sweats and workout gear. They'd only done some light sparring as a warm-up before charging headfirst into Celestial Light training.

Within seconds, they were glistening in sweat and trying to catch their breath. Minisc looked marginally better than the other two, being able to push his body slightly further than his friends. But even so, he was utterly exhausted only minutes in.

Don stood just a few feet away, looking on with his arms crossed. His voice carried through the open fields like a drill instructor as he spoke to the young trainees.

"Okay, let's try this again. Remember, you have to clear your mind of all thoughts. Remove all of the worrying and negative that might be flowing inside you. Then feel your element coursing through you. Treat it as an extension of your body. Use it to strengthen your muscles. Let it heighten your awareness. Once you've done that, start to take your maximum power and treat it like you're about to attack, but hold it inside and let it spread through you."

This time, Minisc stood back and watched as his friends attempted to follow the instructions again. Lily and Jules both began emitting the same vibrant shine as Minisc, with small, glowing lines appearing all over their bodies. Jules' arms had lime green lines running up and down them, while Lily's were sea blue. The grass below their feet began to sway from the wind before clinging to the ground for cover.

Minisc stood in amazement, but he was far less shocked than his father, whose eyes were growing wide with each spark of energy in the air.

It was a stunning sight indeed. Then again, channeling energy was only the first step to Celestial Light. Anyone could build up power. The key was using that power in everyday movements and making it second nature in battle.

About to understand a lesson Minisc had already learned, Lily and Jules both felt the intense heat attempting to melt the insides of their bodies. Their faces became covered in distress, and after a few seconds the aura of power around them flickered on and off before exploding into thin air. They dropped to their knees, gasping for air while their hearts pounded through their chests. Lily squeezed her eyes shut in agony as Jules fell onto his back, looking to the sky.

"That's...impossible," Jules panted. "How could...anyone hold that amount of strength... through their entire body..."

"Everything feels like it's on fire. Even my water can't cool me down," Lily moaned, taking a sip from her bottle. Her muscles continued to spasm long after the three of them had stopped.

Minisc walked up to his friends, examining them with a less than subtle and sarcastic grin.

"I tried to tell you, but nooooo—somebody just had to prove that anything I could do, they could do better," he teased.

Lily glanced up with fiery eyes. "If I could stand up right now, I'd punch you so hard for that."

"Yeah, we're just getting started. After some practice, we'll both master this," Jules added.

Behind them, Don smirked, watching Minisc and his friends bicker. It warmed his heart to know that his son had such loyal and determined friends by his side. As a father—and as The Hero of Light—he recognized that his son would be forced to take up his place as their city's defender. But he could breathe a little easier knowing that Lily and Jules would always be at his side, continuing to push him forward and support him.

# CHAPTER 3
## CONFLICT OF INTEREST

NOBODY HAD FORGOTTEN THE DAMAGE CAUSED BY Luminosa, nor would they anytime soon. The vile group had taken so many lives unnecessarily and wreaked havoc on many more still. But in the months since their heinous crimes, the damage done gradually faded to the background of people's minds. Their leader, Dusk, sat behind bars in Penatang, never to be released. And with his heir apparent nowhere to be found, the old phrase "out of sight, out of mind" definitely rang true.

That was not to say that Brooklyn and his group weren't preparing their revenge. On the contrary—it just meant that it would be all the sweeter when they succeeded. And with The Hero of Light now forced into retirement, their chances of victory were astronomically higher.

Deep past the outskirts of town, the zombie-like teen with an uncontrollable head of hair and equally uncontrollable temper sat in a large but mostly desolate shack. Brooklyn was surrounded by furniture that was either old or ripped to shreds, and the smell of musty rotten wood refused to dissipate. Although, it was the best he could expect for the time being considering the circumstances. They needed to lay low and remain away from the public, buying time until they could strike.

In his hands he held a magazine with a picture of The Hero of Light plastered on the cover. Stamped across the iconic man's face was the word "RETIRED."

"All that work to rid the world of that nuisance, and I didn't even have to soil my own hands to do it. That idiot Ignis actually came through in the end, and now even he's out of the picture. Soon this world will be bowing at my feet."

"If you're so confident, what are we waiting around here for? The Hero of Light's gone. Now's the perfect time to strike." The high-pitched yet miserable voice came from Bex, a diminutive monster of an Elementalist with a short temper and a deadly touch. She licked her cut lips like she was cleaning blood off her jagged teeth, and her pale-blue pigtails stretched down to her hips.

Brooklyn turned his freakish complexion toward the girl as she stood in the far corner of the room next to a few wooden crates. All the boxes were filled with old wartime supplies that could be used to survive for months. He watched her crack open a lid on the nearest box, then stretch as far in as her small body would allow until her feet left the floor. Once she stopped fishing through the contents of the box, she pulled out her hands, her feet again returning to the ground. Holding some sort of rectangular bar, she sank her vampire-like teeth into the gravely texture. What she was eating could only be loosely called food. It was one of the many old protein bars stored away, but it tasted like saw dust and was just about as filling.

"You know damn well why," Brooklyn fired back. "We have no funds, no resources, and no people. Lacking those things, even without The Hero of Light around, we won't get far."

Bex pitched one of the protein bars to Brooklyn, who then ripped away the wrapper and tossed it on the ground.

"The doc doesn't have any of the equipment to boost our forces either," Brooklyn continued, taking a hefty bite of the snack. "Not with his lab gone. So until Bronx gets back here with some good news, we're staying put."

"That's…strangely rational of you."

"Shut it. As long as it's still just us, we're not doing anything."

"Where is Bronx anyway?" Bex asked.

Brooklyn finished the protein bar and said, "I sent him to do some sleuth work for us. He's still got connections around this city, and if he can get us some supplies to start rebuilding then we'll be in good shape."

Just as their conversation ended, the rusty, bronze door handle on the other side of the room twisted. It screeched open, and in strolled their black-cloaked comrade.

"Took you long enough," Brooklyn chided.

"Well, sorry, but it's not exactly as simple as asking my next-door neighbour," Bronx shot back. "I was working all across the city to find even crumbs." He tossed off his cloak, revealing a long dangling frame and a painful scar over his left eye. His silver hair was pulled into a ponytail. Bex tossed him a bar and he peeled it open.

"And? Don't tell me you came all the way back just to whine about getting a workout in."

"Have I ever failed you before?"

Bex prepared to open her mouth, but Bronx glared at her and said, "Shut it. Point is, we have someone who might be willing to help us out."

"Who?" Brooklyn and Bex raised curious eyebrows.

"Don't flip out, but the Adenji gang approached me. It seems that they're interested in making a deal with us. But…"

"But what?" Brooklyn was getting more annoyed.

"But they refused to let me hear them out. Their new leader made it pretty clear that he's only interested in negotiations with you...something about getting their old leader killed. Seems like they might still be holding a grudge over that one."

"Well, fat chance that's happening. They're probably just trying to lure me out so that they can chop my head off. I'm not wasting my time with a bunch of unintelligent thugs like that anyway. You can tell them to choke on it."

This time, Bronx stopped his chewing and glared at the new Luminosa leader. "Like hell we are. Now that Dusk is gone and we're dying for resources, you'd better hear what they have to say. I didn't bust my ass all around the city just so you could blow off the only offer we got for help. Now they're expecting all three of us to meet them at their compound tomorrow."

"Excuse me? You did that explicitly without my permission," Brooklyn growled, the purple claws of his shadow element popping out of his knuckles. They pulsed in time with his increasing heart rate.

But Bronx showed no concerns with this threat. "Chill—this is just something that we're gonna have to do, whether you like it or not."

Brooklyn paused, snarling at Bronx. Then he turned his attention to Bex and griped, "I hate dealing with people..."

The next day, Brooklyn, Bex, and Bronx sat in a room that could only be described as a drastic increase in luxury. There were two couches in pearl white, and between them a glass coffee table with food that gave off the scent of a fresh home cooked meal, something they hadn't experienced in years. Around the room were expensive vases, plenty of books, and portraits of various people all dressed in dashing clothes. The entire place resembled a mansion, and Brooklyn wondered where these people got their funds from.

"Why didn't you drag the doc with us?" Bex asked.

"What use would he be here," Brooklyn retorted. "Just 'cause he gave himself an element doesn't mean that he's any use in a fight. And if this whole thing goes south and he gets himself killed, we're all screwed."

Brooklyn sat in the middle of the couch with Bronx and Bex on either side of him. Bronx had his feet up, leaning back and enjoying the much-needed comfort, while Bex scarfed down as much food as she could handle before the meeting started. Brooklyn was far less enamored with their amenities, his arms on his knees propping up his chin.

The Adenji gang was one of the best known Elementalists gangs in Toronto. Throughout the years of their existence, they'd clashed with the EC on numerous occasions. But no matter how often the leader of the gang would be stomped out, another would rise and take their place, making sure that the group never extinguished. For the most part, they were known for having deep roots in the underground world while also maintaining a heavy presence in the waterfront section of the city.

When they committed crimes, those crimes weren't about attacking Humans or causing mayhem just for the sake of it. The Adenji gang was interested in making money. They were in deep with a number of questionable businesses, which brought them more funds than any gang had a right to. They were a secretive group, lurking in the shadows but always thinking in terms of the big picture. Connecting them to most of their crimes was a near impossibility.

Over the years, a number of their members were handed life sentences in Penatang for their roles in different events. But, as is the Adenji code, they refused to spill any secrets or shift blame to their brothers and sisters.

All their beliefs were instilled and enforced by their original leader Marek, a man who grew up on the streets and spent all his time looking for a family. He formed the Adenji gang to fight what he believed to be a growing infection in the world.

Thanks to their shady dealings with some of the city's richest patrons, they carried a strong influence under their thumb. Not only did this allow them to live more freely with money but also to stand in the public eye, unlike Brooklyn and his group who remained stuck in hiding.

The last time Brooklyn met with the Adenji gang was before the Tournament of Elements. Although those negotiations happened on his terms, the meeting grounds took place in a mutual hideout, and it was only between himself and the Adenji's former leader. This time wouldn't be the same.

Since being tricked by Brooklyn to participate in a revenge scheme at the Tournament of Elements, which led to the current leader's imprisonment, the group was less than keen to be played for fools again.

Thanks to those events, the Adenji gang was left without a number one in command and without direction. This was something the well-established group didn't appreciate.

Finally, through the door walked a tall, thin man who was far from intimidating. Considering that the former leader mirrored a professional wrestler, this new head of operations stood out like a sore thumb. He wore a maroon tailored suit with a black tie, a stark contrast to the shine of his baldness. The only hair on his head was a small black goatee. However, his confident saunter suggested that he was in total control.

On either side of him stood a man and a woman. The man was shorter, but with a fair bit more muscle definition. His face was weathered and ghostly white. Sunglasses concealed his eyes, but he wore a similar suit to his leader.

The woman on his right was just as tall as the leader and she wore a long, elegant dress with gaudy jewellery around her neck and wrists. She grinned devilishly as she flicked her long, blood-red hair back, and her eyes sparkled with malice. At a glance, men would likely fall for her in an instant, but that was most certainly a trap.

"What is this? Are we negotiating or going to prom?" Bex muttered.

The leader paid no mind to her comment. "I like for my followers to look professional. Regardless, I'm glad you decided to give us a visit. I believe that we can make you a most compelling offer, leader of Luminosa."

Brooklyn glared at the man and raised an eyebrow, examining him from head to toe. "And who are you?" He could pick many Adenji members out of a crowd, but the three in front of him were a mystery, with the exception of one of them having the title of their new leader.

The man gave a half bow. "Please excuse my rudeness. Allow me to introduce myself. I am Dominos, thirteenth leader of the Adenji gang. These two are my advisor's, Marco and Kari." Dominos took a seat on the couch across from Brooklyn. His smile was convincing, but Brooklyn refused to buy it.

"So, you're the new leader. You don't look like much," Brooklyn sneered.

He wasn't wrong in his blunt assessment. Dominos' pencil-thin frame lacked dominance, and his two advisors beside him didn't appear much different. And yet, the three of them were now in charge of Canada's biggest Elementalist gang.

Bronx leaned in and whispered, "Why don't you try...oh, I don't know...not pissing them off? We're sitting in the middle of their territory here."

"You have quite the nerve to be judging us by appearance," Dominos said, his voice calm and steady. "I would say you're not much to look at yourself."

"I'll slice that chrome dome of a head into bloody pieces if you'd like," Brooklyn said through clenched teeth, hardly keeping the same calm composure. He gripped the couch with a glowing hand, ready to strike.

Bronx and Bex both stared at Brooklyn, wondering if he was about to make good on his threats. Kari, on the other hand, wasn't willing to wait and see.

"Your friend is right. I'd watch your tongue if I were you."

"That's enough," Dominos said. "We're here to discuss a deal, and that's what I intend to do. Tell me, does this look familiar to you?" He gestured to Marco, who tossed some folders on the table in front of them.

Bronx leaned forward and flipped one open. Inside was a grainy picture of a strange-looking creature, covered in some kind of grey goop. "Are these...are these the bioweapons the doc created?"

"That they are. And I'd like to know a bit about how you did it." Dominos said.

"How am I supposed to know that? You'd have to ask the doctor. All we did was get some humans—he's the one who turned them into those mindless piles of slop."

The word "humans" caught the Adenji gang's attention first. And, much to their surprise, Marco was the one to speak up. "The reports said that the bodies were missing for months. How did you keep them alive?"

Dominos raised his hand, summoning the elder man to cease speaking, but it was too late. Brooklyn latched on to the issue.

"So that's what you're really after here—you're trying to preserve bodies. But that begs the question: why?" Brooklyn drummed his fingers on his knee.

"That's not relevant," Dominos interjected.

"Oh, I think it's very relevant. Without knowing that, we're not making a deal."

Dominos eyed Marco, taking a breath. "All right, what about

this? As leader of the Adenji gang, I have access to some of the best equipment on the planet, along with a wealth of funds — two things I'm sure you'll use to move forward now that The Hero of Light is gone. I'll grant you full access to those funds and equipment if you give us access to this doctor of yours."

Both Bronx and Bex took a quick glance around the luxuries surrounding them, then back to Brooklyn, and said, "Give them the Doc. He's no help to us anyway."

Brooklyn stroked his chin, still not satisfied. "I don't think so. Sweeten the pot."

"Excuse me?" Kari asked, bitingly.

"If you're taking the doc, that means that we can't use him to rebuild his lab and help us. Seems sort of pointless to get all the equipment if we have no big brain to operate it."

Then something interesting happened. Marco and Kari both looked at Dominos. Their leader shook his head and said, "I suppose you have a fair point. All right, here's my new proposal then. You give us this doctor for our purposes, and we'll not only give you access to our equipment and funds, but we'll also allocate some people to build you that lab you seek. We have plenty of useful people who are more than capable of that. And when we're done with what we need from the doctor, you can have him back. Is that satisfying enough for you?"

Brooklyn shrugged, feeling the burning stares of his partners on his cheeks. "I still say it's a lousy deal, but fine. We meet here tomorrow before sunrise. But just remember, if you try to pull anything, I'll be the one giving you your next haircut," Brooklyn threatened.

Kari sneered. "Listen, kid…"

"Take it easy," Dominos said. Then, to Brooklyn, "We have no intentions of anything shady. But also, don't believe that I'm unaware of what happened the last time you made a deal with the Adenji gang. I will not be falling for the same tricks."

Dominos stood up and walked out of the room.

# CHAPTER 4
## HARD-TAUGHT LESSONS

THE MOST RECOGNIZABLE BUILDING TO PERISH the night of Dusk's return was the Elemental Council headquarters. In an act of cathartic poetry, Dusk personally turned the building into a pile of rubble through his efforts to capture Minisc. The battle that ensued—involving The Hero of Light and his son against the former leader of Luminosa, Dusk—left no remains of the once grand structure.

Like Elemental Academy, putting all available resources behind rebuilding the EC helped restore the structure so that it looked even more monumental than before.

It wasn't all bad, though. For the Elemental Council, a wave of youth was injected into their forces, with the EA students helping as their school underwent construction. Many students from all four years of the school were enlisted to help with the council's city rebuild efforts, while also repairing the damage psychologically to Humans and Elementalists alike. They continued to smooth over relations, and although tensions were sometimes high, strides were being made each day. Humans and Elementalists came together in an act of solidarity to fix roadways, build new homes, and reunite families.

Despite Luminosa's constant attempts to drive a stake between the two races, they refused to take the bait, even without The Hero of Light around to keep them united. Life was far from perfect for the two groups, but noticeable progress could be seen everywhere.

After being given the week to decide on their apprenticeship, Minisc, Lily, and Jules, stayed true to their original decision, preparing to join Yuri and learn under his tutelage.

When the time finally came, the three stood at the bottom of the massive marble steps admiring the outside of the EC.

"They really cleaned this place up," Minisc said, as he and his friends headed up the steps.

"It's way nicer than the last time we were here, that's for sure," Lily added.

"Yeah, Yuri said that the final touches on the outside were done last week," Jules noted. "Some of the rooms on the inside haven't been finished yet, but that shouldn't take too much longer."

They weren't wrong. Just a short month ago, much of the EC was still under constant construction. There were different machinery and vehicles driving in and out every day to drop off supplies or help move the concrete slabs for the walls. Even the banners that hung from the rooftops looked more vibrant and crisp than the previous ones. It was hard to believe that the updated, sleek building came together so quickly.

Inside, the EC looked as lavish and elegant as one would expect for a building of such high importance. There were multiple staircases leading up to the higher floors, all lined with pristine red carpeting. The walls and pillars around the main lobby gleamed like pearls. It was evident that no expense was spared on the rebuild, and with good reason.

Since the population of Elementalists gradually increased year over year, and with younger Elementalists preparing to join, the building needed to be ready for the shift in generations.

Lily and Jules had spent a fair bit more time in the building than Minisc and were accustomed to the lavish adornments, but for Minisc it came as quite the shock. Even the air in the room smelled fresh, like a new car.

Men and women all wearing similar uniforms hurried up and down the stairs, and a few of them even had students following close behind.

"Guess we should get moving. It looks like everyone's already starting their apprenticeships," Lily said. The two boys agreed and they all made their way up the largest middle staircase, which led directly to the third floor.

For all of Yuri's efforts in the fight against Luminosa and his years of service in the EC, President Zale Osiris had awarded him with a wonderfully large and lavishly decorated office on the third story. It was certainly fit for someone that was so instrumental in many different battles against Luminosa.

Although Yuri was no longer capable of harnessing his element due to those battles, his smarts and experience were still tremendous assets, which the EC sorely needed in their investigative unit.

Jules flung the door open to his brother's office with a joyous grin. "Hey Yuri!" he called out loudly. Breathing in deeply, he inhaled the new leather smell of the office furniture.

Ever since Yuri had left his old firm and began working out of the EC's main building, the office was one of Jules' favourite spots to be. He loved being in the building and seeing all the various people that he'd one day call co-workers. A couple of other council members even knew him by name at this point.

"Jules, you can't just barge in like that—have some manners, for goodness sake," Lily scolded as she and Minisc lagged behind him.

"She's right, you know. It's not good manners," Yuri said from behind his desk, "Nice of you three to finally show up." His desk was full of paperwork, alongside a mug of fresh, steaming coffee, the smell of which filled the room and added to the richness of the atmosphere.

"Blame Minisc — he slept in," Jules revealed.

Minisc rubbed the back of his neck, caught. "He might actually be telling the truth on that one."

"Well, that's all right — you're here now." Yuri said to the three, rising from his desk. "Come on, we don't have any time to waste today."

"Oh, do we have something going on already?" Lily asked.

"Nah, not really, but I just wanna make sure that you guys get the most out of your weeks here. Learning under those in the EC is a critical step to your success."

But before they could do anything, they heard a knock on the door.

"Hey Yuri, here's the paperwork you requested."

Standing in the doorway was a girl slightly older than the teens, taller than Minisc with shoulder length deep blue hair, a few free strands of which fell along her round face. She had a glimmer of opaque blue in her eyes and a strut of confidence about her. Under her arm were a couple of folders.

When Minisc stared at the girl, for some reason he had the strange feeling that he should recognize her. He tried to be subtle about his confusion but, try as he did, he just couldn't put a name to her face.

He glanced at Lily and Jules to see if they looked equally confused. But much to his surprise, he witnessed something that he never thought was possible.

Jules' eyes were glazed over as if he'd been struck by cupid's arrow, and Minisc swore that he could see hearts in his eyes. "No way…did Jules just fall in love?" Minisc gawked under his breath. Only Lily heard him, and she quietly giggled, "I think he did."

Jules tried to mask the amorous awe all over his face, while Minisc and Lily fought to hold back their laughter.

Yuri walked out from behind his desk, placed his hand on Jules' shoulder, and looked at the girl. "Perfect timing, Adelle. Allow me to introduce you to our new team. This is my little brother Jules, and his friends Lily and Minisc."

Adelle tossed the folders on the nearby chair and offered a half bow, somewhat of a curtsy. "Hi, it's a pleasure to meet you guys. Yuri has told me a lot about you."

"Adelle here is freshly out of EA, and was top of her class for all four years. Since she's now a full-fledged member of the EC and you guys have done plenty of your own work with us in the past, it seemed like a good idea to group you up. This way, you can learn from someone who was in your position a bit more recently than myself."

"That sounds great," Lily beamed. "It's way more fun having another girl in the group anyway." She and Adelle both smiled.

"Wait, does that mean that you're not coming with us?" Jules asked his brother.

Yuri chuckled. "Don't worry — I'll be tagging along for sure, but I can always use a second pair of eyes on you guys. And after working with Adelle over the last few weeks, I figured that she'd be the perfect fit for our group. Oh, and before we leave, you guys are gonna need some more official clothing for the week. Here are some fresh uniforms," he said, pulling them out of the bottom drawer in his desk. "I know that your last ones got ruined pretty badly in all the battles. Now go and get changed and then we can head out."

He handed Jules and Lily uniforms before turning to Minisc.

"Sorry, Minisc. Mr. Howland doesn't wear EC uniforms."

"Uh, what? Who's Mr. Howland...?" Minisc trailed off, raising his eyebrow. Dread befell him as he saw Yuri's always encouraging smile flinch. Yuri's face drooped with concern, and Minisc knew that he was hiding something.

"Yuri? What are you not telling me?"

Yuri sighed. "Sorry, Minisc—I had assumed that your father had already let you know, but I guess not..."

"Let me know what?" Now Minisc could feel his heart quickening and a sinking feeling in his stomach.

"You'll be working under an EC member named Mr. Howland for the next two weeks."

"What?" Jules asked, unhappy. "But we need Minisc. He's part of the team."

"Yeah, Yuri—we all wanted to work together," Lily added.

"I know, I know, but it's by special request. I didn't have a say in the matter."

Minisc frowned as he looked at Jules, then at Lily.

"Don't worry, I'm sure it'll be fine," Lily encouraged him with a pat on the shoulder.

"It's just down the hall and around the corner," Yuri instructed. "You'll see his name on the door. And I'd suggest that you get a move on—Mr. Howland isn't a fan of tardiness."

Taking a moment to process his new orders, Minisc nodded, accepting his fate. He was disappointed at not getting to spend the week working with Jules and Lily, but he tried to adopt a positive attitude.

"Okay. Well—good luck, guys. I guess I'll see you later." Minisc was unsure of what to think. Who was Mr. Howland, and what did he want with him? Whatever the answer, he had a sneaking suspicion that his father played a role in this sudden switch, which meant that there was no complaining about it. He'd just have to follow orders and assume that his father had good reason for pulling him away from his friends. Still, Minisc wondered: *Why wouldn't he mention it beforehand? And how is a member of the EC so freely allowed to disobey dress protocol? What am I about to get myself into?*

With everything decided, Lily and Jules both hugged their friend tight and went their separate ways.

The walk to Mr. Howland's office was short, but for Minisc it felt like an eternity. It was a lonely road. The halls were silent enough for him to hear his own heartbeat—not a good sign. As he made his way there, he tried to picture what Mr. Howland would look like and what kind of person he'd be. What kind of a teacher was he, and what sort of experiences did he have?

When Minisc got around the bend, he stopped in front of the red and white door. "Mr. Gordon Howland" was engraved onto a gold, eye-level name plate.

*All right, here goes nothing.* Minisc took a deep breath and knocked on the door. No answer. He waited a second, not wanting to barge in. But if nobody was around, he'd feel stupid just waiting.

Realizing that his knock would remain unanswered, he took the brave route and cracked open the door, peeking in. The lights were on and the windows were open, but still no reply.

"Hello? Mr. Howland, are you in here? It's Minisc. You requested to see me?"

When Minisc entered, he was surprised to see that he was standing in an office twice the size of Yuri's. There was a furniture set to his left, a desk at the back, and a large steel cabinet twice his size along the right wall.

But something was missing.

He shifted his eyes around the room, noticing scattered papers, fresh coffee, and a jacket hanging on the wall, and yet he saw no one. "Mr. Howland..." he said again, this time clearly knowing that he'd receive no response.

Then he heard the door close behind him, followed by a definite locking sound. He spun around and grabbed the handle, but it refused to budge.

A robotic voice sounded from all four walls, counting down. "10…9…8…7…"

*What's going on?!? Is this a trap?* Minisc's eyes darted around the room, and he held his fists up defensively. The voice swirled around him, making it impossible to determine where it was coming from.

"6…5…4…3…" As the voice counted down further, chills ran up Minisc's spine. He stepped backwards, his back now against the wall to try and narrow his blind spots, but still he had no idea what was happening.

"2…1…0."

Suddenly, the lights shut off, leaving Minisc in total darkness.

*Seriously — what is happening?* Before he could think, a streak of light came sailing through the darkness toward him. He jumped out of the way, dodging the attack, but then he crashed with a thud, smashing his shoulder up against something heavy and unforgiving.

Then another voice sounded, this one male and much more human than the countdown voice. "You were given ten seconds to learn the layout of the room. When in battle, you never know the scenario you might be presented. You must take notice of every detail in whatever time is granted, and then be ready to strike."

"My surroundings? What're you talking about?" Minisc yelled into the void, remaining on guard for a second attack. Then he saw another streak of lightning, but this time more clearly as his eyes gradually adjusted to the sudden blackness. It was a lightning bolt with a faint yellow glow trailing behind it. He held his hand out, firing a ball of light. The flash illuminated the room for a brief second, but Minisc still couldn't locate his attacker. If he had a moment to breathe, he could use his element to light up the room, but bolts of lightning continued to fly toward him in waves. He tried to roll again, and then he crashed into something else, but he had no clue what it was.

*What's going on here?!? I show up for a meeting and I get ambushed into a fight? Why is nobody running to help? They must hear what's going on in here!* Minisc pushed to get to his feet but struggled as he grabbed something that felt like loose papers instead of a sturdy object. *I need a place to hide so that I can launch a flare. If I pull that off, this guy's done.*

An image of the room that he recalled from before darkness befell him flashed in his mind. He was slightly disoriented from jumping around, but if his memory served him right, then the desk was only a few feet in front of him. If he could get underneath it, perhaps he'd have a chance.

Minisc scrambled to his feet and ran forward. Praying that his mind's eye was accurate, he slid until he seemingly crashed into a wall, but it wasn't nearly as solid as it should have been. He quickly determined that it was the back edge of the desk's underbelly. He reached his hand up and smacked the roof of his confined space. He had nowhere to go, but at least the lightning bolts had stopped.

*Time to shine some light on this sociopath.* Minisc's entire body began to glow a bright gold, which finally revealed the room to him once again. He crawled out from beneath the desk, his vision now restored. He was ready to turn the tides.

But the room still remained empty. The bolts of lightning had ceased, but Minisc remained on guard. Feeling a surge of electricity in the air, he spun around and fired a blast of light toward the tall steel closet. The ball exploded into a puff of smoke, but through the shadows Minisc spotted the doors of the closet opening. A man's silhouette came flying out like the grim reaper and grabbed Minisc by the face, pinning him to the ground.

"I was beginning to wonder if you'd ever find my hiding spot." It was the voice of an older man — he sounded like he was in his late 60s — but it still carried a menacing level of authority.

Minisc struggled to free himself from the man's grasp, swinging wildly in a panic. Then his body began to shine even brighter, which blinded his attacker. Lines of gold formed on his arms, and he managed to push the unknown assailant off him. He scurried to his feet and fired a ferocious blast in his direction, with no regard for the damage he might cause in the office.

The man smacked the fiery blast to the side, and it exploded into the open steel cabinet.

Minisc prepared for the next strike, but before they could return to blows the man held his hand out like a stop sign.

The assailant said, "That's enough for now. I've seen all I needed to see from you." He clapped his hands and the lights of the room once again turned on.

Minisc gritted his teeth, his power still overflowing and his fists twitching for a fight, but he lowered them when the lights granted him sight again. He began sucking back wind as the light from his arms faded and his body caved to exhaustion.

"Looks like that fool of a student taught you some decent moves after all," the man said, "but your instincts are dull and predictable. Even so, I guess it was good enough to pass the test."

Minisc looked at him in bewilderment. Then his words sunk in and he started to freak. "Wait...test? What're you talking about? Who *are* you?"

"I am Mr. Gordon Howland."

"Mr...Mr. Howland..." The whole ordeal had been Minisc's test. Now that it was over, Minisc took a second to breathe and get a good look at the man standing in front of him.

Mr. Howland was toweringly tall, and Minisc was utterly tiny in comparison. He also had a grizzled, snow-white beard that blended into his equally white hair. Thin, round spectacles sat on his ridged nose, and weathered wrinkles lined his forehead. Unlike the customary EC uniform that almost everyone in the building wore, he was dressed in what looked like a self-tailored, black and blue uniform. A zipper shaped like a lightning bolt fastened his jacket. Any other man of this age should've been well past his prime, but he was lean and built, and Minisc had already learned firsthand that there was power in those archaic bones.

Mr. Howland walked up to Minisc and started to examine his body as Minisc attempted to introduce himself. "Uh, hello, Sir…I'm Minisc Prem—"

"Minisc Premier, I am well aware of who you are. You are a second year EA student who is here to study for the next two weeks in what the school is calling an apprenticeship program. Your father told me everything I needed to know about you." Mr. Howland stood up and took a step back, glaring at Minisc. "Normally I would never bother with a second-year student such as yourself, let alone have them working with me, but I am considering this a favour."

"Huh? A favour?" The pieces were slowly starting to fall into place.

"Yes. Working for the EC is not the same as EA…or even the same as what you students did over the summer. When you are on my team, you are dealing with the real world, with real lives at stake. Every move you make has consequences, and you will not be bailed out by your enemy. I cannot risk my operations by putting an ill-prepared child on my team who will cause more harm than good."

Minisc frowned, then appeared puzzled. He knew he was young, but to be called an "ill-prepared child?" That was an insult. He could guarantee that nobody in all four years of EA faced the same fights he had in the last year alone. The clashes against Dusk, Ignis, Bex, and so on were more than most EC members faced, for that matter. And, just for good measure, he came second in his first Tournament of Elements. He had talent and strength. But all of that wasn't enough for Howland, who seemed to regard The Hero of Light asking for a favor as some sort of burden.

Of course, when he gave it more thought, he realized that nobody knew about those fights, as his father had claimed all the glory. Not that Minisc wanted any fame—he made the decision himself to avoid any kind of intense spotlight, but the insults still filled him with a bit of anger. Anger that wasn't unnoticed by Mr. Howland, though he hid his smirk well.

*Yes, this boy does indeed appear to be a younger version of his father. Don said that he was more like his mother, but, as per usual, I'd say that he was wrong in his assessment. The way he fought when I had him pinned, the quick thinking to hide for cover...and he also clearly has some fire in him. He thinks that I don't know about his accomplishments, and yet he still refuses to blurt them out and prove me wrong. Interesting.*

Though fired up, Minisc remained silent. To prove a point, he refused to reveal his involvement against Luminosa to Mr. Howland. That was the past, and he was here to prove that he was ready for the future.

"Sir, with all due respect, I understand what I'm getting myself into."

"I'm sure that's what you think, but we will see about that. Take a moment to clean yourself up, I'll be back momentarily. There is a bathroom next door."

# CHAPTER 5
## NEW DOG, OLD TRICKS

WHEN MINISC RETURNED, HE WASN'T GREETED BY Mr. Howland, which felt like a blessing by that point.

But to his surprise, the room was being cleaned by a boy around the same age as him. He was dressed casually, and his wavy, green-tinted hair was a mess. Though he was doing mundane cleaning, which had nothing to do with the other boy, he had a jubilant smile on his face, humming tunes while he worked.

Luckily, none of the pieces of big furniture had suffered too much damage in Minisc's test, but, even so, papers were scattered, furniture was flipped, and floors were scuffed. There was a fair bit of work to be done.

"Oh, hey—you must be Minisc," the boy said cheerfully, neatly stacking the papers on the desk.

"Uh, I'm sorry, but do we know each other?"

The boy shook his head and laughed. "No, but I know about you. You're Minisc Premier, son of The Hero of Light, and you're here to work with the one and only Mr. Howland."

Minisc's eyes narrowed. He wasn't sure how to react.

This was hardly the first time he'd experienced uncomfortable encounters with an unfamiliar person. Playing the role of The Hero of Light's son his entire life had led to many strangers approaching him at random. He often hated those moments of dealing with the intrusive questions and silly requests, but something about the way this boy spoke—with no desire to dig further—kept him relaxed. Or at least relaxed enough.

"'The one and only?'"

The boy laughed again. "Come on, you can't tell me you've met anyone else like him before. Who else would ambush you like that in a work setting?"

Minisc grimaced as the words sank in. "Wait, you know about that? Don't tell me…"

"Oh, you bet. And let me tell you, I didn't fair nearly as well." The boy walked over to Minisc and shook his hand. "Hi, I'm Robin. I work under Mr. Howland, too. I imagine we'll be working together quite often for the next two weeks."

"Oh. Okay—well, it's nice to meet you Robin, but you shouldn't really be the one cleaning up. After all, I made the mess here."

"Oh, don't worry about that. Mr. Howland likes things in particular spots, so I just went ahead and took care of it."

When Robin finished flipping over the couch, he took a seat and gestured for Minisc to join him. He did so, sitting across from the older boy.

"So, Minisc, what made you decide to go to EA? Did you wanna follow in your father's footsteps, or did you have another reason?"

It was an innocent enough question, posed by a seemingly innocent enough boy. And a question with a rather straightforward answer, but Minisc still tripped over it.

"Um, actually…my mother was always big on bringing Humans and Elementalists together and helping push society forward to be more accepting to us, and I wanted to help make that dream a reality. That's why I chose to go to EA."

"Wow, I never would've guessed. I just figured that you'd be striving to be like your father, but that's a pretty cool goal, too!" Every word Robin spoke had a powerful aura of positivity to it.

"I mean…don't get me wrong — my father's done some amazing things for sure. And no doubt he's helped bridge the gap between Humans and Elementalists, too. But to be honest, I'm not really much of the Hero type. I'd rather stay away from the spotlight and the publicity that comes with it. Anyway, what about you? I assume that if you're working with Mr. Howland, you went to EA as well?"

"That I did. Graduated last year. Top of my class, too." Robin placed a fist over his chest with pride. "Well, my friend Adelle tied with me, but still. She's actually working here as well, with Yuri and your friends."

"Wait, how do you know all of this?"

"Mr. Howland is rather thorough in his research of things. It was all in the paperwork on his desk. But, to answer your question, it's not much different than your reason for going to EA. I wanted to help people as best I could. Especially seeing all the destruction and sadness that Luminosa has created recently. There are so many people in this world that live in fear. Humans especially still have fear when they see a bad Elementalist on the news or committing a crime that they have no way of protecting themselves. Now that your father's retired, people need someone they can look up to. Someone that can stand strong and tell everyone that it's going to be okay and that they're going to be safe. So for the past four years at EA, I've been working tirelessly to make that my top priority."

Despite having just met, Minisc was starting to feel comfortable around Robin. There was an infectious aura around the boy, and it reminded him of his father in some ways.

Before they could continue, Mr. Howland finally returned to his office.

"Good, I see you took the liberty of cleaning things up. Thank you for that Robin." He glanced toward Minisc. "And I see you've met our newest member, so I'll spare the introductions. Robin, I need you to run these files over to the other offices. I'll take it from here with Minisc for a bit."

Minisc shot his new friend a plea that said, *Please don't leave me alone with this old kook.* But Robin was oblivious to the cry for help.

"Of course." He bolted upright with a grin, took the papers, and smiled." I'll see you later, Minisc! It was nice meeting you." But as he passed by Minisc, he whispered, "Don't worry — he's not as scary as you think."

Mr. Howland headed for the couch, sitting where Robin had been previously. He poured two cups of tea, placed one on the other side of the table, and then glanced up at Minisc.

"You may relax. This isn't another test…"

Hearing those words, Minisc snapped out of his confusion, shook his head, and worked up the courage to muster a faint smile. He grabbed the cup, and the scent of lemon filled his nostrils as he took a sip of the tea. The warm drink slid down his throat, leaving behind a sour taste.

Mr. Howland blew onto his own tea to cool it and said, "I would like to discuss Celestial Light with you."

Minisc froze. The words "Celestial Light" were the final piece of the puzzle that Minisc had yet to solve. Now he understood why the man had called his apprenticeship a "favour."

"Your father explained your disinterest in the public spotlight, so I assumed that this was not a conversation you wished to have with Robin in the room. And I would say that he was right based on your refusal to mention your fierce battles against Dusk and Luminosa when I called you an ill-prepared child earlier. Though harsh, I wanted to see how you would react. Since those moments in history have yet to become public knowledge, I too believed that it best not to share them. If one day those events were to spread across the country, that will be your choice to make, not mine."

Minisc bowed his head. "Yes, all of that is correct…and thank you, Sir. I appreciate keeping that a secret. For the time being, I think it's best if my father continues to take the credit. I doubt I could handle that level of attention. And besides, I'm the furthest thing from a hero. I just did what I could to help. If not for my father, most of those battles would've ended poorly." Minisc tried to downplay his involvement in the fate of Elementalists, as he was more interested in getting to the point of the topic. "But how do you know about Celestial Light? Did you work with my father at some point?"

"So, he never told you." Mr. Howland briefly appeared disgruntled, then resumed his calm demeanor. "Some would say that I am the creator of Celestial Light."

Minisc blinked a few times, his mouth agape. After a brief pause to process this information, he said, "Back up a sec, I always thought that my father created it? Aren't he and Dusk the only two who could ever use it?"

Mr. Howland held his hand to his head in disgust. "Of course that's what he told you. I might not be able to use the technique to its fullest potential anymore, but to claim that I am not its creator…well, my protégé certainly has some nerve."

"Hold on, what do you mean your 'protégé?'" Minisc's eyes widened again. "You were the one who trained my father? No, that can't be right. How come I've never heard of you before?"

Mr. Howland took another sip of his tea with a small smirk. "Well, I guess I might've been a tad bit harsh on him in his younger years, but yes—I taught him everything he knows. Without me, there *is* no Hero of Light."

It finally dawned on Minisc. *Now I understand what Father was talking about the other day. He must've asked Mr. Howland to train me instead of himself.*

"So, tell me—how much do you know about this technique that you desire to learn?"

Minisc's shoulders slumped, knowing that his answer would be lackluster. "I thought I knew nothing about it before, but now I'm starting to think that I might know even less than that. My father's only ever described it as 'a state of being that enhances your power to great lengths.' For the last month or so, basically since my father officially retired, he's been convinced that I can learn it, but I haven't had much luck. He just keeps saying, 'Clear your mind and let your element flow through you,' but nothing seems to be working. It's like I grasp the power for a second, and then in a flash it's gone. I'm guessing that's why he sent me to you instead."

"I see. Yes, that does sound about right from when we talked on the phone. I can see why frustration might set in. Your father was a natural as far as Elementalists are concerned, and so, admittedly, learning Celestial Light for him was relatively easy compared to others who have tried." Mr. Howland took another sip of tea. "Allow me to shed some light on the subject then. I know the name 'Celestial Light' is synonymous with the power that guided The Hero of Light, but that in itself is a bit misleading. It was called that because your father is a light Elementalist. Under hypothetical circumstances, any Elementalist could learn the skill."

"That makes sense. I did know that Dusk was the one other Elementalist to master the power."

"Correct. Aside from your father, Dusk was the only other Elementalist with the level of strength required to master the technique. He happened to believe in the same power-enhancing philosophy that I was studying at the time."

"Hold on…does that mean that you never mastered your own technique?" Minisc asked, grasping his tea up with both hands.

"That is a complicated matter. No matter my efforts, I have never possessed the power that your father and Dusk did, so even though I created the technique, they were the ones to perfect it in time. See, your father is right, in a sense, when he told you that it was a state of mind. Think of it like an amplifier. As I'm sure you already know, an Elementalist's body can only produce so much power from their element. Some of that can be chalked up to good genetics, while other factors involve the development of your element, the same as developing a muscle. Celestial Light works by turbo charging those elemental cells in your body. From thousands of hours of studies, when the element cells are stimulated to an extreme degree, you can reach a heightened state of strength, speed, and awareness that your normal state could never pull off. To put it more plainly, it makes your element produce twice as strong and twice as fast. When you learn to let that level of strength flow to the rest of your muscles, increasing other physical traits, that is when you complete the full mastery of the technique."

"Okay, I guess that makes sense…"

"That being said, there are a few drawbacks from being in such a state. The reason that your father continued to preach that you clear your mind is because of the strain that the power puts on your muscles. Think of it like this: when your mind begins to race with anxieties or fears, your heart rate increases and your muscles tense up. Achieving Celestial Light causes a similar effect, but if you lose focus while using the power, it can have catastrophic consequences. It is extremely dangerous to use."

Minisc nodded in silence, doing his best to take in all the information Mr. Howland was offering.

Next, Mr. Howland showed more of a human side as he

sighed, frowning. He hesitated, and then, "The other drawback of using this power…is that eventually it will erase your element altogether."

Minisc lowered his head. "Like Father."

"Yes," Mr. Howland agreed. "Harnessing this power takes a tremendous toll and can have a severe negative impact on the growth of your body's elemental cells. Because they are forced into overdrive, they die faster, and the longer you use the skill, the harder it is to replenish those cells until they are no more. But now it appears that your father believes that you are the *only* one with the capability of learning this state and of making good use of it as the next Hero of Light." Mr. Howland paused, placed his tea down, and looked into Minisc's eyes. "So, before anything else, I must ask you…are you prepared to lose your element in order to take up your father's battle against Luminosa?"

Howland spoke with a straight face and wasn't mincing words. Even so, Minisc was all too aware of the consequences.

He and his father had never once discussed the effects that learning Celestial Light would have on him. In a way, they didn't need to. Minisc could see the prime example before his very eyes every day. Perhaps that gave Minisc enough time to come to grips with his choice—even knowing the risks, he smiled somberly and said, "Yes. I'll confess that I really have no desire to be the second coming of my father. Actually, the idea of that prospect is torture for me. But I've seen the damage that Luminosa can cause…the divide they create between Humans and Elementalists, all while taking innocent lives in cold blood. They've hurt me, my father, and my friends. I refuse to let that happen anymore. If Father believes that I can put a stop to Luminosa, then I won't let him down. And if this costs me my element somewhere down the road, so be it. I'd rather live in this world with no element than in one where Luminosa achieves total control."

Mr. Howland could hear the same subtle determination in Minisc's voice that had always followed Don when he'd talked about stopping Luminosa. It filled him with hope for the future.

"All right then. But I warn you—this will not be easy. To ensure that your body is capable of achieving such power, you will have to train far harder than what I'm sure you've done with your father. You will not simply learn this during weeks of an internship—it is something that will take time. Are you still prepared?"

"I don't have a choice, Sir—I must learn it. If it's the only way I'll be able to stop Luminosa, I'll do whatever it takes."

"Then the decision is made. Starting tomorrow, I want you here at the crack of dawn. We will start with training, then you will work through your apprenticeship, and after that we will train some more. Also, tomorrow I will have a schedule written out for you to follow."

The intensity in the man's voice forced Minisc to pause and reconsider. Was this a mistake? After all, just the mere introduction between them had been scary enough. He could only imagine what training under Mr. Howland would be like. But regardless, he agreed to the terms.

After his chat with Mr. Howland, Minisc was sent home for the evening. Overloaded with information to digest, he swung open the door to his house. Entering the newly built Premier home, he headed straight into the workout room attached. In his old home it was just an unused office space, but now it had been transformed into a home gym.

He knew that he'd likely find his father there. Despite no longer being capable of using his element, Don was adamant about staying in great shape. He was still just as diligent with his workout routine as he'd ever been.

Just as Minisc predicted, he found his father sitting flat-backed on a workout bench, lifting weights. Minisc tapped on the door, causing his father to stop and sit up. He saw the disgruntled glare on his son's face and gulped. The price to pay for misleading his son had come due, and he knew it.

Minisc stood with bruises on his arms, disheveled hair, and even a few marks on his forehead for good measure.

"Hey, you're home early," Don said casually. "How was your—"

But Minisc cut him off abruptly. "Mr. Howland." He stared down his father, watching a bead of sweat drip from his brow. It easily could've been from the intense workout, but Minisc knew better. He could see the look of dread, the look of fear, the look of someone who'd been caught. For a man known to stand on death's door more times than he cared to count, the name "Mr. Howland" caused a flinch reflex in him like no other name could.

It was always going to turn out this way. The second that Don placed a call to his former mentor and threw a wrench in Minisc's plans, he knew that he'd have to bear the brunt of his son's anger. Luckily for him, Minisc didn't have much of a temper and was far from a shouter by nature. His son would no doubt have some words for him—just in his own way.

"Yeah, thanks for the heads up on that one…" Minisc snapped sarcastically, leaning up against the door frame.

Don swallowed the pity he felt for his son and said, "I know…I wanted to tell you about it, but Gordon demanded that I stay quiet…"

Minisc eyed his father sharply for an explanation, and so Don took a seat on the workout bench. Minisc walked over and sat across from him.

"He wanted to test you firsthand," Don explained, "to see how you reacted to situations and unpredictable circumstances. But if I'd told you about his…let's call them teaching tactics…then you would've been more on guard and prepared, so it would've voided the info he wanted to gather. I'm sorry I had to pull one over on you, but I promise that it was for a good reason." He was almost pleading with his son.

As a recipient of the revered Gordon Howland training regimen himself, he was all too aware of the torture that he was getting his son into.

"So what crazy test did he set up for you?" Don asked, his mind flipping through various flashbacks of all the clever ways Mr. Howland had forced him to train. In the end, the man's methods worked, as Don went on to become the greatest Elementalist the world had ever known. But some of the tactics were excruciating—and that was an understatement.

Minisc explained the entirety of Mr. Howland's test, along with meeting Robin and the rest of the day. Don grimaced when he heard about the training tactic.

"Yeah, he got me with that once as well. He actually knocked me unconscious and I was out cold for a few hours," Don chuckled.

Minisc shook his head. "Who is this guy anyway? I always thought you were the one who created Celestial Light, not some old EC member."

"He is one of the original Elementalists."

"Well, yeah, I figured that. The guy is like 60—of course he's a first generation Elementalist," Minisc said, stating the obvious.

"No, Minisc—I mean that he's one of maybe the first ten Elementalists ever to have been born. He's also the first Elementalist to ever wield an electric element. He's the first of his kind. He's seen everything, and for the most part has been a part of everything an Elementalist has gone through since the time when elements started to sprout up. When Luminosa first formed, he was still training me, but he had no intentions of showing me this secret technique he was developing. Eventually, though, there came a point where he knew he'd taken the power as far as he could, but he still believed that it could go further. When the world started to collapse, he finally decided to impart that strength onto me in hopes of stopping Dusk. And, as they say, the rest is history. That said, throughout his years of wisdom, he's become one of the wisest Elementalists alive."

Minisc was shocked. "I had no idea. I could tell from talking to him that he was knowledgeable, but to be one of the first Elementalists born…" Minisc looked at his father as an interesting question sprang to his mind. "So if you both were at your peak, would he be stronger than you?"

In his own way, Minisc was needling his father. They both knew the answer, but even asking the question would be a small jab to his father's ego.

"No chance he could take me. Not that he'd ever admit it, but no. I would win."

"Oh, really. Then why did you start sweating when I first said his name?" Minisc prodded further.

"I wasn't sweating from that! I'd just finished working out."

"Oh, yes you were. The second I said his name you looked like you'd seen a ghost. I mean, really — you hadn't looked that pale when Dusk returned."

"Not the point," Don said, trying to get the conversation back on topic. "Gordon Howland is the creator of Celestial Light, and with his unmatched wisdom of the skill, he'll be a good teacher for you. I have no doubt that he can show you everything you need to know to pull this off. But I won't lie to you — with his… shall we say, methods…you'll be in for a bumpy ride. Still, I promise that if you listen carefully and learn from his wisdom, he'll take you to heights you could never have imagined. The Hero of Light would've ceased to exist without his guidance."

Although Minisc still wondered if the words his father spoke were true, he had no choice but to believe him. Mr. Howland had demonstrated both strength and wisdom in just a few hours of their meeting. And if he'd trained The Hero of Light, then who better to learn under? Also, Robin seemed like a good person, someone solid who he could learn with. Even if he wasn't working with Lily and Jules for a week, an invaluable chance was being presented to him. And it was one that he needed to take full advantage of.

# CHAPTER 6
## ROCKY WATERS

YURI WALKED OVER TO HIS DESK AND PICKED UP SOME loose papers. With Minisc leaving Lily, Adelle, and Jules behind, Jules asked "So what are we doing today?"

"We're heading to the lakefront. As I'm sure you're aware, most of that area is patrolled by the Adenji gang. Over the last few weeks, we've been gathering intel on different shipments of strange materials coming in, and the names of those ordering the shipments don't add up. We're pretty sure that the Adenji gang are up to something, and we also know that they're not big on confrontation, at least not in the public eye, so we're gonna make sure they know that the EC is around the area and watching over them. We might not be able to make arrests, as that's only for the police to do, but if the Adenji gang starts to see us patrolling, they'll be forced to back off for a bit, giving the police more time to gain evidence and warrants for arrests. After all, a big part of the EC is being visible for people. The sight of authority often deters criminals. As for what you three will be helping me with, we have word that one of these strange shipments will be coming in at 10am sharp, and we've already secured warrants to search those ships before they unload."

Yuri handed the papers, tied with a small string, to Adelle, as she was technically a full member of the EC. He kept the other set of papers for himself.

The south end of Toronto was known as the city's Lakefront. Outside of admiring the sparkling water each morning or enjoying the refreshing lake air, viewing the homes there often fascinated people, as they were some of the most expensive in town. Aside from the affluent neighborhood, docks were scattered all across the city's lake front, and most of the time those docks were filled with towering ships stacked to the brim with different metal crates full of various supplies. Mostly imported food from other countries, but occasionally they carried other products as well.

Of course, that wasn't the only thing that the Toronto Lakefront was famous for. Due to the large amount of money that the people living there were worth, crime rates tended to be higher in that part of the city, and the Adenji gang carried a large presence there. They patrolled the waterfront like it was their own version of the EC, dictating much of what happened in the area. Although they didn't commit the same heinous crimes in the past as Luminosa, they liked to flex their muscles when need be.

After Minisc departed to work with Mr. Howland, that left Jules, Lily, and Adelle in the care of Yuri. The group was excited about their upcoming mission, but Jules and Lily were still disappointed that Minisc wouldn't be alongside them. After all, they were a team.

"Hey, Yuri—who is this Mr. Howland anyway, and why did Minisc have to go with him instead of us?" Jules asked as they left the EC building.

"To be honest, the request took me by surprise, too. Mr. Howland almost never takes anybody under his wing. But when Minisc's father called me and said that he was going to make different arrangements, he didn't specify why. Mr. Howland taught me for a year after I graduated EA as well." Yuri shuddered at the thought, shaking his head. "He's one tough teacher, I'll say that much. But he's also one of the wisest Elementalists I've ever met. Minisc will be in good hands…hopefully."

Walking beside Lily, Adelle added, "He'll be working with my friend Robin as well, I'd imagine."

"Robin?" Jules asked.

"Yep, we were in the same class at EA. He's actually the reason I ended up going to EA in the first place, but that's a different story. Anyway, after we graduated and started applying for people to study under, he was requested by Mr. Howland personally. It's quite amazing, really. I remember our first year together when he didn't have much talent at all. He was short and sort of scrawny, but nobody in the school worked harder or studied longer than him. And, more than anything on the planet, he wants to help people. He'd give his own life if it meant saving just one single person—even a complete stranger. He really is one of a kind."

"Actually, that sounds a lot like Minisc," Lily giggled. "Well, doing whatever he can to save someone, but not so much the studying part."

"Yes, I'd imagine that those two together would make quite a formidable team," Yuri added before muttering under his breath, "If they survive Mr. Howland's antics."

"It's probably for the best that Minisc isn't here anyway," Lily continued.

"Oh, and why is that?" Adelle wondered.

All three of the others gave the same response in unison: "Minisc hates water."

"He can't swim to save his life, he gets seasick super easily, and even when training with me, he hates if he gets hit by my water element. It's quite humorous to watch him squirm, actually." Lily laughed as everyone else joined in.

Soon the group reached the waterfront and headed down the docks. Lily approached the edge of the water, deeply breathing in the morning lake air. Exhaling, she smiled and said, "I love the smell of the lakefront in the morning."

Adelle agreed. "I know, and look how beautiful the water is. I love the way the sun glistens off it every morning. It's so romantic."

The arching sun reflected upon the lake with an orange hue, and the scene was just like a painting. There were no waves, no swimmers, and no incoming boats. The water calm and motionless.

As the three continued down the pier with Adelle cooing over the enchanting view, Lily nudged Jules, shooting him a look. But all he mustered in response was a simple, "Yeah, it looks nice." The words came out flat, and if Lily didn't know any better she would've thought he was being sarcastic. Luckily, Adelle didn't think the same way.

Lily tried to hide the mocking giggle under her tongue as she heard Jules' pitiful responses. It reminded her of the first day she met Minisc on their way to EA. His struggle to even choke out a word that morning on the train always made her smile; it was the awkward charm of a shy, modest boy. But Jules had never been shy or reserved like Minisc. In fact, seeing him at such a loss was rare.

Yuri led the group to the end of the cobblestone path, reaching the last docking station. Unlike many of the other docks stretching only moderately into the water, this last one crawled nearly 100 feet into the depths. It also had close to 40 feet of clearance from any of the other docks, for which there was good reason—it was designed for ships far bigger than an average freight boat.

Beside the pier was an elongated warehouse matching the length of the boat. It was closed off with a large white garage door and a small side door to the left.

Yuri came to a stop. "Jules, I want you to go with Adelle and search the boat. Make sure that you check every crate they have and anything else that might seem suspicious. Lily, you're coming with me. We're gonna do a sweep of the warehouse. If anyone tries to stop you from looking through the ship, show them your warrant papers. If they still refuse, then you're to call me." He looked directly at Jules, "You're not to engage. We're not here to start a war, we're here to inspect."

Jules averted his gaze down to his feet, pretending not to be the subject of Yuri's orders.

"Adelle, you're in charge. You remember the procedures I taught you?"

"Indeed I do."

"Good, glad to hear it. And Jules, please—for the love of my sanity, try to stay out of trouble."

Adelle turned and snickered at her partner as Jules said, "It's not like I go looking for it! Things just happen!"

"Sure. Regardless, stick close to Adelle and treat her as if you were taking orders from me. That means no adlibbing or trying to play hero, understood?"

"Yes..." Jules bemoaned in response. They both knew that sometimes he had a habit of trying to do too much. Jules never doubted his ability, which was important, but he still needed to believe in the people around him if he was to succeed.

Adelle and Jules were about to take their leave when Yuri said, "Wait. Before you go, I almost forgot." He reached into his other pocket and pulled out three rectangular steel objects that looked like cell phones. He handed one to each of his team.

Jules took the device and looked it over with confusion. He tapped the center of it and watched the screen light up with a big green button that read, "Talk." Underneath was another buttom that read, "Emergency Signal."

"What is this?" he asked. He looked over at Lily who was also fascinated by the new device. But before Yuri could answer, Adelle piped up, wanting to show off some of the knowledge imparted to her from her mentor.

"These are what the EC likes to call our 'communicators.' They're essentially walkie-talkies, and they can be paired off with other communicators as well so that we can talk to each other with the click of a button. It also allows the EC to track its members and emit a frequency to alert others when someone is in potential danger or needs backup."

"Why can't we just use our phones to communicate?" Jules asked.

"You guys will learn quickly enough that in this line of work, your smartphones break a lot," Adelle told them. "Luckily, the EC will cover that for you, but these things are way more sturdy and can survive a far greater beating."

Jules and Lily looked at each other with the same flashbacks playing in their heads. One after another, memories of each time they'd shattered, melted, froze, or destroyed their phones danced in their minds.

"Good point," the two of them said in unison.

Yuri slid his own device into his pocket. "With that out of the way, let's hurry. It won't be long until the boat starts trying to unload and the pier gets busy, so we need to get this done before we start agitating the workers around here."

The four split up into their teams and headed for their locations. Jules followed close behind Adelle, beaming with unmatched levels of excitement.

Normally, he would've preferred to work with his brother,

but being on a team with Adelle was a nice change. Unlike her partner, though, Adelle's mood had become a tad more stern. She took her job seriously, and she also understood the threat of being in Adenji territory. It wasn't something to be taken lightly.

Attached to the end of the boat was a large metal ramp that led up to the main balcony, and standing at the bottom were a man and a woman, both wearing white and grey sailor uniforms. They had their arms crossed as Jules and Adelle headed their way.

Adelle walked up to them and flashed her papers, breaking the couple's stoic stares into an accepted gesture to go on ahead, while Jules continued to marvel at his surroundings in awe.

The boat was massive and unlike anything he'd seen up close before. It had a red base that barely floated above the water, and unlike some of the other cruiser boats, there were no windows on the sides. There was, however, a captain's deck and a huge chimney stack in the middle.

Jules and Adelle climbed up the ramp, the rattling metal clanking with each step.

Once they hopped the edge of the boat, they got a true scope of just how big an effort their search would be.

"Holy, this thing is massive," Jules gawked. "It could take hours to search everything around here."

From the back of the boat pushing forward, there were dull green containers stretching long enough to fit a large car inside of them. Each one had a number of wooden crates inside. The two were surrounded by the steel, making it hard to see much around the corners.

At the far end of the ship was also a large wooden hatch that led to the bowels of the ship below.

Adelle made her way to the crate closest to them. "You're right—it might take a long time, so we'd better get started. The sooner we get out of this place, the safer everyone will be."

Her arm started to glow a pale blue and a layer of ice attached to her hand, jetting out like a switchblade. She jammed her hand into the thin crevasse of the lid and sliced it as if she was cutting open a letter.

"Oh, cool—so you're an ice Elementalist then?"

Adelle finished carving through the box. "Yeah, what about you?"

"Wind—just like Yuri was. So if you can crack open the boxes, I'll pop the lids off with ease and we can speed this up considerably."

"Good plan."

Jules walked up to the crate, and with a simple gust of wind he pushed the heavy metal lid to the side. Then he leaned over until his feet left the ground.

"Anything suspicious in there?" Adelle asked.

Jules started digging through. "No…just a bunch of dead fish. Smells awful, though." Jules dropped back to the ground, holding his nose with his left hand. "Let's crack open a couple more and see what we can find."

The two inspected crate after crate with hopes of finding something nefarious inside, but each one led to little more than fish, fruits, and a few random materials like nets and ropes. Nothing of substance by any means.

After opening a few dozen crates, Jules finally stopped and asked, "Hey…do we even know what we're looking for here?"

"Not really," Adelle replied, stabbing another crate as they got closer to the front of the boat. "When it comes to the Adenji gang, they're rather strategic in their plans. They don't have much interest in Human extermination like Luminosa. In fact, there've been rumors that on occasion they're actually willing to work with Humans. Well, at least the ones willing to fund them. But like Yuri said, they hold a lot of control over the waterfront area. They have sailors, construction workers, and some even say a few police officers and EC members in their back pockets, which is how they avoid getting into trouble with the law so often. It's a strange group, though. In a sense, they're one big family that protects each other…at least if you don't try to leave them."

They both kept working away, but Jules was listening intently.

"Lately," she continued, "it seems like they've been gaining more wealth and taking control of a number of businesses — or so the reports say — which means that they must be up to something big since Yuri and I have been investigating them for weeks now. Not that we've found much."

"Odd. I wonder what they could be planning? I guess we'll know if we see something other than this mass of fish I've been digging through."

Once Jules finished checking the last crate on the top deck, he joined Adelle by the hatch leading inside.

"Guess we head below?" Jules asked.

"Seems like it," Adelle replied. "We should probably let Yuri know that we're moving into the lower part of the ship, though."

"True." Jules pulled out his new communicator and held his finger against the screen. It lit up with the giant talk button he saw before, along with a series of names underneath. They were pre-registered contacts for him to choose from. He clicked on his brother and waited for the device's screen to turn blue.

Once it did, he heard his brother's voice. "Jules? Are you and Adelle okay?"

"Yeah, we're fine. We just finished checking the top deck of crates and we're moving to the lower part of the ship. Still haven't found anything. Well, minus a bunch of dead fish and some other random supplies. Can you give us any clue as to what we're looking for?"

"Wish I could, but I gave you all I knew. Just keep looking, and if there's anything that isn't in line with the haul of fish then take note and let me know. And remember, stay alert. The Adenji gang has eyes everywhere."

"Will do. Jules and Adelle, out." He slipped the device back into his uniform pocket as Adelle lifted the wooden hatch open. It let out a rusty screech. The entrance was nothing more than a void of darkness.

"Well, that looks ominous," Jules said unenthusiastically.

"It's too bad that Robin isn't here. He'd be able to light this place up no problem."

"Yeah, Minisc too, although getting him on a boat like this would be next to impossible."

Jules hopped down, using his wind element to carry him before lending a hand to Adelle as she dropped in next.

The two started down the belly of the boat and through the lines of even more crates, these ones slightly smaller but more abundant in numbers. The metal underneath them scraped loudly and as they continued to move deeper away from the hatch, the faint ray of light disappearing into the shadows.

"How're we supposed to see anything around here?" Jules asked. He was holding his hands out, gradually running his fingers across the slick walls, using them as his guide.

"Like this." A thin beam of light shone forward, cutting into the darkness that consumed the ship.

"Wait, is that your communicator?" Jules asked, pulling out his own device.

"Here, check the bottom of the screen. If you swipe left, it'll bring up a little button that looks like a flashlight."

Jules followed her instructions, and with a click he had a guiding light of his own to follow.

Since they were now free from the shadows, Adelle walked over to one of the crates and noticed that it was already open. She bent down and examined the word spraypainted near the bottom, reading it aloud. "Sandbags?"

Jules joined her, reaching into the box and feeling its contents. He noticed how light the brown sacks were.

"Hold on," he said. "There's no way these bags are full of sand." He pulled one out and heard a strange rattling noise inside.

"Okay…sand doesn't sound like that…" Adelle added.

Curious, she made a small cut in the bag, and a few grains spilled out. She noticed a translucent object inside.

"Well, this probably shouldn't be here." She reached in and pulled out a plastic bottle, half filled with a strange, green chemical.

She handed it to Jules, who shined his light on it for a better look. The first thing he thought of was when he and Minisc found those slime monsters in the sewers. It looked like the same colour of liquid that filled those containers.

Adelle kept digging. "There's more. And they're all sorts of colours, too…I think they're chemicals, but I'm not sure…nothing is labeled."

She held up a blue tube, filled with liquid. Because the tubes were unmarked, they had no way of knowing what was inside without testing them. Not that they should be experimenting with mysterious substances, and they knew this. They'd found something of interest, and now they needed to report it.

"Right, just give me a minute," Jules said. He was cracking open another crate and reaching inside. But when he did, he yelped. "Ow!" He fell onto his butt and grabbed his thumb.

Adelle spun around. "Are you okay?" she asked with worry.

"Yeah, I'm fine, but there's something sharp in this bag… and it's not the sand," Jules said curiously, wiping off the small trickles of blood.

In a subtle act of retribution for Jules' sore thumb, Adelle stabbed the heart of the bag, ripping it clean open. She watched as small grains of sand spilled out like water, but then she caught a glimpse of something else. More cautiously than Jules, she cleared out the mess and found a series of strange utensils. Surgical utensils. Needles, scalpels, and plenty other tools. She hurried over to the other bag and did the same thing, but this time she found plastic masks, more needles, and other strange items that looked like they belonged in an operating room. She cracked open one final crate and discovered even more chemicals.

"It's a full-on hospital lab down here," she said in wonderment.

"But why would all of these things be hidden in boxes down here?" Jules asked.

"I guess it could've been a bunch of medical supplies that were mixed in with a different shipment. Then again, I don't think they do chemical shipments…at least not like this. I mean, this stuff is unlabeled, in plastic tubes, and hastily sealed. I think it's fair to say that someone was using this ship as a hiding place for their tools. As for why, it's hard to say, but we should definitely tell Yuri about it."

"Right!" Jules reached for his communicator, but suddenly he heard heavy stomps begin to shake the ceiling. Dirt fell to the ground like rain and the boat began swaying. Jules stumbled onto his butt as Adelle grabbed the side of the crate for balance.

A wretched grinding sound pierced their ears, and Jules could feel the swaying of the floor underneath him as he tried to stand. "What's going on? Are we moving?"

"Looks like we weren't the only ones on this ship," Adelle said nervously as she grabbed Jules and lifted him up.

Worried, they quickly rushed back to the hatch in the ceiling while Jules continued to call Yuri on his communicator.

They came to a sudden halt, looking up at their escape hatch. "Wait…we didn't close the hatch, did we?" Adelle asked, though she knew flat out that they hadn't.

"Definitely not."

Jules shot up with a gust of air, throwing his shoulder into the hatch, but he was met with incredible resistance. The lid above failed to budge, and he came crashing down beside Adelle, rubbing the pain out of his shoulder.

Suddenly from Jules' coat pocket, they heard Yuri's voice. "Jules? Adelle? Are you two okay? I heard some sort of crashing. What happened?"

Jules grabbed his communicator. "Uh, we're not okay, no. We found a bunch of chemicals and medical supplies down here, but we think the boat is starting to move and we're trapped below. Someone sealed off the exit."

"The Adenji gang must've anticipated that we were coming. Be on your guard and see if you can find another way out. Remember, do *not* engage anyone unless they act first. I'm on my way."

"Yes, Sir." Jules put the device away and looked at Adelle. He could see the wheels spinning in the mind of the brilliant EA graduate.

"Jules — do you think you can fly both of us up if I can break through whatever is covering up the hatch?"

"Yeah, that's easy enough. But if I had to guess, they moved one of those metal crates over the top, and I don't know how you're going to break through it."

"I'm a lot stronger than I look. Just hold me up, okay?"

"Uh…okay," Jules said tentatively, but he did as he was instructed. Wind started swirling under his feet until he began to levitate, then he grabbed Adelle by the waist and hoisted her up to the hatch.

While Jules did all he could to keep Adelle steady, she began to punch the door as hard as possible. Chips of ice flew off her hand as it grappled with the metal, but even though she could feel progress being made, it would take far too long to escape.

"Damn it!" she huffed as Jules brought her back to the ground.

"How could we fall for such a stupid trap? They wait until we head underneath, lock us down here, and now will probably try to kill us. Then they can toss our bodies overboard and nobody would be the wiser."

Jules refused to give in so easily. "Not if I can help it. There has to be another way out of here. Let's head to the other end of the ship and see if we can find anything."

Left with no other choice, the two hurried back past the crates they'd opened and down the dark hall.

Along the way, they began to hear faint footsteps heading in their direction.

Acting fast, Adelle shut off the light from her communicator while also putting her hand over Jules' device. "We need to hide," she whispered, grabbing Jules' arm and pulling him into the empty crate to their left. They grew more and more anxious as they squished together in the cramped space.

"I can't move," Jules whispered as he wiggled his free hand loose.

"Shhh—just stay tight and be quiet."

Jules held his breath, his heart pounding as Adelle's head wedged into his chest. Their legs were trapped together, and in no way was their cramped quarters an ideal situation, but they were forced to make do. There was simply no time to fend for more breathing room.

Outside of their hiding spot, they could hear the thunderous footsteps growing louder. Except they quickly realized that it wasn't just one person walking toward them—it was two sets of footsteps, one of them a bit gentler than the other. The steps came from their left and continued along past them, but before they got far enough away for Jules or Adelle to feel safe, silence.

*Why are they stopping?* Jules thought feverishly. He peered over at Adelle, who tried to meet his eyes. The two were squeezed so close together their noses were almost touching. When the two locked onto one another, they realized they'd made one critical mistake.

Communicating only through looks of concern, they both said to each other, *We never cleaned up the sandbags.*

A deep voice bellowed, "Hey Serge, take a look at this." They could hear him kicking around the contents of one of the bags.

"Looks like we've still got some rats aboard. Hurry up and find them. The sooner we dispose of the waste, the sooner we can get this shipment back to the boss."

The two men, clearly part of the Adenji gang—and the reason Jules and Adelle were locked inside the ship—began walking again.

Seeing was impossible, but thanks to the clanking of their unexpected company's steel boots, Jules could at least predict where they were—and it was getting uncomfortably close to the duo's hiding spot. Each clamouring step sent signals of impending danger through Jules' spine.

He wanted to whisper to Adelle, but it was too risky. The men were practically on top of them.

Jules knew the orders handed to him. He was not to engage with anyone from the Adenji gang if at all possible, but it seemed inevitable at this point that they'd be found out. He needed to react while they still held the element of surprise.

He shot Adelle a confident grin. She didn't understand what it was supposed to mean—not until her partner began to squirm his way free.

"What are you doing?" her mouth said in silence, but there was no use trying to read lips in the dark.

The steps came to a sudden and jarring stop. This was his chance. Jules popped out like a jack in the box, his hands thrusting forward. A flurry of wind pulsed out, sending his opponent flying backward. The man crashed into another crate, crumpling to the ground. But unfortunately, Jules had made a grave error.

Unlike what he'd expected, only one of the men had been coming toward him. The other had been standing a few feet away checking another crate, and when Jules attacked, he whipped his head around to see the commotion. Of course, what he saw was Jules standing upright, hands positioned for an attack on his partner.

Unaware that he'd been spotted, Jules took a bolt of lightning to the face, sending him flipping over the edge of the crate and onto his head.

"Trying to hide from us, you dirty rats? Big mistake," the first man growled.

"Damn it, Jules, what were you thinking?!?" Adelle yelled. She leapt out of the crate, crossing her arms and encasing them in ice. More bolts of lightning ricocheted outward, but they did little to penetrate her defenses. She broke her shield and went on the attack. Pillars of ice flew forward, striking the man in the stomach and sending him tumbling backwards.

Her composure as an EA graduate who worked under Yuri was beginning to shine through. She grabbed Jules by the arm, yanking him up. "Come on, we're out of here!" Her generally polite and kind demeanor flipped like a switch into someone ready to take action.

They ran down the hallway, and with each step Adelle took, a trail of ice sprouted skyward, forming small walls behind her. The ice narrowed down the radius for their opponents to attack while she and Jules ran.

"Where are we running to?" Jules huffed, still rubbing his face from the pain.

"These two must've come in from another entrance, right? So that means there's another way out of here! And we're gonna find it."

After a minute of full-on sprinting, they saw a sign of hope.

"Up ahead! I see a door…that must be where they came from!" Adelle picked up her pace and soon reached the door. But when she ripped on the handle, her hopes were quickly dashed.

"Oh, come on—this is locked too!" Her eyes narrowed and she slammed her shoulder into the door, which refused to budge even more than the hatch. She was exasperated, but then she noticed the little lock slot on the door. An idea was forming in her head, but behind her and Jules she could hear the ice shattering and the thundering stampede of their killers approaching.

"I think I can pick this lock, but I need you to hold them off for a minute!" Adelle ordered.

"What? Do you even know how to do that?" Jules gawked, panic-stricken.

"We'll talk about that later—just cover me!"

"Right, I'm on it." Jules got into combat position while Adelle formed a miniscule shard of ice, just like a lock pick, and jammed it inside. Normally, there'd be the risk of having such a thin object break, like a lock pick, but in this case she could just keep reforming her ice until she succeeded.

"We've got you now," the man with the deeper voice said ominously. A bolt of lightning flew through the darkness like a rocket, striking Jules before he could react.

Jules yelled out in pain, holding his left arm as he fired an errant pulse of wind in retaliation.

"You okay back there, Jules?" Adelle frantically asked as she continued to tinker with the door. Despite a strong desire to turn back, she focused her full concentration to quicken their escape.

"I'm fine—I can handle this! Just keep working on the door!"

"You sure about that, kid?" said the man with the higher pitched voice. A burst of flames came rushing toward Jules, but this time he reacted, using his wind to disperse the fire. But once again, Jules' haste had brought about unforeseen trouble. Though he'd managed to shield himself from being burned, his surroundings weren't quite so lucky.

The flames sprung from crate to crate and soon started crawling up the walls. The fire attacks came to a stop, but the entire interior of the boat was quickly flooding with smoke.

With one final attempt, Adelle heard a click of success and kicked the door open. A burst of the cool lake breeze hit her face and she got to her feet. "Come on, Jules! We're out of here!"

As the two raced out the door, leaving the smoke and flames behind, they came to a skidding halt after realizing that they were on the lower base of the deck, which meant that they were only a foot or two above water. Water that was washing up onto the ship's dock. And to the left and the right, even more water.

"Looks like Yuri was right! They'd planned on shipping us out to sea!" Adelle said, nearly breathless.

"Well, I'm not letting that happen. Here!" Jules reached out his arm and grabbed Adelle's hand. With a gust of wind, the two launched high into the sky, then descended onto the main deck. Jules gasped for air, his hands on his knees as they landed.

"Are you all right?" Adelle asked, also slightly out of air.

"I'll be fine…doing that just…takes a lot out of me…but we should be safe now…for the moment, at least."

"I wouldn't go that far — we're still stranded in the middle of the lake on a burning ship!" Adelle reminded him. She definitely had a point; they were far from what anyone would consider safe.

During this lull, Yuri's voice could be heard from Jules' pocket.

"Jules, can you guys hear me? Are you okay? Your distress alarm is going off. Just hold on a little longer!"

"Better make it quick, Yuri!" Jules yelled back into the communicator. "Everything is on fire and we have nowhere — "

Before he could finish, the device was struck out of his hand by another bolt of lightning. Then a wave of fire rushed in from behind, but Adelle dove and knocked Jules to the floor of the ship. They could feel the heat from below, radiating up as if they were sitting on a stovetop.

"Not so fast. You two aren't going anywhere."

They looked up and saw their two attackers climbing a ladder to the top deck—one floor higher than where Jules and Adelle were standing.

Now that there was a bit of midday sunlight, the men's appearances could be seen clearly. Of the two, the one with the deep voice was bald and hefty. The other was skinnier and taller, but both of them were wearing sailor uniforms.

The heavyset man had significant burn marks on his arms and clothes, but that didn't stop him from casting flames down at Jules and Adelle.

Walls of fire surrounded the two, cutting off any path of escape. They scrambled to their feet, keeping their eyes on the two men while also feeling the waves of sizzling heat behind them.

"Looks like we have no choice but to fight," Adelle said. "Stay back—I can handle this one."

"No way! I'm still able to fight, and I can help," Jules argued, getting ready as a bolt of lightning streaked toward his head. He cast his wind outward and tossed the attack to the side.

"I'd let him fight, girly—you're gonna need all the help you can get." The larger man jumped off the top deck, crashing down with a thud hard enough to make Jules and Adelle stumble.

With sparks flying off his body and shooting out in all directions, the man began throwing his heavy fists at Adelle. He was expecting an easy fight, but that only allowed Adelle to demonstrate the skills she'd worked so hard to develop. Displaying years of intense training and extreme mastery of technique, she blocked the man's blows with ease. But Adelle also had something more distinct about her style—she was able to read the man's moves like a book, almost as if she'd fought him before.

Adelle moved with grace, chopping the man in the neck and dropping him to the ground. Casting her hand downward, she covered him in a layer of ice. She knew it wouldn't last long due to the intense heat, but she needed to buy all the time she could.

Spinning in the direction of the other man, she watched as Jules continued to battle against the fire Elementalist. His wind powers struggled to hold the flames at bay, and he was losing ground to the wall of fire behind him. Finally, he became overwhelmed and dropped to the ground, forced to dodge again.

"The boss warned us to be worried about you guys, but I guess this is the best the EC has to offer these days" the heavier man mocked.

Jules was seething. He got up and rushed furiously ahead, using his wind as a motor to increase his speed. He came face to face with the brute man, and with all his might he sent a blast of wind into his gut…but nothing happened.

The man scoffed. "This is the real world, kid. Weak attacks like that are nothing but a nice refreshment." Then he cocked his fist and punched Jules in the chest.

The breath shot out of Jules as he sailed a few inches above the deck, skidding to a crumpling halt beside Adelle. His eyes watered as he fought to breath.

Adelle heatedly bent down and helped Jules to his knees. "Are you okay?" But Jules just shook his head back and forth, struggling to speak.

Realizing that she was on her own, Adelle stood up with a menacing glare. "Why don't you try picking on a real member of the EC, you scum!"

But just as she was ready to go into battle again, she saw the other man getting to his feet.

*I know that I could handle these two on my own no problem, but trying to keep Jules safe at the same time is slowing me down…*

She was at a loss. Until suddenly, tidal waves of water gushed in from behind and began flooding the boat, dousing the flames that had been trapping them.

"Jules! Adelle! We're here!" Adelle whipped her head around, and from the stern of the boat she saw Yuri, running through the steam and smoke toward them. And he wasn't alone—he had five EC members with him as well, all of which appeared to be of the water variety.

"You made it!" Adelle beamed as Yuri dropped to his knees and picked up his unconscious brother. "Don't worry—he's alive. He's just a little stunned."

"All right, let's hurry to the boat and get him some medical attention. Leave everything else to the others."

Thanks to Yuri, and with help from the other EC members nearby, Adelle and Jules were safely escorted back to land. On the way, Adelle did her best to recap the situation and report on what they'd found, but that only brought up more questions than answers.

They did manage to recover a few of the supplies, but not many, which meant that investigations once again stalled. The two men in the Adenji gang were also pulled from the ship and taken into custody, but as was a common law of the Adenji gang, neither man said a word about the incident. No amount of bargains or reduced sentences would make them rat out their brothers and sisters of the Adenji.

On the way back while sitting in the boat, Jules lay on a stretcher. His burn marks were nothing severe, but the extreme heat and the punch to his chest had left him in a world of hurt. He was strapped down but conscious, and he could hear the brief conversation between Adelle and Yuri.

"I'm just not sure he's ready for this," he could hear Adelle saying. "I know it's an apprenticeship and all, but we're fighting real-life criminals here. The Adenji gang won't hesitate to kill him if they get the chance. I just don't want to see him get hurt."

He could hear that Adelle wasn't angry or frustrated—actually, she sounded concerned more than anything else—it still cut Jules deep. He recalled what she'd said on the boat while fighting: "Why don't you try picking on a real member of the EC?" The words were nothing more than a battle cry, though for Jules they represented a harsh truth. He wasn't a real member of the EC, and for good reason. Once again, he'd faltered when it had counted most, and he'd had to be saved by someone else.

# CHAPTER 7
## A COURAGEOUS HEART

AS ADELLE AND JULES HEADED OFF TOWARD THE PIER with their warrants in hand, the morning sun sparkled on the horizon.

Yuri watched, as a small group of butterflies fluttered in his stomach. No matter how hard he tried to shake it, he couldn't help but worry. Although his brother had grown considerably since starting EA, and had certainly found himself with far more real-world experience than he had any right to have, every time Jules joined a mission, Yuri would have the same lingering feeling of anxiety following him. Still, knowing that this was what his brother wanted, he had to accept the risks, and, in a way, that meant not sheltering him anymore. At least he could take comfort in Adelle being by his side.

Luckily, Lily was there to pull him out of his worries. After all, they had their own job to handle.

"They look so romantic walking together," Lily cooed, hands atop her heart.

Yuri smirked slightly as he started to walk, but not before saying, "Yeah, sort of like you and Minisc." He didn't bother to glance back, but he could feel the heat emanating off Lily's cheeks.

On their way to the warehouse, Lily asked, "So why'd you send Jules with Adelle anyway? Not that I don't enjoy getting to work with you, but I figured that you'd want to keep Jules from…well, from causing trouble."

"I thought about it. But in all honesty, Adelle knows more about the Adenji gang and their tactics than I do. I wasn't sure how she'd handle being part of the EC at first, but she's smart, driven, and strong. And more importantly, she's managed to do it through discipline, not just strength alone. We know that Jules is plenty strong, and he's certainly crafty, but he often acts without thinking. That's what gets him into so much trouble. I think that working with Adelle will give Jules a new voice to listen to instead of his brother lecturing him all the time."

"Hmmm, interesting. And yes, Adelle does seem like she's got a good head on her shoulders. Hopefully the two will be good for each other."

"And what about you?" Yuri asked with genuine interest, and maybe some slight concern.

"What do you mean, what about me?" Lily looked at him, perplexed.

"Well, if you're gonna be learning under me for the next few weeks, I think it'd be good for me to know what it is you're hoping to get out of your apprenticeship. I know that those two crazy boys drag you into a lot of trouble, but I've never heard you say that you want to be the strongest Elementalist like Jules, and you don't have the burden of expectation that Minisc carries. So what's your goal for the apprenticeship?"

Lily tilted her head and put her finger to her chin, tapping it. "Um, I guess my goal is just to keep learning. To keep improving myself little by little so that when Minisc and Jules do drag me into trouble, I won't be a burden. When I started school, it seemed like they were getting themselves hurt protecting me in every class, all because I couldn't defend myself. It always felt like I was just dead weight they were forced to carry around, not that they'd ever say that. But I don't want them having to worry about me all the time. I want to be able to defend myself. I want to be able to defend them too, and to be there for them with a smile. That's really what my goal is."

"I see. Well, I can certainly say that you've grown a lot since I first met you. And as for those two knuckleheads, they'd be lost without you, that much I'm sure of. So just keep doing what you're doing. I have no doubt you'll be every bit the reliable teammate you want to be."

At the end of the pier, Yuri and Lily reached the warehouse. Yuri took a brief look around; there was nobody nearby. He led Lily past the giant white garage and toward the door on the side of the building.

"So what are we looking for in here?" Lily asked as Yuri opened the door for her. She went to walk in, but the respected EC member held out his hand to block her.

"Not so fast. We need to be cautious. I know that the warrant allows us to be here, but that doesn't mean that if an Adenji spots us they'll be pleased to know we're snooping around. You need to stay on your toes at all times."

Lily paused to let his words sink in. With her life returning to normal, her constant paranoia of the worst happening was slowly decreasing, but she needed to remember that this wasn't school. She was back in a role with the EC, which meant having her eyes and ears open at all times. She needed to be prepared for anything.

She looked back at Yuri and nodded. "Right."

The two took a cautious peek through the door, first to their left and then their right. They noticed a massive amount of wooden crates stacked on top of each other, almost touching the lofty ceiling. They were stacked nonsensically, making the room look like a maze. Hanging lights were everywhere, and small pockets of sunlight crept in from open windows at the back of the room.

"I don't know quite what it is we're looking for, but just keep your eyes peeled for anything suspicious," Yuri said.

They started to the left, and after making their way past the first few crates in their maze, Lily gagged slightly and pinched her nose. "What's that smell? It's like dead fish! It's making my eyes water." She was correct—the pungent smell of thousands of dead fish piled on top of each other wafted through the warehouse like the lingering odour of death.

"If I had to guess, I'd say that this is where they store all the shipments that're loaded off the docks," Yuri said with a wave of his hand, directing Lily to follow as he walked down the far-left row of crates. "Just try to ignore it for now. Hopefully we won't be here long."

Once they reached the end, he stopped and whispered, "It doesn't seem like anyone's in here…" But he refused to believe that they were in the clear that easily.

They stalked up and down the rows looking for anything inconspicuous, but they saw nothing. No workers, no red flags, and certainly nothing of note.

After a good 20 minutes of searching, Yuri felt a small buzz in pocket. He reached for his communicator and saw his brother's name on the phone. "It's Jules," he said, tapping the button. "Jules? Are you and Adelle okay?"

"Yeah, we're fine—don't worry. We just finished checking the top deck of crates and are about to move to the lower part of the ship. So far we've found nothing but a bunch of smelly fish and some other random supplies. What is it we're looking for anyway?"

"We don't know exactly. Just keep searching and if there's anything that isn't fish related, or anything that looks unusual, then take note and let me know. Also, remember to stay alert. The Adenji gang has eyes everywhere."

"Will do. Jules and Adelle, out."

Yuri tucked the device away and he and Lily started moving once again.

It wasn't long before they heard a door close behind them. Lily came to a stop and a chill crawled up her spine. She spun in the direction of the sound and whispered, "Did you hear that? It sounded like a door."

"Be on guard. We're definitely not alone."

Lily's eyes darted back and forth, looking from the towers of boxes to the large three bladed fans spinning above them. She searched every suspicious nook and cranny she could find.

There wasn't much of note, but then Yuri yelled, "Lily, look out!" He grabbed her and they dived to the left. Lily let out a sudden cry from the tackle, and they both crashed to the ground, Lily landing heavily on Yuri's chest. Stacks of boxes began toppling down around them like dominoes. They smashed into pieces, and wooden splinters shot out of them that could easily puncture the two.

Stuck on the floor with Yuri holding her down, Lily slipped her left arm out and created a water barrier in front of them like a giant bubble. The sharp javelins of wood absorbed into the water, becoming soggy and wilted and not nearly as threatening.

Now safe, Lily dispersed the water as the broken shrapnel fell lifelessly to the ground.

"Thanks. That was a close one," she whispered.

"Yeah, you too. That was quick thinking."

Yuri pushed himself off the cold hard floor before lending a hand to Lily, who sprung up no worse for wear. She brushed off her uniform and examined the room, looking for the cause of the avalanche.

"That was no accident," Yuri said, following Lily's lead. Their eyes bounced around the room until Yuri caught a strange silhouette of a man from the top of another box tower. He took off without a word, hot on the trail.

"Whoa, where are you going?" Lily shouted as she began to chase after him.

The two sprinted through the long aisles created by the crates, whipping around the corner before seeing a door close by.

"This must be the back exit. Hurry!" Yuri said, ripping the door open and dashing through it.

As they chased the man down, they soon found themselves surprised to be in a far more crowded area with a decent sized group around them. Gasps and cries sounded, drawing even more attention as they watched the fleeing man shove people out of his way to escape.

"Faster—don't let him get away!" Yuri yelled again, following the same path the man had created.

Much to their shock, where they ended up appeared to be a public docking area with small motorboats all along the pier.

The man came to a skidding halt, his feet barely touching the edge of the wood before everything fell to water. He spun around, and was wearing a rather inconspicuous outfit that helped him blend in with others. If not for a glimpse of him back in the warehouse, Lily never would've figured him to be the man they were chasing.

"That's far enough," Yuri said. He and Lily closed the man off, leaving him with few options to flee. He could dive in the water, but that seemed pointless, as there was nowhere for him to swim to, not to mention that it would leave him defenceless. He'd either drown or be caught.

That didn't mean that he was beat, though, and this was a

lesson that Yuri knew all too well. The EC veteran stepped in front of Lily. "Stand back."

"What? But we have him!" she whispered.

"Remember, an enemy with their back against the wall is un-predictable...you don't know what he might do."

Yuri prepared for some sort of response from the man. Instead, the man dropped to his knees and bowed his head, clapping his hands together. He actually started to grovel. "Please, I beg of you. I don't want to go to jail. I was just doing what the boss told me to. It's not my fault, I swear."

"What on earth...is this guy serious?" Lily gawked. She'd never experienced a scenario where the perpetrator simply gave himself up. She glanced at Yuri, looking for some sort of leadership on the matter.

He whispered back, "Don't fall for his lies. He's up to something."

Lily nodded, on guard for any tricks.

Behind them, the crowd began to gather, with what felt like even more people than before joining to see the commotion. It was the last thing the two needed in that moment, but they had no time for crowd control.

"If you really want to give yourself up, then you can wait right there until the police arrive," Yuri ordered.

The captured man on the ground lifted his head, tears beginning to stream down his cheeks. Then he tilted his head to the left, starting to laugh. It was a slow, confident laugh, soon turning into a full-on cackle.

"What's with this guy? Has he completely lost it?" Lily asked. His high-pitched laugh made her throat tighten and she started sweating. She glanced to her right, wondering what had caused the hysteria, and then she understood. Far off in the distance, she could see a boat, freely floating toward the horizon. That ordinarily wouldn't be an unusual sight, but this boat was spewing smoke like a volcano.

"Yuri, look!" She pointed in the direction of the boat. Yuri's eyes grew wide as he shifted his focus toward the open body of water. And to make matters worse, he and Lily both felt their communicators violently begin to vibrate. "It's a distress call from Jules."

"They played us!" Yuri growled. He clenched his fist in a rare display of agitation and said, "Somebody must've tipped them off. They set us up!"

The Adenji man's laughing stopped, but a sinister smile remained on his lips. His eyes narrowed as he got to his feet, hunched over like a zombie.

"Don't you know that this is Adenji territory? We don't take kindly to EC members snooping around our business. So now you have a choice to make," the man said, lifting his head to look directly at Yuri. "Either you let me go free, and rush to save those who were checking the ship, or you allow them to die while you deal with me. So what's more important to you, those of your so-called family, or completing the mission?" His smugness was palpable.

Even though he'd posed the question, he didn't care what answer came of it. In truth, regardless of a response, the Adenji member had no intentions of being caught. He wanted to have his cake and eat it, too.

He raised his hand parallel to the cobblestone dock, unleashing a ferocious wave of fire. The crowd around them gasped, with some dropping to the ground in terror.

Lily countered, spreading her hands apart to create a wall of water big enough to scale the width of the dock. She absorbed the fire with ease, protecting Yuri and the crowd behind her.

The moist spray of her shield floated through the air. The flames holding steady, she said, "Yuri, you need to call the police and save Jules and Adelle. Leave this guy to me. I can handle it."

Yuri looked pensive and, for the first time, he questioned what to do. The thought of his brother being hunted by the Adenji gang petrified him, and if not them, then being swallowed by the lake would be his fate. But he had Adelle there to help, and surely she could handle things. But how big of a risk was this? She was still green too, and if he rolled the dice wrong and lost his brother, he'd never be able to live with himself.

When it came to working at the EC, he knew that he needed to trust those around them to do their job. But in most cases, that didn't mean abandoning Lily, who wasn't even a true member of the EC, to try and handle an Adenji on her own, not to mention protecting a crowd of petrified people behind her.

With all the different scenarios swirling in his mind, Lily could see that he was stuck. So she hastily made the decision for him.

"Stop worrying about me and go save Jules and Adelle right now!" She barked the orders with authority rarely heard coming from her. Those in the crowd were surely wondering who was actually in charge by hearing her brash tone. Not that she wanted to force Yuri's hand, but she knew that he could never arrive at a conclusion in good conscience if it meant leaving her behind. Jules was blood and his beloved younger brother, but in his eyes, Lily was as much a family member as anyone—she was like his little sister. Leaving her in such a dangerous situation would bring him no comfort.

The fires ceased, and Lily dropped her barrier, the remaining flickers dancing by her.

"I've got this, Yuri. Go save Jules."

Finally snapping out of his dilemma, Yuri nodded. "All right. But remember, if things get too dangerous, protect yourself and let this guy go free. I'll send help as soon as I can."

Yuri took off like a bullet, leaving Lily, a frightened crowd of people, and an Adenji flame Elementalist to resolve their issues without him.

*I guess it's up to me now*, Lily realized. *I just hope that Yuri can make it to Jules and Adelle in time.*

She fixed her gaze across the pier, sizing up her opponent. Based on his opening flamethrower move, his attacks were nothing she couldn't handle.

Then again, it was possible that had been another acting job, causing, seeds of doubt to sprout in her mind. What if this was part of his plan, to get her alone and the Adenji to freedom? If the gang had such insight, knowing that Jules and Adelle would be searching the boat and herself and Yuri the warehouse, then perhaps their foresight extended further. Had they been played again?

Although she couldn't be sure, it wouldn't make a difference in the end. Jules and Adelle needed to be rescued, and she needed to stop this guy from escaping. That was her task, and nothing could keep her from accomplishing it.

Behind her were mounting whispers of petrified Humans. None of them were leaving, and she couldn't understand why.

"Everyone, you need to get out of here right now—it's too dangerous to stick around!" she hollered, channeling her inner Hero of Light.

What would come as a surprise to her friends and those who knew her best, however, was far from a spur-of-the-moment reaction. The usually kind and joyful girl had spent countless hours with The Hero of Light, training in secret. Not only on her skills as an Elementalist, but also on projecting a ray of hope to those in fear.

Nobody had ever worried about the Hero of Light. Whenever he'd arrived on scene, it was a foregone conclusion that the criminal would be stopped, that those around him would be safe. She wanted to create the same sense of comfort, even if she herself had doubts about her abilities.

Unfortunately, her demands were instead met with another laugh from the man in front of her, rife with mockery.

"Didn't anyone ever teach you, girly? Bystanders make great bargaining chips. Nobody's going anywhere."

The man spread his hands wide and surrounded the pier with walls of fire. More gasps and cries rang out, and any chance of escape evaporated.

Fire wasn't particularly an issue for Lily, but to extinguish the flaming walls would leave her open to the Adenji. She refused to take her eye off the slippery gang member, knowing the risks that would present. It also made maintaining everyone's safety far more difficult.

Smoke rose to the sky and, for a split-second, Lily prayed that help would arrive in the form of someone in the crowd—perhaps an Elementalist who could use water to the level needed in this situation. That would allow her to focus on the Adenji, and the Elementalist could douse the flames.

Seconds passed, and, unlike the flames, her hopes were slowly being extinguished. Everything fell onto her shoulders.

With the cage of flames all around and the only escape being into the water, the Adenji man concentrated his fire element into his hands. From under the sleeves of his jacket sprang two long whips, making him look like a lion tamer. He channeled the flames into his whips, smacking them off the ground emphatically.

*He's using his element to create a weapon now? This might be a problem.*

While Lily silently stood deep in thought, the Adenji member chose to berate her.

"What's wrong, girly—cat got your tongue? Remember, you chose this by chasing after me. What was it that you told that other guy? Not to worry about you? Well, it's time that you try and back that up."

He shot forward, swinging his flaming whips at Lily, forcing her to dart out of the way.

"You're in over your head, girly!"

The heat from the whip warmed Lily's face as she feverishly leaned back, narrowly dodging each hit. The second whip cracked through the air in her direction, but she managed to hold her hands up, the water from her element enveloping them. With the rope gripped tight, steam formed, helping dull the smoke beginning to surround them. The makeshift weapon lost its luster, and with a fierce rip of the whips, Lily pulled the ropes, her opponent tumbling forward like a puppet. She dropped the ropes at her feet and then shot the man a proud look of confidence.

"I said that I could handle this and I meant it! I'm not letting you get away." She raised her hands to the sky, and multiple bubbles of water formed around her. "Here's a new one for you!" She threw her hands down and hundreds of water balls surged at her opponent, crashing into him before exploding like a heavy rainstorm.

Lily refused to wait around while the man did his best to defend himself from the pelting. She kept up her water assault, doing all she could to force the man into defeat. Multiple hits later, he dropped to his knees again, pounding the stone below him.

Lily could feel the gazes of people standing behind her, silently cheering her on, and it filled her with motivation. To them, she was an official member of the EC — they didn't know that she wasn't the strongest of the world's Elementalists. All they knew was that this young water Elementalist put her life on the line in the name of justice and to do what she knew in her heart was right — protect the innocent and take down this criminal in the process.

With her opponent forced to his knees, she prayed that the police and other EC members would arrive any second. She refused to show fear, but the sooner their fight was over the better things would be.

Besides, she not only lacked the legal power to make an arrest, but she also lacked the tools to ensure that it was done safely.

The man started to panic, suddenly struck with hysteria. "No! I can't let this happen. I can't be taken to that place again! If I do, the boss is gonna kill me. He knows that I'll crack this time — they all know it."

*Is he doing his acting job again? No, something is different this time. I think he's really snapped.* Lily kept her guard up while still glancing at the crowd with her peripheral vision. They'd all remain stuck there, either until help arrived or until the Adenji member was down for good. Only then could she safely free them. Until that happened, she was responsible for the well-being of them all.

The man stood up again, his head twitching nervously.

"I can't. I won't. Not again. I won't go back to that cell. The Adenji are my family now, and I'll do whatever is necessary to please them."

Flickers of a flaming spiral started to form around him.

Lily gulped, feeling the increase in his power. A heavy thud pounded in her chest with anxious anticipation. Then the man made his next move.

"I refuse to let my family down. Not this time!" He raised his hands and spat out droves of fire, each more ferocious than the last. "Infinite hell flames!" he shouted, beckoning his fiery weapons.

Once again, Lily created a barrier of water stretching far beyond what she was comfortable with, but she had to protect everyone around her. The flames crashed into her shield, the collision shoving her back a few feet.

"Give up, girly — you'll never be able to extinguish my infinite hell flames. Just like the name says, they'll never run out. I can keep this up all day," the man laughed with another dramatic mood swing.

*He has to be bluffing. Nobody has infinite energy. I just need to hold on!* Lily bit down, drawing a drip of blood from her pink lips. She refused to be pushed back any further. The soles of her shoes were being ripped apart as she dug her heels into the cobblestone. If she could just continue to hold strong, then she'd be able to test the man's bluff.

Being defensive used far less energy than producing an attack of such ferocity, so if she could wait him out, the man would have no strength to fight back. At least, that would've been the case if she wasn't creating such a large shield to cover everyone. This was taxing her as much as, if not more than, the man's raging flames. Not that it mattered, however. There was no choice to be made. She couldn't narrow the shield and risk people being caught in the crossfire...unless they narrowed the width for her.

From behind the water barrier, Lily began to plead with those she was protecting. "Everyone, I need you to get closer to me. Please, get as tight together as you can so that I can narrow my shield and focus on deflecting the flames. Hurry!" The cries for help began to murmur through the crowd as her message was passed along.

Some were working to huddle in, but they lacked the urgency that Lily was requiring. Every second mattered. Frustration was setting in, until finally a booming voice of a sailor began yelling from the back.

"Everyone listen to the girl! We need to huddle together and stay behind her!"

That caused another man to yell similar commands, and before Lily knew it, the warmth of those she was protecting surrounded her. A group of Humans, most of whom had no connection to one another aside from waiting to be engulfed by flames, came huddling in with locked arms. They stood directly behind Lily, allowing her to focus her shield.

"We believe in you, girl! You can beat this monster!" said one of the same men who'd made orders earlier. He coaxed the crowd into a series of chants, encouraging Lily and filling her with hope. She had aches in her arms and tension in her body, but with their support she could shove it all to the background and continue her fight.

"Thank you, everyone—I promise I won't lose!" Lily took a step forward as the rising steam created an ominous fog around the pier.

Nobody behind the wall of water could see the strain on their attacker's face or the pain ripping his body apart from the inside out, but Lily could sense it. She could feel the man's strength beginning to waver, and with it, her opening would soon come.

And then it did.

The flames exploded into the sky like fireworks, sparks flying violently through the air. The man dropped his arms to his side, his face contorting in angst. He was struggling to breathe and desperately trying to keep his body from finishing him off internally. But he was having little luck.

Sweat dripped from Lily's bangs as she stared down her opponent.

Then the Adenji changed his tune once again. Lily watched him drop to his knees and begin begging, "Please don't hurt me! I was only doing what the boss ordered. I didn't want to do it, I swear. This isn't my fault!"

Lily stomped her feet into the ground and clenched her fists. "I've had just about enough of your wild temperament. First you talk about not letting your family down, then you throw them under the bus by saying that they made you do all this. Nobody made you do anything! Quit trying to blame others and take some responsibility for your actions."

The man kept his head down, still pleading for his life, which left Lily unsure of what her next steps should be. Anything beyond what had been done already would be considered excessive force, though she needed to remain on her toes.

Then she heard Yuri's voice from her hip pocket.

"Lily, are you there? Are you okay? The police are on their way any moment!"

"I'm okay, and everyone's safe. What about Jules and Adelle?"

"Don't worry, I have them with me. We're fine. Once the police arrive, let them take things from there, okay? We'll be back soon."

Just as Lily tucked her communicator away, she finally heard the marching footsteps of the backup she'd been waiting for. The waves of water came crashing through the back wall of fire, dousing them into oblivion.

"Finally," Lily sighed. At last she could take a step back, as six men, two police officers, and four EC members came rushing through the crowd.

It was over.

With the Adenji man taken into custody, Lily looked out toward the lake. The boat remained in the distance, giving off a cloud of smoke while also lighting up the water and sky with an orange glow. Lily knew that her friends were safe. She could breathe easier now, but until they were back in front of her, a heavy lump would continue to sit in her stomach.

Luckily, she'd have a host of new fans talking over each other to distract her for the time being. They wanted to thank her, to tell her how great she was and how glad they were that she stood up and protected them. Each compliment filled her with a loving warmth, and she smiled at the group in return.

*I don't get why Minisc hates this so much. It's actually pretty cool.*

# CHAPTER 8
## STARTING OFF SMALL

DAY TWO OF MINISC'S APPRENTICESHIP STARTED much earlier than the first. He agreed to meet Mr. Howland before work to do some introductory training on Celestial Light.

Putting aside his hatred of early mornings, today his stomach jumped with anxiety for a different reason. The thought of working with Mr. Howland and training with such a revered Elementalist brought a lot of uncertainty. What could he expect from Howland? One thing he did know, however, was his new teacher wouldn't be going easy on him.

Minisc still had doubts about his own ability to learn the technique, but he knew that he had no choice. This is what his father expected of him — to protect everyone. Especially after the events that took place the day prior on the waterfront.

Lily had told him about all the details that night, which only raised his anxiety more, knowing that his friends had been in danger and he wasn't there to help. Of course, he was more than glad that Jules' injuries were minor, but it only meant he needed to learn Celestial Light that much faster. If he didn't know, how would he be able to stop his friends from getting hurt?

Behind the EC was a stadium the size of a football field, with a white-domed roof that looked like a bubble. It was another new building that had come about recently.

When Minisc walked through the front doors of the bubble, a wave of nostalgia overcame him. In many ways, the inside of the building felt much like his short-lived stint in *The Underground*. He could tell instantly that some of the technology that *The Underground's* lead scientist Reynn and her team had implemented in that secret training facility had finally come to the surface. It made him smile, knowing that the woman's hard work had borne fruit. Now, hopefully, his would do the same.

The inner walls of the stadium were silver-chrome metal, with bars climbing up the roof like a grid. Multiple fields were laid out horizontally from one end to the other — Minisc counted eight in total — and each of them was surrounded with satellites. Those satellites produced barriers to ensure that any attacks from various training sessions wouldn't blend into each other. To the side was a fully loaded gym similar to EA's facilities.

*This place is incredible. But it's so…empty.* Minisc tried to find another soul within the building, but to no avail, most likely due to the sun having not yet risen.

When he peeked into the window along the wall of the gym, he finally noticed the only other person crazy enough to be up at that hour. The man was doing push-ups rapidly. Minisc's eyes bulged once he realized that it was his new mentor: Mr. Howland.

*You've gotta be kidding me. What is he doing working out this early? He's gonna give himself a heart attack.*

Not sure if interrupting Howland was a wise move, Minisc decided to tiptoe into the gym, but the creaking of the door drew his new mentor's attention. He stopped mid-push-up and glared up at Minisc.

"Hello, Sir…" Minisc said with a lackluster wave. He was trying to mask his fatigue, but there was no hiding it; five in the morning was just too early for him to function properly. Even his father had never forced such a torturous hour on him.

Howland dripped with sweat, his face hardened and unreadable. He got to his feet and said, "Good — you've finally arrived. We have no time to waste. However, before getting into the crux of Celestial Light, you will need to loosen up. Start with 100 push-ups, 100 sit-ups, and 100 chin-ups. Then you will do a five-mile run. That should be enough to get your body suitably warmed up."

"Warmed up?" Minisc gawked. *This guy is gonna kill me.* But before he could lodge another complaint, the glare he received from Mr. Howland was enough to shut down any further argument.

The workout alone was enough to make Minisc's bones ache. Yet just as when he started with his father, and again with Ms. Wright, he concentrated on the bigger picture. The workout itself wasn't too far off from what he'd been asked to do in the past. The difference this time was that there was more to come. He should've been done, sitting on the couch with ice taped to his limbs, not preparing for round two.

After he completed the warm-up routine, Mr. Howland took Minisc to one of the training fields. It was covered in dirt, just like the one in which he'd fought against Ignis at EA, and it also had a few painted white lines around it.

"Now that you're sufficiently warmed up, I believe that it's time to see exactly where you're at. I will need a baseline of your power. So try to achieve Celestial Light right now, the exact way your father taught you."

"Okay — here goes nothing, I guess." Minisc sucked in a deep breath. He relaxed his body, trying to put any early morning aches out of his mind. He closed his eyes and let his element flow through him as best he could. His insides were already burning, and feeling his power bubble up only intensified the sensation.

Mr. Howland stroked his beard as he stared at the boy. It was like he was watching a lab rat. Even so, he could sense the power emanating from Minisc. It was palpable.

Minisc's body began to shine, and gradually he began taking the familiar form. He was glowing majestically, his hair flying all over the place as wind around his feet propelled outward.

Mr. Howland had to fight to conceal his jaw dropping. *I can't believe it. At his age, he's actually reaching his peak while tapping into Celestial Light. And he's maintaining it. Perhaps his father was right?*

"There, that's…that's as far as I've got…" Minisc said, breathless. He was fighting the intense pain brought on by aiming to hold such power. In a battle, however, he'd be borderline useless.

He held strong for a few seconds, but eventually the light exploded like fireworks and he collapsed to his knees—just as he had done all those times at home.

"Come on, I really thought I had it that time…" he complained, feeling defeated.

Minisc got to one knee and then glanced up at Mr. Howland, seeing the confused expression on his mentor's face. "What happened? Did I do something wrong?"

"Not you exactly, but it's clear that your father has done a lousy job in teaching you. I can't say that I'm surprised, though. He achieved that skill far easier than he had any right to."

Confused, Minisc asked, "What do you mean?"

"This is not how one is to approach Celestial Light. What you just did there, although miraculous, is not sustainable."

Minisc furrowed his brow. "I'm still confused."

Mr. Howland sighed. "Let me explain it this way: It's clear

that what you have been trying to do is achieve Celestial Light at 100% power, something only your father and Dusk have managed. I dare say that seeing you hold the power for as long as you did was quite shocking, but it's clear that in a fight you would never survive."

"Of course I was using my full power—what else was I supposed to be doing?"

Mr. Howland shook his head. "Remember, this state acts as a power multiplier. And not only that, it does it exponentially. This means that at its peak, you are far stronger than you could possibly imagine. Trying to combine your maximum power while using Celestial Light at 100% is far too much for your body to handle. In all honesty, it's a bit of a miracle that what you've been doing so far hasn't killed you. You need to start on a much smaller scale. Let's try this again—but this time, you will follow my lead."

Mr. Howland closed his eyes and sparks started to fly off his body. A dancing aura of electricity formed around him. The waves rippling through the air were enough to push Minisc back.

"This is what it is like using Celestial Light at 5% of my power. The two mixed together increase my element far past what I would normally be able to achieve on my own." Then Howland disappeared in the blink of an eye, suddenly appearing behind Minisc. "My movement, my strength, and my senses are also increased, and because I am not multiplying my energy beyond my means, I can hold the state for much longer."

Minisc spun around, shocked. It was like he was staring at a completely different person.

"Now I want you to try tapping into Celestial Light. However, begin with only 1% of your maximum power."

"Only 1%?"

"Yes. Concentrate. Repeat the same internal feelings from when you were in Celestial Light, but focus on regulating your energy before it has a chance to build. Only let it bubble inside you for a moment, and then cut it off like creating a dam to block water. Suppress your energy in that state to only about 1%."

"Uh…okay. I guess I can try that." Minisc followed the same routine that he'd done over a hundred times by now. As his mind relaxed, he felt the change in his body. But this time, instead of attempting to stoke those flames to their fullest, he capped his power. Once he opened his eyes, he looked down at his arms and saw no signs of glowing under his skin. He looked normal, and he also *felt* normal. His body still tingled with the warmth that was brought on by achieving Celestial Light, but in terms of strength, he noticed no difference.

"Did…did it work? I don't feel any different."

Mr. Howland rubbed his temples as he watched Minisc wave his arms up and down, trying to see if he could notice any changes.

"Allow me to remind you that this is only 1% of your strength. Of course you feel no different," Mr. Howland sighed. "In this state, the change in your body is negligible. If you are keen to feel a difference, then let's take it up a notch. Try repeating that process, but aim for something a little higher—say, 8%. See if you can do that without putting too much strain on your body."

"Okay, here we go." Suddenly, Minisc was filled with confidence. He dropped his power down to zero, and then repeated the same steps as before. This time, through deep concentration, he began to allow his power to surge just a little more. Admittedly, he was guessing at what an arbitrary number like 8% of his power actually was, but he knew that there was no chance of him being bold enough to bring that up. So once he felt comfortable but not overwhelmed by the burning strain in his muscles, he relaxed and capped his power.

He definitely could feel a difference. It was strange—he felt lighter on his feet, like he was floating. For good measure, he looked down; as expected, his feet were still firmly planted. Also, he felt more in tune with his senses. The smell of the dirt at his feet, hearing even the smallest movements from his arms…even his vision seemed crisper.

"Whoa, this is amazing! And it was so easy," Minisc said, attracting another sharp look from his instructor.

"Again, you are only at 8%. I assure you that anything past 10% won't have you thinking this is easy."

Minisc immediately realized his mistake. "Right…sorry. So now what? Should I try and go further?"

Mr. Howland shook his head. "I don't think that will be necessary. You might not feel it now, but your body is chewing through energy at a rate you're not yet accustomed to. It will be best to hold this state for the rest of the day…if you can. Let your body become acclimated to it. Then once I believe you're ready, we can try upping it to higher levels. That said, it would be ill advised to send you into the world without at least letting you explore your strength beforehand." Mr. Howland looked at his wristwatch. "We have another hour until Robin will arrive to take you on patrol. I think that now would be best to do some self-training."

Mr. Howland watched and made his assessments as Minisc trained. *For someone so young to actually reach that level of power… wow. And not only did it not kill him, but he was also able to maintain it for a moment. Even his father was not that gifted. His technique isn't quite where his father's was when I began teaching him, but the boy has that same unwavering commitment. Although, he's not as brash and forefront in his convictions — he's much more like his mother in that sense. But still, I can see the fire in him. He's prepared to see this through to the end.*

The next hour of training pushed Minisc to his limits. He

wanted to rescind any idiotic thoughts he'd once had of Celestial Light being easy. Once he was done, his body wanted to keel over, and the day hadn't even really begun yet.

When Mr. Howland left for his office, Minisc took a few minutes to relax and rest his overworked body. But the incredible difference in his power could still be felt. His movements were quicker, his element brought about an explosive power that he'd never experienced before, and for the first time, he began to truly realize just how strong his father was.

Minisc heard the door to the training facility open and he scrambled to his feet. He looked across to the entrance and saw two people heading in his direction. Unsurprisingly, Mr. Howland was returning a few minutes before the facility actually opened, and beside him was Robin, with his jovial smile and bright enthusiasm along for the ride. Even the early hours couldn't bring him down. *How does he do it? I'm still a zombie.*

Robin threw his hand in the air with a big wave and called out, "Good morning, Minisc!"

Minisc raised his hand with slightly less enthusiasm as they approached, but still he returned the smile.

Then he noticed a set of clothes in Mr. Howland's arms — a new uniform from the looks of it. It matched the clothes that Robin was sporting.

Mr. Howland handed him the uniform. "This is yours now. Try not to damage it."

"Okay, thank you." Minisc took the uniform and headed for the change rooms right away. When he returned, Mr. Howland had disappeared again, leaving only Robin to wait for the boy.

"Congrats, Minisc. Now you're officially part of Mr. Howland's team — uniform and all. Looks good, too!"

Minisc smiled sheepishly. He always felt strange wearing the gaudy uniforms of the EC, but he was slowly growing accustomed to it. At one point, Lily even offered to make a few adjustments to his clothes for him, but he declined. There was no way he wanted to stand out the way she did.

That wasn't an issue with Mr. Howland, however. These uniforms weren't the standard red and white threads of the EC. These were navy blue, with minimal embellishment to them. They did have a patch on the arm with the universal symbol for light Elementalists, but that was about it.

"Where's Mr. Howland?" Minisc asked.

"Oh, he went off on his own for a bit. Guess it's just you and me today. But don't worry, we're just doing some patrol on the west end of the city. If we hurry, we can catch the next train and get there within the hour."

Minisc was happy to be working with Robin for the day. Mr. Howland might've been a tough and forceful teacher, but Robin struck him as the complete opposite. Kind, nurturing, and a positive ray of sunshine. Working with the EA grad would definitely teach him things that Mr. Howland never could. Also, the young graduate was top of his class, and both Yuri and Mr. Howland obviously thought very highly of him.

Once they reached the west end of Toronto, the two started walking around the main streets, keeping an eye open for anything of note. Robin waved at everyone, from kids to the elderly, which was quite the opposite of what Minisc was wanting to do. He'd never been big on drawing attention to himself. But around Robin, much like being with his father, it appeared to be inevitable.

"It's such a beautiful day," Robin beamed. "I think that this is one of my favourite parts of the job—getting to walk around and enjoy the sunshine, meeting all these new people. It just makes me feel so connected to the world." Robin kept talking while Minisc remained quiet, simply observing. He couldn't help but be fascinated by the aura that drew people to Robin.

But apparently, Robin was more perceptive than Minisc gave

him credit for. The EA graduate stopped and turned back to look at Minisc, noting his lack of enthusiasm. "Sorry—I guess this isn't exactly your cup of tea, is it?"

"What do you mean?"

"You know…stopping and talking to everyone we see. You strike me as more of the quiet type, the kind of guy who just wants to go about his work. Sort of like Mr. Howland."

"Oh." Minisc wasn't sure if he liked the comparison, but Robin did have a point. Ingratiating himself with strangers just wasn't his forte. "Yeah, I guess you're right. It's just…growing up, I had a lot of strangers pestering me, trying to get the scoop on my father and stuff, so I'm a bit on the cautious side when it comes to dealing with strangers."

Robin laughed but understood. "That's fair. I guess I never really thought about it like that. Well, don't worry. It's not for everybody. But personally, I think for me to be like the Hero of Light, I need to be visible. I want people to recognize me and know when I arrive on the scene that they'll be safe."

Minisc had to hand it to his partner. In many ways, Robin was incredibly similar to his father, a fact that made Minisc feel strange. In one way, it brought him relief. To know that people like Robin existed and that they were eager to fill the massive void his father's retirement had left was comforting. On the other hand, he wondered why someone like Robin wasn't being taught Celestial Light. Minisc made a mental note of that question for later.

A few more minutes of walking around the city, and then suddenly Robin came to a stop.

Minisc asked, "What's up? Why'd you stop?"

"I smell smoke. Hurry!" Robin took off like a charging bull, leaving Minisc stunned. The young Elementalist whipped his head around, trying to find any sort of smoke signal, but there was nothing in sight.

Minisc chased his partner down anyway, but even while using Celestial Light he failed to keep up with Robin's athletic prowess. It was a marvel to watch.

Eventually, he noticed a small apartment a few blocks away, with streaks of smoke rising from it and up to the sky. Outside stood a group of people hollering and pointing to the higher floors of the building. Minisc could hear fire trucks in the distance. But when he finally managed to arrive at the smoldering building, Robin was nowhere to be found.

As the flames spread further, Minisc looked around for a water Elementalist to help. The fire trucks would arrive soon, but there might still be people stuck inside, and time was of the essence.

Before he could panic, Robin shot out from the top story window, much to the shock of the crowd. In his arms were two small children. Everyone gasped as he sailed through the air, his majestic glow and bright smile still intact. He grabbed the branch of a nearby tree and swung downward to safety.

The crowd of people came rushing over to the area, including Minisc, while Robin looked down from his perch.

Minisc stood in awe of what he'd just witnessed. Again, it reminded him so much of his father. The sharp instincts, the sheer bravery. Minisc barely had time to blink before it was all over. There was no denying that Robin lived up to his status as the top graduate out of EA.

Robin dropped down from the tree, grinning from ear to ear. In his arms were the two children, both beaming with excitement. There was no fear at all on their faces, no doubt a by-product of Robin's infectious attitude. Even in the face of danger, he brought joy to people.

Robin handed the kids to their joyous mother while graciously accepting the thanks being heaped upon him.

When the day finished, Minisc returned to the EC, ready to

continue his training of Celestial Light. Although before that would happen, he wanted to talk to his new mentor about something.

Howland was preparing to leave his office when he tossed out a simple question to Minisc. "Did you learn from young Robin today?"

Minisc lingered on the man's question, speaking in a reflective tone. "Yeah, I actually learned a lot. I can see why he graduated at the top of EA. He's incredible. We came across a burning building—he smelled the smoke from a few blocks away and took off before I could even react. By the time I'd arrived, he'd already saved the children inside and escaped unharmed." Minisc paused for a moment. "But it's not only that—he brings out the best in people. He makes them feel safe wherever he goes. Honestly, while watching him today, it struck me that he's more like my father than I've ever been..." Minisc trailed off, looking down for a moment.

"And you're now wondering why I am teaching you Celestial Light instead of him?"

Minisc's head shot up, not sure how to respond. The man's tone implied a trap, even though he was correct in his assumptions.

"I guess you could say that. Don't get me wrong—I don't want to stop, but wouldn't it be better if he learned it too? I mean, if I can learn Celestial Light, then surely he can as well, right? Then Luminosa wouldn't stand a chance."

"Yes, indeed that would be ideal. And if it came so easily to others the way it did to you, I would imagine Luminosa would be learning it as well. But in the real world, life rarely works out that way." Mr. Howland pulled out a binder from his drawer. "You see, I've kept tabs on every student in their third and fourth years of EA ever since the school opened. I do it so that I may select the top graduate each year, and then take them on as a student of my own. Some years, I've even forgone selecting one because I could not in good conscience trust them to join my line of work. However, in Robin's case, I watched him at the Tournament of Elements in his first year, and I have been monitoring him ever since. I, too, thought that if there was anyone on this planet that carried the strength to make full use of Celestial Light, it would be him. I had hoped that would be the case well before your father prepared his retirement."

Mr. Howland turned to face Minisc, his tone becoming quieter. "Although, as incredible as Robin is, he struggled mightily to grasp the power. We spent an entire year training his body and his mind, but no matter what we did, he didn't appear to reach the necessary level—not the way you did so easily this morning. He never even came close to approaching 100% power, let alone by accident. It's fair to say that he was not blessed with the gifts that you were granted. As your father described it to me, there is a wealth of untapped potential inside you that appears to manifest at certain times, like when you were facing your old friend Ignis. Robin does not have such potential locked away. At least not that I have been able to determine."

Minisc was surprised by the mention of such a private fight, but he safely assumed that his father had informed Howland of every important detail over the last year and a half.

"It's not necessarily fair that you're the one who should be burdened with this reasonability just because you were born with this incredible strength stored inside of you, but it has become increasingly clear that this is the case. What you did this morning—it was uncanny, even at 8%. Only one with a blessed ability could pull off that feat. It would appear that the genes of your father have evolved into you."

"I see..." Minisc trailed off. He knew as The Hero of Light's son that certain advantages were handed to him as an Elementalist, and the blessing of power appeared to be one of them.

Not to discredit his work ethic and training, but learning under his father matched with a gifted ability did perhaps mean that he was the only one ready to pick up where his father had left off—even if Robin was more of a fit when it came to personality.

"You can feel the pressure, can't you?" Mr. Howland asked. "Your father mentioned that you might be struggling with everything that's happening and knowing that you're the only one capable of learning Celestial Light. It's an enormous responsibility, trying to be that beacon of hope he stood for during all those years."

Minisc lifted his head and nodded. "Yeah. It's just…after seeing Robin today and how far ahead of me he is and how bright and loving his personality is, he feels like such a better fit for the role instead of me. I appreciate what my father represented, but I've never wanted to be like him. Sure, I want to help people, but the publicity and fame that comes with being a symbol… well, I have no interest in any of that."

"You're probably correct on the matter," Mr. Howland said bluntly. "Robin is far more suited than you to bring calm to people. Still, that doesn't necessarily mean that you're not fit for this role. Your father represented many different things to many different people, so it's important for you to carve your own path. And I'm sure that will come in time. For now, your first objective should be continuing to learn Celestial Light. Prove you are able to master it. Without that power, the rest of your worries in regard to your father are irrelevant anyway."

Minisc still looked less than convinced, so Mr. Howland took a different approach, one he wished that he'd taken more often with his previous pupil.

"Look, Minisc. I know it's a lot. Truly, I do. I can't even begin to imagine what it's like to be 16 and have the burden you've been handed. But you can't get too far ahead of yourself. There is no shortage of talent at the EC, and they are here to help you in your fight against Luminosa. Perhaps learning Celestial Light falls onto your young shoulders, but you are not alone in this. Trust in your father's belief, and also in the belief in yourself. With that, you will find your way."

Minisc smiled slightly. For the first time, he'd seen a hint of compassion in his new mentor.

"Thank you, Sir."

# CHAPTER 9
## A SECRET OUTED

THROUGH THE YEARS, THE ADENJI GANG HAD FOUND themselves with a number of enemies—not only from the EC, but also from various smaller gangs lingering in the shadows.

Not that they cared. For the most part, they had nothing to worry about when it came to small-time threats. Thanks to their large size and the strength they possessed, they were considered the top of the food chain in the underworld. But for a man like Brooklyn, that was simply a speed bump on his way to the top.

Normally, he'd never bother with such trivial minded grunts who lacked the foresight of his plans, but after meeting with the Adenji gang's leader, Dominos, and cutting a deal to help his own needs, they should've been on good terms.

But that couldn't be further from the truth.

Because the EC managed to discover the incoming shipments, which carried much of the requested supplies from their deal, Brooklyn knew that their agreement was about to fall through.

There was only one problem: The doctor was already fulfilling his end of the deal.

At the moment, Dr. Jarrad resided somewhere in the Adenji compound, working on something that required a genius mind, all while Brooklyn and his team were sitting idle and gaining nothing for it.

"Why are we doing this again?" Bex asked, pulling on her pale-blue pigtails in frustration.

"Because we're not giving the doctor away for free, and since the Adenji gang refuses to play nice after failing our deal, we're doing things the old-fashioned way," Bronx replied.

They peered down from the nearby rooftops. Along the horizon stood the Adenji compound, a symbol of self-indulgence if there ever was one. Concrete gates stretched ten feet tall, locking in the mansion—a horizontal structure with a flat roof, certainly much different than a traditional house. The palace spread back until it connected with a massive forest that went on for miles. The trees were towering, filled with thick leaves that made seeing any further impossible. Getting lost in that forest would mean traveling in circles for hours, not that the Luminosa members cared.

Only a few days ago, they were invited into the Adenji compound, their second visit to the luxurious palace wouldn't be nearly as welcoming.

Bex glared at the mansion, her hair flapping in the wind. Her oversized black coat dragged along the ground, becoming torn and ragged. She cracked her knuckles in disgust. "This is stupid. I hate having to sneak around like some sort of rat. Why can't we just storm the place and kill them all?" A mist of ice formed from her fist in anticipation of meeting an unsuspecting Adenji.

Bronx held his hand to his head in annoyance. "How exactly would that not get us killed? Besides, it'll be better if we don't make a scene. Once we find the doc, we're gonna have to flee and stay low anyway. If we don't, chances are the Adenji will start hunting us, too."

"And it's not like the EC will be coming to our defense."

"Considering the EC's the reason we're here in the first place… yeah, I'd say so. And if we don't come back with the doc, Brooklyn might never listen to my ideas again."

"Oh, and what a shame that would be. You're the reason we're in this mess in the first place."

"Shut it," Bronx snapped blithely.

"We don't even know where that lunatic doctor is, and this place is massive," Bex complained, crossing her arms. "I don't suppose Brooklyn gave us a map?"

She made a valid point. They were going on almost no information. The one thing they did know was that the Adenji gang were trying to preserve bodies, though it didn't seem like it was for experimentation. So then what was it for?

"No clue. If I had to guess, the doc must be wherever they're storing those bodies. If we find the bodies, we'll probably get some answers about their plans, too."

Bex shrugged. "Guess we'll just have to figure it out once we're inside. Now let's get a move on. I'm sick of waiting."

Bex waved her hands, creating a slick ramp along the side of the obscure building. With the go ahead, she hopped on her slippery path, sliding down like a stealthy snowboarder. Bronx followed close behind until they dropped into a small alcove between the buildings.

After they reached the side of the Adenji mansion, Bex peered up at the towering concrete gates blocking their path. "So, Mr. Stealthy, how do you suppose we get over these walls without getting caught?" Compared to her diminutive stature, they looked like mountains in her path. Then again, she only had one simple option. Scaling them would be easily done by jamming a few icicles into the walls and using them to climb. But without knowing what traps lay on the other side, it seemed risky.

For good measure, there was also electric wiring wrapped around the tops of the walls, which Bronx took notice of. Those would pose an issue as well.

"Maybe there's a way in through the back?" he wondered.

The two began cautiously moving along the walls, trying to find a crack in the infallible armour that was the Adenji mansion.

"Seriously, this place is so much better than any of the hideouts we've been in before," Bex noted. "Brooklyn really needs to up his game. These guys are living rich while we're spending most of our time in caves or sewers. A girl can't live like that."

"Feel free to join these ingrates if you want, but when Brooklyn finally does achieve his world of Elementalists, I highly doubt that you'll be welcomed back with open arms. He's not exactly a forgiving person."

Bex held her hands up, shaking her head. "Whatever. Let's just remember that he's the one sitting with his feet up while we're doing the dirty work here. And if he's not here to tell me what to do, then I say we're doing this my way now."

Before Bronx could fully grasp what she meant, Bex turned to look at the wires all around the compound. She licked her lips with a demonic smile as her body began to glow.

"What the hell are you doing?" Bronx whispered forcefully. But it was too late—the devil child had already set her plan into action. Icicles began to fire outward, slicing the wires and sending them snapping back to their tethered ends. Sparks rained down from above, as Bex took out the electricity bit by bit. "Hurry up and blow the biggest hole you can in the concrete— that'll draw everyone's attention," she demanded.

Bronx remained in a state of shock, confusion, and anger. He fought the urge to pound his partner into the ground, but knowing that she'd carry out her plan regardless, he stuck his palms out and mustered all the strength he could. A shadow ball exploded into the concrete base of the wall, blowing chunks of debris everywhere through the smoke and dust.

"Okay, genius—now what?" he seethed.

"We run!"

"That was your grand plan?!?" Before Bronx could explode in frustration, Bex took off to the back of the compound. Bronx hightailed it behind her, his pulse quickening to an unhealthy level. They turned the corner to find even more compound walls, but doubly concerning was the roaring stampede of Adenji on the other side of them. Only a slab of concrete, maybe ten feet tall, kept them from a hoard of Adenji gang members who were ready to kill without hesitation—not that Bex and Bronx wouldn't return fire with just as much gusto.

Bex glared at her partner, yet she also looked quite satisfied with herself. "See? Now that we've drawn the guards away, we just need to get inside. Then we can start looking around."

This time, Bex jammed some ice pegs into the wall, clinging on to them before tossing herself recklessly over the top.

"And what if your little plan didn't draw away all the guards?" Bronx shot back, still following his new, diminutive leader.

"You mean like this guy?" Before them stood an Adenji member, his head affixed to the wall like some sort of abstract human painting, his eyes and mouth frozen before he could even react. "Then we just turn him into art," Bex cackled with glee.

"Fine— let's just hurry and get inside."

After penetrating their first layer of defense, they began moving with more stealth, looking for anything resembling an entrance. It was slim pickings, but once they reached the back of the compound, Bex pointed to a series of windows on the second floor. But instead of providing a beautiful view of the outside world, the indents in the concrete were entirely sealed with what looked to be vines. An unorthodox and odd solution to say the least.

Before they could make a move, Bronx held his finger to his mouth. "Shhh! Do you hear that?"

He picked up on the shouting of orders coming from different directions, along with a stampede beginning to surround them.

Bex huffed, "Let me just kill them already!" But Bronx refused a head-on assault once again.

He held his hands to the ground. Waves of pitch-black fog began to spew outward, plunging the morning sun and every-thing else around him into shadows. "Seal off the paths with your ice. We're going through the window," Bronx ordered.

Following his instructions, Bex stretched her arms parallel to her body and created thick walls of ice on either side of them. "There—that should seal off any path to us. But we better act quick…that ice isn't going to hold up for long."

Finally, with a second to think, Bronx turned his aim toward the vine-covered window overhead. Another shadow ball rock-eted off his fingertips, crashing through the window.

"Hurry, let's go!"

The entrance firmly secure, Bex jammed a series of ice picks into the wall, climbing up them like an acrobatic monkey. Bronx took a more methodical approach, scaling the wall like a moun-tain climber and using the picks to hoist himself up. They heard their makeshift barriers shatter below, followed by a deafening boom, but it made no difference. They were finally within the Adenji compound.

Now inside the room, Bex turned around and, thinking quick-ly, blocked their impromptu entrance with a similar wall of ice.

However, doing so left them in eternal darkness. Through the shadows, they heard small, precise, machine-like beeps.

"What is this place?" Bex asked. "It's not like any bedroom I've ever seen."

"Who cares? Come on—there's gotta be a light switch around here somewhere." Bronx, being more adjusted to the dark thanks to years of maneuvering his own fog, made his way to the back of the room and flicked a switch.

The lights in the room turned on, but they were dull and underwhelming.

"Well, that was useless," Bex muttered. The ceiling lights barely lit up the center of the room, let alone illuminate the corners. But it was enough to at least gather their bearings and figure out where they were.

The two tiptoed around, trying not to blow their cover as the wood below their feet creaked slightly.

"This wasn't what I was expecting," Bex said, examining their dim and disheveled surroundings.

"No kidding. You'd think that he could afford to clean up his guest room a bit."

Bronx picked up a photobook from a nearby dresser, and he almost felt small pangs of empathy while flipping through it. Each page revealed pictures of a younger Dominos. A happier Dominos. He was all smiles, giving hugs to a woman who Bronx could safely assume was his mother. She was rather tall with long, curly black hair and a beaming smile. But as he continued to flip through the pages, gradually the woman started to appear frail and brittle. "I think I know what he's trying to do," Bronx said.

"And that would be what?"

"Revive the dead."

"Are you kidding me? That's just stupid. Nobody is reviving any dead people—even the doctor can't make that happen."

Bronx nodded in agreement. Bex was right; the idea was absolutely absurd. There had to be another explanation.

Giving the room one final check, Bex cracked open the closet door. Piled-up clothes tumbled to the ground, most of them dresses and skirts.

"I think Dominos might have some explaining to do," Bex

surmised sarcastically. But in the back of the closet, she spotted a faint light that stretched deep into a long pathway.

"I don't suppose you brought a flashlight, did you?" she asked Bronx. He turned around, wondering what his partner was going on about, but suddenly saw that she was gone.

"Bex? God, I swear this girl is going to be the death of me," Bronx sighed, rubbing his temples. Feeling like an accidental babysitter chasing down a restless tot, he walked on through the dim tunnel, following Bex toward the faint light at the end.

The tunnel spiraled deep underground, lights only partially paving the way. When Bronx caught up to Bex and they reached the bottom, it was like they were in a different place altogether.

But it certainly wasn't an ordinary place, nor was it underground caves. It was a hospital—a dark, dreary, and abandoned hospital. There were doors on each side of them, and tons of pipes and wires climbing the walls.

"A hospital floor," Bronx observed grimly.

Bex whispered, "Okay…maybe this lunatic really *is* trying to revive the dead."

Unsure of where to go, the two started walking down the hallway. Suddenly, the threat of the Adenji gang retreated to the back of their minds. They were more curious about what they were seeing.

Bex tried the first door, which squealed open. The hinges were ancient and rusty, and the two were lucky that the door didn't fall off.

"Guess we know why he wanted to preserve bodies," Bronx said.

Inside looked much like an ordinary hospital room—if it had been waiting for an apocalypse. The lights were depressing. Much of the room was empty. Holes were rampant on the walls, and the floor tiles were broken and dirty. The only thing of note was the bed and equipment. Or, more specifically, the person laying in that bed and the equipment that was binding them to it.

Bex came to a stop. She raised her hands with that killer glare of hers, but Bronx stretched his arm out to block her.

Curious, Bronx approached the bed. What triggered Bex's reaction was the sight of an elderly woman, laying tucked underneath the sheets with her eyes closed. Her brittle, silver hair was spread out across her pillow, her hands intertwined like she was in a deep stasis.

By looking at her, she didn't seem threatening, certainly not with the cords wrapped around her head and arms. There were a series of tubes that ran in and out of her as if she was a science experiment. Each tube had a different set of fluids pouring into the woman and was attached to machines that were the source of the constant beeping. On the table beside her were a handful of bottles filled with pills, alongside tubes of thick, red liquid that looked like blood. It matched one of the tubes that dripped into her motionless body.

"I get it now," Bronx said, eyes widening. "He's not reviving the dead—he's trying to keep his mother alive. But hey, I was pretty damn close." He smiled smugly.

"Yeah, yeah, who cares about some woman? We need to find the doc, remember?"

"Right. He must be close."

They exited the room, opting not to touch the equipment. If the woman was related to Dominos, he'd probably be alerted somehow if her pulse came to a sudden stop.

Back down the hall they went, cracking open more doors. It was the same scene behind all of them: more bodies clinging to life. It was exactly like a hospital.

When they finally turned the corner, they heard nonsensical groaning and fiddling about.

Bex flung open the door to see their prize. "'Bout time. Hurry up, doc—you're coming with us."

The scientist spun around, stumbling backwards. "What're you two doing here?" he asked, gobsmacked.

"Deal's off. We're taking you home."

Dr. Jarrad, dressed in white and looking horribly weathered, pushed his glasses up from his stubby nose and stared skeptically at the two, thinking about his goals. He turned to the decrepit body he was currently examining and stroked his goatee. "I was hopeful that by taking this job I'd find what I need for my research, but none of these bodies are of any use. They're infected with common Human diseases, just waiting to die. They're no good to me."

"Good, then we're in agreement. Brooklyn wants you back with us," Bronx stated bluntly.

They all hurried back into the hall preparing to make their leave, but before they could depart, 10 members of the Adenji stormed down the stairs. They stopped at the other end of the hall and locked eyes with Bronx, Bex, and Dr. Jarrad.

Dominos flanked the rest of the members, his fist gripped and the veins in his forehead bulging.

"I knew I never should've gotten into bed with people like you. You're only out for yourselves. So be it. I'll make this place your grave."

Dominos cast his hand forward, and thorny vines from under his sleeve shot outward and darted toward the three.

"Bex! Ice!" Bronx commanded.

"On it!" She summoned a protective wall stretching the width of the hallway. From behind the wall, Bex hurriedly asked Bronx and the doctor, "Okay, now what's the plan?"

Luckily, Dr. Jarrad had a solution. "There's another entrance that'll lead us to the forest. It's how Dominos has been smuggling in the chemicals he plans to use for keeping these bodies alive."

"It's a start. Let's go." Bronx gestured for the doctor to lead the way. Heavy blasts smashed the ice wall behind them, but as they rushed to freedom, Bex touched the walls every few feet or so, summoning pillars of ice. She was creating an obstacle course that would be tough for the Adenji to break through, nevermind gain ground on them.

Whipping around another corner, they passed through an open gateway. Bronx and the doctor rushed up the stairs while Bex flew by like a bullet. She could see a sliver of daylight up ahead.

"Take this," Dr. Jarrad said, tossing up a key card from his pocket. Bex caught it, sliding it down the middle of the slot and turning the light green. After a beep, the three found their entrance and escaped.

"Well, that was a close one…" Bronx panted, his hands on his knees.

"Yeah…but look around. We're not free yet," The doctor reminded them.

The three managed to escape the compound, but they were still lost. Surrounding them were mammoth trees that succeeded in shrouding them in darkness.

"Guess this is the forest behind their compound?" Bronx asked.

"Looks like it. Hey Doc, you know a way out of this place, by chance?"

Dr. Jarrad stroked the whiskers on his goatee, staring thoughtfully at the trees above. "Based on our location in proximity to where we were underground and our distance from the compound…yes, I know which way to go. Follow me."

# CHAPTER 10
## SOMEONE IN NEED

FOR MINISC, MUCH OF THE WEEK WENT BY JUST AS IT had begun. Up before the crack of dawn, he'd spend his mornings working on Celestial Light, training his body and mind to the extreme. He was also growing accustomed to the intense strains being placed on his muscles.

Once he understood just how much wisdom Mr. Howland carried from his decades of experience, as well as the gradual comfort of learning Celestial Light, the dread of his mentor's training began to dissipate. At least a little.

The first week of his apprenticeship flew by, and Friday arrived before he knew it. Based on how Monday had started, he never imagined that the time would pass by so quick. There was so much more for him to learn—not only from Mr. Howland, but also Robin.

The boy with whom he spent much of his week learning under was the very definition of positive influence. And, much to Minisc's surprise, he found himself enjoying working with the

Hero of Light fanatic. Still, he was looking forward to seeing Lily and Jules again, though Lily continued to spend most days after her apprenticeship helping redecorate Minisc's new home with Don.

Minisc always found it strange and yet somewhat comical how much his father seemed to have in common with Lily. She was like the daughter he never had.

Jules, on the other hand, kept rather quiet about his experiences. That was fine by Minisc, though — it gave him the ability to focus on his goals for the time being.

Since he'd be continuing with his training of Celestial Light long past the end of his apprenticeship, he wanted to take advantage of his time in the EC and learn all that he could in the process. There was much to be educated on, from the way Robin carried himself to the way he interacted with those around him. Those were invaluable traits to learn, and what the role of the EC was truly about.

One facet of the job Minisc had already learned about was how much of priority the EC placed on visibility. That meant daily patrols along the city streets, being seen in public, and the ability to react to issues at a moment's notice.

For two rookies, tasks such as patrol were more than enough to keep them busy, even if the streets they repeatedly walked along remained quiet all week. But that only gave Minisc more time to observe Robin in action. There was so much about the Hero of Light hopeful that fascinated him.

Everywhere they patrolled, Robin always took to waving and smiling, if not full-on stopping to chat with strangers on the street. This was obviously a far cry from Minisc, who attempted to stay quiet and mind his own business. The more the two worked together, the more Minisc could see Robin's desire to create a world of peace for all those he met. It didn't matter if they were Humans or Elementalists — Robin treated them all like family.

Part of Minisc envied the boy's easy-going nature. He'd love to be that relaxed all the time. Nothing ever seemed to bother Robin, and he was always ready for the next challenge.

Handling publicity was one skill that Mr. Howland could never teach. Much like Minisc, he avoided the spotlight with an incredible degree of effectiveness, so much so that most of the younger members in the EC probably didn't know that he worked there, or of his incredible knowledge. Even for Minisc and Robin, who he was supposed to be in charge of, seeing the man for more than an hour at a time was a rarity. He'd give them their orders at the start of the day and then disappear for his own investigations. Being on the streets or otherwise visible to the public in any way were the last things that the veteran Elementalist worried about. He had bigger fish to fry.

Robin had a little more information on the investigations Mr. Howland continued working on, but even he didn't have very much intel. They were patrolling Etobicoke for a reason, of that they were sure. But after four straight days of visiting different areas and seeing nothing, it was hard to even fathom what the man could be digging so intently into.

After his morning training finished, Minisc joined Robin in Mr. Howland's office. The two were waiting to receive their orders and close out the week.

Minisc took a few moments to relax, and soon Mr. Howland returned to his office. Like usual, he wore an expression of keen focus and strict determination as he blew past them and straight to his desk. He opened up the drawer, forgoing any acknowledgment of those in his charge, and pulled out two small folders, placing them on the table.

Figuring that they were important, Robin grabbed the top folder and opened it up for him and Minisc to glance at. On the first page of the lengthy document, there was a picture of a man in his early to mid-thirties, bald and with a small brown goatee on his chin. He wore a sharp suit, his face was scrunched in anger, and his eyes were shifty. Even though it was just a photo, it seemed as if he was watching them.

"Um, Sir? Who is this?" Robin asked. He held the picture up to eye level, examining any scarce details and expecting this to be some sort of a test, but that was far from the case.

Minisc answered the question as he read at the information on the next page. "'Dominos…Last Name: Unknown…Age 31… Element: Earth…'" Minisc read off the man's profile like he was reading a baseball card, until he reached the bottom that said, "Affiliate: Adenji Gang." He read those final words again making sure he wasn't misreading them. "Wait…the Adenji gang?"

Thoughts of the Tournament of Elements flashed into his mind. He recalled the former leader of the Adenji gang being obliterated by his father's Solar Impact. But, more recently, he knew that Lily and Jules were investigating them as well with Adelle and Yuri.

Robin put the paper on the table. "Are they not the group that controls the lakefront? I thought they were just a bunch of money hungry Elementalists who tried to rule the underground and black markets?"

"You would be correct in that assumption," Mr. Howland said, his tone softening. "Over the decades' long history of the Adenji gang, they've always stayed somewhat out of the forefront, sticking to the areas they have claimed as their own in the lakefront district. However, as you're both aware, the former leader of the Adenji gang, Marco Lindell, was defeated by the Hero of Light during the attacks on the Tournament of Elements by Luminosa. Now he resides in Penatang for the rest of his days. Though that was good for society, it also left a large hole in the gang's leadership—a void that, over the last year, has been filled by the man in the picture: Dominos. Since he rose to power within the group, they've taken advantage of the distractions caused by Luminosa, lurking in the shadows and out of sight from the EC. There has been much more activity from the group in the last few months, and if we continue to ignore them, we could find a new, formidable foe to worry about before long. It's better to quell this threat before it becomes a bigger issue."

Robin flipped through a few more of the notes, glancing over them. "He was last seen in Etobicoke? So that's where we think we can find this guy and stop him?"

Mr. Howland glared over his glasses, hanging low on his nose. He directed a cold and terrifying stare toward the boys.

"This is not a man you are to engage in battle with. Understand? He is a supremely dangerous threat, and he will not hesitate to kill those he sees as a roadblock in his plans. Unlike the former leader of the Adenji gang, this man holds no ethical standards. I am giving you these folders so that you can keep your distance from him. If you are to run into this man as you patrol the streets of Etobicoke today, then you're to get as far away from him as possible. If he chooses to follow you, one of you are to call for help immediately. I cannot stress this enough: You are only to engage in a fight if you are defending your lives. Our goal in going to Etobicoke is to look for any oddities around and to let our presence as the Elemental Council be known. We are not looking for a fight with Dominos or the Adenji gang. Are we clear?"

"Yes, Sir." Minisc and Robin said together bleakly. If Mr. Howland, a man who'd witnessed every threat that faced society, was making this demand, then there was no question that it was for their benefit. But did that mean that Dominos himself was even stronger than Luminosa? Minisc decided that it was probably best to not find out.


Etobicoke was a massive part of Toronto's west end. It was

a quiet area of the city, and the Adenji gang's presence was definitely felt there. This was especially true near the lakefront, where the gang held a strong and influential presence—even more so now that Dominos had taken over as their new leader.

Back when Luminosa had set its sights on attacking different areas of the city, even they didn't bother going near Etobicoke, which remained relatively unharmed. One of the reasons for this was because they had no interest in being forced into a turf war, as that would only detract from their goal. Also, the area was clear of most Humans—not many of them wanted to live in an area where a gang of Elementalists ruled the land.

Overcast clouds lined the horizon, but the sun still tried to fight through the afternoon sky. The smell of a fresh lake breeze permeated the air as Minisc and Robin walked down one of Etobicoke's many streets. As for their mentor, Mr. Howland had opted to take a different route, leaving the two on their own.

After a few minutes and seeing nothing of interest, Robin decided to make conversation, as he often did. "Have you ever been to Etobicoke, Minisc?"

Minisc looked around to the many small buildings surrounding them, trying to recall any remembrances from his youth. "Not that I can think of. What about you?"

Robin laughed, throwing his hands behind his head as he walked. "Yeah, actually. I grew up here, right up until I applied for EA. Then my parents decided to move a little closer so that I could get to school easier. It's been a few years since I've returned, but I still remember these streets well."

"Really? I never would've guessed. But I suppose that's a good thing, though—at least you can keep us from getting lost."

"Yeah, that shouldn't be an issue. Walking around this place still feels like second nature."

As the two continued talking, they walked past a local shopkeeper who was brushing the dust off his front porch. The elderly man glanced up from his broom, his eyes lighting up followed by a bright greeting.

"Robin, my boy! What are you doing here?" He waved for the boys to come over.

"Hey, Mr. Matthews—yes, it's been a few years, hasn't it?" Robin said wistfully as he and Minisc headed over to the man. "I hope Rascal has been keeping out of trouble these days!"

As if on cue, out from the front door of the shop meandered a fluffy, orange cat. It let out a soft purr and trotted over to Robin's leg, rubbing up against him. Robin reached down and picked up the feline, the soft fur brushing against his chin as it snuggled into his chest.

"Aw, you missed me! I missed you, too." Robin cooed.

After reminiscing for a moment, the man turned and fixed his gaze on Minisc, who was standing by somewhat awkwardly. He watched the interaction entirely confused, but he could see Robin's personality shining through. The EA grad had left Etobicoke just a few years ago, and people still remembered him fondly.

"You know, Robin?" Mr. Matthews said. "Everyone here still talks about that time you beat up those robbers who stole from Mrs. Coco's store when you were a kid. You should really drop by there and see her. I'm sure she'd love to know that you're around for a visit."

"Oh, that would really be awesome. But right now, me and my partner are actually on patrol for the EC."

Mr. Matthews studied the boys' uniforms, not recognizing the untraditional EC garb. Even so, he grinned wide and said, "So you finally did it. You actually made it to the EC. Edin must be so proud of you—nobody wanted to see it happen more than him. How is he doing these days, anyway?"

"Oh, he's doing what he can. He's a fighter, that one. That's for sure." Robin said with a small laugh, but Minisc detected a bit of sadness.

"Good, good. Glad to hear it." Mr. Matthews said, taking the cat out of Robin's hands. "Well, I don't want to take you or your friend away from keeping us safe, so go on and get out of here. Just remember—if you're ever around for a visit, feel free to drop by. For you, the full menu is on the house."

Robin smiled and bowed graciously. He waved goodbye to the man and started off, Minisc following behind.

"What was that all about? Who's Edin?" Minisc asked.

"Oh," Robin said quietly. "Edin is my little brother."

"I didn't know you had a brother."

"He's seven years younger than me. In truth, he's the real reason I went to EA…why I want to be the peace bringer of the world. It was his dream. He loved elements, and we both loved The Hero of Light. But unfortunately, he was born with a weak heart, and he's constantly been in and out of the hospital ever since."

"That's awful. I'm sorry to hear that."

"It's been hardest on my parents, never knowing if and when they might wind up back in the hospital. But he's a fighter—he refuses to give up. He makes me proud every day to be his brother."

Minisc thought back to his conversation with Mr. Howland. He knew that he was the one tasked with Celestial Light, not Robin, but if he had to picture someone who completely fit the mould of what his father's successor should be like, Robin was it. He was skilled, smart, dedicated, and personable. He embodied these things while also carrying an enormous weight on his shoulders, and he handled it all with perfect grace—far more than Minisc ever could. It made him wonder: Was the young EA grad *really* incapable of learning Celestial Light? For a moment, Minisc thought about broaching the topic, but ultimately decided against it.

They walked a little further down the street until they came to a bend in the road. It split off into two directions, one to more houses and the other to a parking lot with a nearby grassy area. There was nothing of interest in terms of the houses, but the grass-filled park was a different story.

"Minisc, Robin…are you there?" The voice belonged to Mr. Howland, but it was coming from their communicator devices.

"We're here, Sir — what is it?" Robin asked.

"We have a report of an injured child near South Park, close to your current location. Can you guys check it out?

Minisc and Robin looked at each other and nodded. "Yes, Sir — we're on it."

It didn't take long for them to find the area in question. When they reached the park, Minisc said, "Look, laying on the grass," gesturing to a body in the distance. But it was hard to tell if it was the injured child without getting closer.

"Maybe he's the one Mr. Howland was talking about. Come on, we should check on him," Robin said. He took the lead and the two hurried over, determining that it was, in fact, a collapsed child.

Robin dropped to his knees and placed his fingers on the boy's neck. It was ice cold, and there was a red rash that looked quite painful.

"He has a pulse," Robin determined, and they both breathed a sigh of relief. "But he doesn't look good."

The two stared at the boy with genuine concern. There was a sickly look about him — his head pointed downward, bandages on his arms, and his overalls tattered with holes and rips. His hair was greasy like it'd never been washed, and his limbs were almost skeletal. He couldn't have been any older than five, but they'd have to wait for the boy to wake from his slumber for that level of information. If, in fact, he was just sleeping and not in a coma of sorts.

"Should we take him somewhere?" Minisc asked. "I mean…

we can't just leave the poor kid here." He glanced around the park and then across the street, but saw nobody around that might be his parents.

"Yeah, let's can take him back to Mr. Matthews. We can treat him there."

"Good thinking. I'm gonna call Mr. Howland too and let him know what we're—"

Suddenly, Minisc's voice became trapped in his throat. He tried to mouth the words, but he couldn't.

Robin began coughing and sputtering, his eyes wincing in pain. Then he dropped to the ground.

The little boy remained on the grass, but now he was awake. And his eyes were filled with bloodlust.

Stabbing the side of Robin's left leg was a jagged spike that had shot up through the grass.

"Robin!" Minisc cried out. He fired off a reactionary Lum Bomb, causing the still groggy boy to scramble to his feet and jump back.

"What is wrong with you?!?" Minisc shouted at the boy. "He was trying to help you!"

The strange child got to his feet and erupted with mockery-filled laughter. "Hey, don't look at me—I'm just doing a job. You guys should be more careful approaching strangers in Adenji territory."

He was short, but when Minisc caught a full glimpse of his face, he realized that he was far older than just a kid. *They set us up! This is bad.*

Minisc tried to keep his eyes on the Adenji member while also monitoring Robin. A small pool of blood was forming from his partner's leg, leaking out from where the spike had punctured him.

"So, what will it be?" the Adenji man asked. "Gonna help your friend here and let me escape, or take me on and let him writhe in agony? It doesn't matter, honestly — there's no right choice here."

"Of course there is," Minisc countered. "That wound might hurt, but it isn't fatal, and I know that Robin would rather that I take you down first." Minisc prepared for battle, but he wasn't ready for what was coming next.

"Stand down, Biggs," a man's voice ordered, carrying the tone of someone in full control. "And go make sure that they have no other EC around. I'd prefer to have this done quietly."

A chill ran up Minisc's spine. He'd never heard the voice before, and yet somehow, he just knew that they were in real trouble now.

# CHAPTER 11
## HARD DECISIONS

THERE WAS SO MUCH RUNNING THROUGH MINISC'S head. Was he dreaming? No, this was real. Things were too vivid, the voice behind him too crisp.

He leapt back next to Robin, who was still wincing and laying on the ground.

A few feet away stood the man they were most concerned of: Dominos. He looked exactly like his picture—thin frame, bald head, simple goatee. And yet his appearance paralyzed Minisc.

Since starting EA, Minisc had stood face to face with many of the evilest threats the world could offer up, but something about Dominos was different. A cold, lingering smell of death followed the man.

In that moment, a number of thoughts ran rampant through Minisc's head. *What should I do? There's no doubt that this is Dominos. It has to be. But what's he doing here?* Minisc took a quick glance around, seeing nobody.

"If there's one thing about the EC, it's that they're predictable." Dominos pulled out a tape recorder, and pressed play.

*"Minisc, Robin…are you there?" "We're here sir, what is it?"*

It was the exchange between Howland and the boys from earlier. Dominos ejected the tape, dropped it to the ground, and stomped on it. "Hacking into your communicators was pretty easy, too. I'd suggest upping your security next time. Not that it matters anymore for you two." He took a step forward, and Minisc shuffled back.

"What do you want with us?" Minisc asked.

"With you? Nothing," Dominos responded before gesturing to Robin, still laying on the ground. "I just want him."

Now Minisc and Robin were both confused.

"What do you want with Robin?" Minisc asked, feeling a hand grab at his leg. He glanced down to see Robin gritting his teeth and trying to push himself up.

Once he got to one knee, he ripped out the thorn from his ankle. "If I'm the one you want, then I suggest you take it up with me." He struggled to remain on his feet, but he refused to fall.

"Well, I must admit—I didn't think you'd be getting up anytime soon. I'm sure that wound is quite painful. I knew that you were something, especially the way that old man praises you, but even so, you're in no position to be threatening me. So I'd choose your words wisely."

The tension was thick, and still nobody was coming to their aid. It appeared that Dominos had secured the perimeter to ensure that there'd be no interference with his plan.

Minisc assessed his options. *The only choice we have is to run. Even if I used Celestial Light, I don't think I could win. But there's no way that Robin can run with his injured ankle.*

Frenzied thoughts continued to absorb Minisc until Robin snapped him back to reality, grabbing him by the shoulder. Somehow—even with a spike digging through his ankle—he kept his confidence, doing what he could to inspire Minisc.

"Don't let this guy intimidate you, Minisc. We can still take him."

Dominos scoffed. "Maybe you're not as wise as I thought you were." He threw his hands forward, and from his fingers shot out vines that smacked into Minisc and Robin, who then crumpled to the ground.

"He's fast," Robin sputtered.

"This is a losing battle. Can you run?" Minisc asked, nearly panting.

"Yeah, I think so. But I'll never be able to outrun Dominos."

"Leave that to me¬ — just be ready to shield your eyes."

"Okay, I trust you."

Minisc got to his feet, helping Robin up as well, and the boys locked eyes with Dominos. He was still toying with them.

"I'll tell you what, kid — I hate having to dirty my own hands for grunt work like this. My time is far more valuable than dealing with a bunch of EC nobodies, so turn over your friend and I'll let you run free. You can even go crying to that old man if you want. I won't stop you."

Now Minisc was really confused. Why would Dominos simply let him free? Was the Adenji boss *that* confident that he was untouchable? Or was he using Minisc to send a message? Either way, Minisc wasn't interested in making a deal.

"I'm not going anywhere. And I'd never abandon Robin and leave him to the likes of you."

Dominos shook his head and rolled his eyes. "You EC are all the same, ready to throw your life away at a moment's notice. You think that you'd understand how precious life really is since you're so gung ho about protecting it. But so be it."

Again, Dominos cast his vine whips forward and directly toward Minisc. Only this time, the boy had a counterattack at the ready.

"Now!" Minisc yelled. Robin slammed his eyes shut. So did Minisc, but not before firing off a massive ball of light. It collided with Dominos' vines and exploded like a solar flare.

They could hear Dominos shouting threats at them as he fought to see through the blinding light. If it had been anyone else, perhaps it would've been a good time to attack, but Minisc chose his only viable option: run.

He and Robin whipped around the street corner, trying to find any source of help or public support. Anything.

With each step that Robin took, blood trickled further down his shoe. The pain shooting through his thigh was unbearable, but as Minisc came to expect, Robin showed tremendous grit. Minisc respected the effort, but they could only go so far.

While they were running, Minisc grabbed his communicator. "Mr. Howland, we were ambushed by Dominos in South Park. We're making a run for it, but Robin's badly injured. We need back up now!" He shoved the communicator away, choosing to not wait for a reply.

When they popped out of the alley and rounded the final corner, they came to the last street in Etobicoke. To their left were six small apartment complexes, though they all looked to be abandoned. The windows and doors were boarded up, and not a single car was parked in any of the narrow driveways.

At the end of the road were sections of grass and a small cliffside. The waves below it crashed violently as storm clouds began to form overhead.

One of the dirt paths led through a group of trees. It would've made for a scenic view of the expansive water below, but when Minisc and Robin glanced in that direction, they felt defeated.

"It's a dead end!" Minisc panicked.

"We need to keep going!" Robin urged, but Minisc knew that the idea was highly unrealistic.

"No, you're too injured…and Dominos will be on top of us at any moment!"

"Then we have no choice. We fight back."

"No, Mr. Howland said specifically not to do that. We'll die!" Minisc argued.

But Robin refused to be shaken. His bravery was shining through, just as it would for the Hero of Light. "I have a plan, but I need you to trust me on this. I promise I'll save us. I'll stop Dominos."

Minisc glanced around, not liking his choices. "All right then—what is it?"

It would only be a few moments before Dominos arrived, and he'd be less forgiving this time around. But that was just enough time for Robin to implement his courageous albeit hasty idea.

Robin stood at the edge of the cliff, doing his best to stay strong. There'd be no running this time, so he needed perfect execution for his plan to work.

When Dominos arrived, the Adenji leader was furious. He marched through the trees, cracking his knuckles as he approached Robin. "So—your friend was finally smart enough to ditch you. Can't say that I blame him."

"I am an honoured member of the EC. It's my job to put the lives of others above my own. But make no mistake: I have no intentions of surrendering to you."

Robin could feel the edge of the cliff below his feet. The drop for a fully grown adult could be withstood, but with Robin's injured leg, getting to shore would be dangerously difficult.

Away from the fray, kneeling down with his back pressed against a tree, was Minisc, fighting his urge to dive in and protect Robin. This was all part of the plan, and if they lost the element of surprise, then Robin—and himself—would be in serious danger.

He tried to peek out so that he could watch as Dominos approached. He found the man's demeanor interesting. The Adenji leader was almost lackadaisical in his efforts. There was no yelling or acting rashly. In fact, his approach led both boys to believe that he was doing whatever he could to avoid drawing attention to the situation. Of course, that made the most sense to Minisc, as someone with Dominos' level of power could easily have stomped out an injured Robin.

With every step that Dominos took, Minisc could feel his body tensing. Yes, Robin was incredibly talented, and the bravery and heroics involved with risking his own life for a single soul was staggering, but Minisc still felt uncomfortable letting his new friend place himself in such a dangerous position.

Although, in reality, neither of them was safe, but Minisc would've much rather been the one distracting Dominos. If a fight were to break out, at the least he could attempt Celestial Light at 8% and fight back. However, the problem was that Robin felt the same way, and they both knew it.

The confidence on Robin's face was unwavering, proving why he was the top graduate in all of EA's history. He would succeed and, even more incredulously, he'd succeed while making sure that Minisc was protected as well. He really was the closest incarnation of the Hero of Light.

There was far too much going on in Minisc's mind to concentrate, but he did what he could to suppress the pit in his stomach.

Robin shouted to Dominos, "If I'm that important to you, how would you feel if I were to swan dive off this cliff?"

Upon hearing this, Minisc's eyes grew wide. Robin had to be bluffing. There was no way.

On the other hand, Dominos showed no concern. "That's a cute bluff, kid, but that's all it is—a bluff."

Dominos took another step forward, and Robin inched back a fraction further as the pebbles at his feet fell to the water below. "You've already seen how I can use my element. If you were to jump, you'd have to trust that I couldn't catch you before you go *splat*...and that's not a risk you're willing to take. But good try."

For the first time, Minisc saw Robin flinch. Their bluff was being called. The debate of whether now was the time to jump into the fray was strong, but he continued waiting.

"I guess we'll see," Robin retorted.

Dominos laughed menacingly, and then offered an evil smirk.

"What?" Robin asked.

"It's nothing…but I think it's only fair that you know…"

Robin's eyes grew wide before tearing up—he suddenly felt another searing pain. He remained on his feet, but now his other leg had a spike from the earth stabbing into his ankle.

"I can create those spikes, too. You're not going anywhere now."

Robin dropped his head. He was struggling, and Minisc could tell. He was done waiting. Their plan was a failure, and he needed to act.

Springing from his hiding spot, he yelled, "Sun Flare!" Similar to before, a ball of light exploded in the sky like a flashbang.

Dominos yelled out in anger, jamming his head into his forearm and trying to shield himself from the blinding light. "Kid, I'm really getting sick of you!"

Robin, also blinded by the light, took a step back in shock, feeling his foot graze the edge of the cliff. He opened his mouth to let out a cry, but no sound escaped. Before he could fall, he felt an arm grab him by the waist. His body became weightless as his feet left the ground.

"Sorry, I couldn't wait anymore!" It was Minisc.

But before he could flee for his hiding spot again, he heard Dominos' voice: "You'll die here too, kid!"

"Minisc, look out!" Robin shouted. Without hesitation, he put his hands together and fired off a blast of light directed at Dominos, deflecting a wave of spikes heading in their direction.

Thinking quickly, Minisc started firing off balls of light all around the forest. He clenched his fist, and all the balls of light moved together like shooting stars, attacking Dominos.

But the Adenji leader was prepared. He dropped to his knees and placed his hands on the ground, and a dome of rock — like a stone wall — formed around him, absorbing the blasts. The damage was nowhere near enough to break through the thickness of the barrier.

"Did it work?" Robin asked Minisc.

"No!"

When the smoke and dust cleared, they watched as the wall of rock crumbled. Dominos stood up and brushed himself off, but his composure was beginning to fade.

"I'm growing sick of your antics, kid! Let me make myself very clear: The green-haired one is coming with me. As for you, you'll be at the bottom of the ocean when I'm through here."

"Any other ideas?" Robin whispered to Minisc.

"Yeah...one," Minisc replied, taking his arm from around Robin. "Celestial Light, 8%."

He could feel his heart pumping rapidly, and he knew that he needed to calm down. He needed to ease his mind of all fears and use as much of Celestial Light as he could muster. Even if that capped out at 8%, that was better than nothing.

One thing was going for Minisc: For whatever reason, Dominos wanted Robin alive. Robin was his best bargaining chip, which granted them a small advantage in their fight for survival.

Minisc's body began to tingle as he recalled his training with Mr. Howland.

The golden light shone through Minisc's body, and Dominos gritted his teeth. "That blasted old man's skill..." The mere sight of Celestial Light caused him to lose all composure. "Why does he always try to get in my way?!? Well, if you're the one he chose, then it'll be all the better for me to just kill you now!"

Dominos stomped his foot, cracking the ground and causing Minisc to stumble forward. As he did, a thin vine shot in his direction. Minisc dodged the first one, then the second, but he was stuck on the defensive. He was working hard to keep the vines away from his partner too, but with Robin being immobilized, it was tough.

Realizing what Minisc was doing, Dominos turned his focus to Robin.

Knowing that the only thing currently keeping him alive was Robin, Minisc sprang for him, but this played right into Dominos' plan. Spikes sailed toward Minisc, who did his best to dodge the incoming impalement, which just narrowly clipped his arm. He fired another blast of light, but before the attack could hit Dominos, another protective wall sprung upward.

Minisc jumped through the air like a flash, throwing a punch at Dominos with all his might. The Adenji crossed his arms and absorbed the blow.

"Using a worthless technique like that won't save you. The most important thing that old fool should've taught you was to not meddle in my affairs." Dominos punched Minisc square in the chest, sending him surging back beside Robin. *Even at 8%, I can't even come close to touching him…*

"This isn't getting us anywhere," Robin winced, still grimacing in pain. "Minisc, I'm sorry…this is my fault." Then he raised his head and looked at his assailant. "Dominos, you win. Leave Minisc. Leave him, and I'll go with you."

Robin tried to gingerly limp forward, but Minisc grabbed his arm, stopping him.

"No! I'm not letting you go! We'll beat him…I swear it!"

"Touching sentiment, kid—but I'm done negotiating. I'll be taking you, and leaving your friend for dead."

From the corner of his eye, Minisc could see a spike sailing toward him. It was about to skewer him, and Robin was too slow to react.

"I can't let you do that, Minisc. I won't let you get hurt because of me," Robin whispered. In a split second, Minisc saw his friend glow a brilliant gold, and as he closed his eyes ready to absorb the wound, he felt his body being shoved.

Robin shoved Minisc out of the way, sending him over the cliff.

The spike flew over their heads, but only because Minisc was now falling over the cliff and into the lake below.

"Robin!" Minisc yelled, holding his hand up to the sky. Out of either desperation or fear, Robin held his hand out toward Minisc as well, almost as if he was waving goodbye, tears trickling from his eyes. Suddenly Minisc saw him disappear, likely into the clutches of Dominos. Minisc felt his heart rip in two.

Even as he fell violently into the water, he fruitlessly called out "Robin!!!" But it was too late. It was over.

He began to sink into the water and further into his own despair. He knew that he was plunging to his death, but he couldn't force his body to resist. All his might and all his will had been drained from him.

And then everything went black.

# CHAPTER 12
## BROKEN HEART

A VOICE PIERCED THE SILENCE.

"Wake up, Minisc. I know you can hear me."

Minisc choked up water as his eyes gradually opened. He lay flat on his back, staring up at the dreary and overcast sky. He felt sand under his hands as he tried to grab at the ground.

He attempted to sit up, but a withered and wrinkled hand pushed him back down. He looked over through blurry, water-logged eyes and was able to make out the white beard of Mr. Howland.

"You're okay. I made it," Mr. Howland said as he looked down at his student.

"Mr. Howland..." Minisc groaned, still sputtering up water. "Where's Robin?" Howland shook his head in disappointment, and Minisc looked to the sky, squeezing his eyes shut.

"I failed. He sacrificed himself to save me."

In a rare display of regret, Mr. Howland's voice sounded equally broken.

"The fault is not yours, Minisc. It is mine. I failed you. I failed you both." Mr. Howland rose to his feet, staring toward the lake's rough waves. "I should have never put you in such a position where you and Robin could even run into Dominos. That was my lack of foresight. Although we are part of the EC and dangers come with the territory, it is still my job as your superior to minimize those risks and bear them myself. I failed you in not doing so."

Minisc remained quiet, lacking the strength to speak. Not because of his battle, but because the only thing in his mind was the look on Robin's face as he plummeted off the cliff, leaving his friend behind to an even more cruel fate. There was no shaking it. How could he? As the son of the Hero of Light—and the one who was destined to replace him—he'd failed. His own friend had been willing to risk his life so that Minisc could live. And Minisc could do nothing to return the favour. He'd failed to save him. He'd been powerless to do anything against an opponent of Dominos' caliber. How could he protect the world from threats like Luminosa if he couldn't even accomplish that?

The more Minisc thought, the more desolate he became. He couldn't ignore the darkest depths of his insecurities and failures, leaving him at a loss.

Minisc would later learn that very soon after he fell off the cliff and began to drown, Mr. Howland arrived. He chose to dive in and save him, swimming more than a kilometer down the lakeside and dragging his student's unconscious body along until they found the shore. But the consequences of such heroism allowed Dominos to escape with Robin.

However, nobody would begrudge the decision Mr. Howland had made—and certainly not Robin himself. It was exactly what he would've done in the same scenario.

Besides, Minisc would've died. They both knew that Robin, although being held prisoner for some reason, would be kept alive. Dominos needed him.

When Mr. Howland had arrived just as Dominos was making his escape, Robin gave a last-ditch effort to save Minisc, yelling for Mr. Howland to rescue him. It was a tough choice to abandon his long-time student, as well as the man he'd been investigating for so long, but he knew that the choice was right.

As for Dominos, he proved to be just as strong as Mr. Howland had anticipated, and what made things worse was that nobody knew for sure why Robin was so important to the Adenji gang leader. They could all agree on one thing, though — whatever he wanted Robin for, it definitely wasn't good.

Twenty-four hours later, the sun shone again, with nary a cloud in sight. Everyone would be enjoying one of the last warm days of the year as winter would soon be closing in, but Minisc had no desire.

Since arriving home the afternoon before, he'd refused to leave his room. The windows and drapes were firmly shut, and not a glimmer of light penetrated his room. He was shrouded in darkness, just as he felt he should be. To him, he didn't deserve to be out in the sun or enjoying the weather on such a beautiful day, not while Robin remained in the clutches of Dominos. If his new friend was denied the sunlight, then he shouldn't have the luxury either.

He sometimes tried to fight his thoughts of despair, but they refused to leave. He was beside himself with grief. Who knew what sort of torturous hell Robin was currently undergoing at the hands of the Adenji gang? And all because he'd failed. He'd failed Celestial Light. He'd failed his father. And he'd failed Robin.

He rolled over, curled up in deep-blue blankets with a mountain of pillows piled atop his head. It was five in the afternoon, and not once had Minisc left his bed. Not to eat, not to say hi to his father, not even to answer messages from Lily or Jules. He couldn't. There was a depressive force around his bed too great for him to overcome.

Eventually, Minisc heard a knock on his door. He remained quiet, only stuffing his face further into the solitude of his pillows. He heard the knock again. It wasn't that he didn't want to talk; in fact, he very much wanted to unleash all the thoughts that continued running through his mind to someone. He could feel them drowning his will to live, just as the water had almost drowned him the day before. The problem was that he didn't even know how to articulate his feelings.

But the door crept open, after which he heard soft whispers.

"Minisc, are you awake?" It was Lily, that much he could tell. Even so, he remained silent, hiding in his cave of blankets and pillows. Part of him hoped that she'd leave while another silently begged for her to stay.

The floor creaked, and then he felt the bed dip slightly as Lily took a seat on its edge.

"Minisc...I know you're under there. You're worrying me. Talk to me."

Lily spoke in a hush, praying for any sort of response. Even in her friend's darkest moments, she'd never witnessed Minisc this distressed before.

In a muffled voice, Minisc muttered something while wiggling his way out of the sheets. When he poked his head out to sit up, she saw that he was a wreck. His hair was greasy and messy, his eyes red and puffy, and even his posture was slouched in defeat. There was no denying the sadness that tormented his heart.

"I couldn't save him...I let him go," Minisc whispered with regret. He stared at the ground, tears welling into his tired eyes. "I'm supposed to bring hope to people...but I was useless."

"Save who?"

"Robin. He needed me and I failed him...I let him slip through my hands. I let him go with that monster…but it should've been me that he took."

The frightful image flashed into his head again, cutting him deeper and deeper. All his instincts told him to bury his head back into the pillows once more and accept that he was a failure.

But before he could retreat into the covers again, he felt the warm, soft touch of Lily's hand on his.

"Minisc…it's okay," she said, still a little in the dark as to what exactly had occurred.

He flinched, pulling his hand away, "No, it isn't. You weren't there. I told him that we were gonna get through it…that I was gonna save us. But I couldn't. It's because of me that he's with Dominos now. He was willing to sacrifice himself to save me, all because I couldn't do it. Tell me, how am I supposed to stop Luminosa if I can't even protect one friend from that monster?"

Lily grabbed Minisc's hand again and squeezed it, remaining quiet. He was getting visibly angry, but then he suddenly buried his head into the nape of her neck, a waterfall of tears flowing freely from his eyes.

She wrapped her arms around Minisc, rubbing his back and thinking carefully about her next words. First of all, she wasn't even sure if she understood the situation in full. She was aware of the events that had taken place, and she understood the pain it was causing Minisc. But to see him taking his failure so hard, harder than any failure he'd ever gone through before, was tough. She couldn't quite understand if the pressure placed on him had finally wore him down or if there was more to it than that. Either way, she stayed quiet and hugged her friend tighter.

After a few silent moments, Minisc spoke up again. "Lily, thank you for coming over, but…I think I just want to be alone for a bit. I'm sorry."

Although disappointed, Lily respected his wishes. She hugged Minisc again and whispered in his ear, "I'll always be here to talk when you're ready." And with that, she exited the room, leaving Minisc to sit in the darkness of his mind once again.

He rolled back into his covers, telling himself that sleep was the only thing that would stop his mind from deteriorating.

The hours continued to pass, and eventually Minisc snapped awake again. His body remained stiff, but he'd been granted a brief moment of energy to roll himself over. He stared at his clock. The neon red lights beamed 11:58pm.

Somewhere deep inside, he found the will to push himself up and then, using every ounce of strength in his injured body, he got to his feet—for the first time in close to 30 hours. The motivation didn't come from some divine revelation, but rather his stomach refused to stop growling. Well over a day had passed since he consumed even a speck of food, and despite the pit in his stomach denying any desire of sustenance, he needed to eat at some point.

There was still one main reason he hesitated, though—the thought of facing his father. He was too ashamed of his failures. His father believed wholeheartedly that Minisc would be the one to bring down Luminosa, and yet he couldn't even stop Dominos.

His angry stomach wouldn't let up, and the growling was enough to be heard throughout the house. He forced himself to stand up, suppress his guilt, and headed toward the kitchen. The lights in the hallway were off, but when Minisc walked past his father's room, he saw that the door was open. Then he noticed the kitchen light on. He approached and saw his father sitting at the kitchen table, head in his hands. Thoughts of turning tail and locking himself in his room surfaced again, though before he could act, his father turned with a melancholy smile and the two locked eyes. There was no going back now. Besides, he'd have to face his father eventually.

Don remained quiet, but seeing his son in such a sorry state was eating at him. Minisc's hair was all over the place, his eyes still puffy and sleep deprived, and he was still wearing his regular clothes, by now completely crumpled and sweaty.

"Hi…" Minisc said lifelessly.

As if someone else was controlling his body, Minisc walked up to his father and just buried his head in the burly hero's chest. It was all he could do. Every waking second, he felt like he was going to crumble emotionally. He had no control anymore.

Don gently rubbed his son's back and said, "I think we need to talk."

Minisc slowly raised his head, suddenly noticing a phone on the table. Then it hit him. Don had already called his former mentor to get the answers that Minisc was failing to articulate.

Don led his son outside onto the back patio, where they sat down on the single wooden step leading to the grass.

Even at midnight, the air was still warm. They both gazed up at the bright moonlight that was coating the grass in a pale, blue light. In the distance, the forest was nothing more than a series of small, planted trees, still decades away from being fully grown. But after Ignis had burned down the burial ground of Minisc's mother—along with their house—all their friends had helped replant in the following months.

Not sure how to begin the conversation, Don said, "Mr. Howland told me everything." He noticed his son tense up and revert to staring at the ground. This increased his concern for his son even more.

Minisc remained silent, and so Don continued. "It's okay, Minisc. They'll get Robin back. You know that Mr. Howland and the EC will not stop until he does…but he can't do it alone. He needs your help."

Stunned, Minisc turned to face his father, shaking his head with tears welling up into his eyes again. Even so, this time he pressed on in a low, hoarse voice.

"I can't. I'm not you. I'm not meant for this." Minisc took a deep breath, finally able to form more substantive words. "I gave it everything I had, but I was too weak. I tried to be the hero you were, but I failed. And it might cost Robin his life." Minisc began to choke up. "Someone else needs to learn Celestial Light. Someone else needs to be you. Mr. Howland needs a true hero, not me. I'll only end up getting more people hurt."

"Minisc, this isn't your fault."

"Yes, it is," Minisc sputtered, his sadness quickly turning into anger. "If *you'd* been there, none of this would have happened. You would've used Celestial Light and defeated Dominos. You would've stopped Robin from going with him. Whenever you said that you'd help people, you always came through. You've never failed like I did."

The words took Don by surprise. Ever since Minisc was born, people had placed heavy expectations on him. However, through all of that, he'd never heard his son compare himself to The Hero of Light.

Don frowned. He attributed part of Minisc's sadness and frustration, on the pressure he was currently facing. Obviously, the scenario wasn't ideal. He had no desire for Minisc to be handed the burden of a battle that he himself couldn't finish, but he had no choice. His son was the only one with the strength to do it. In addition, after talking to Mr. Howland, Don and him both agreed that if there was another living soul on the planet who could master Celestial Light and finish off Luminosa for good, then it was Minisc. No doubt that led to some of Minisc's anger and depression as well.

Silence followed, until Minisc finally took a deep breath, stared at the moon, and said, "I really just came to get some food and go back to bed."

"And I'll let you do that. But first, I have a story to tell you."

"I'm really not in the mood for stories right now."

"Trust me, you'll want to hear this." Don rested his hands on the porch deck and leaned forward, feeling the cool wood underneath his fingers. "Do you remember anything about when Ignis' parents died?"

His attention suddenly captured, Minisc's eyes fixated on his father. For the first time since the incident yesterday, his mind flipped from Robin to Ignis. Once Minisc's childhood best friend, the two were inseparable, right up until the day his parents died in an attack. From then on, Ignis not only hated The Hero of Light but Minisc as well, joining Luminosa and attempting to exact revenge on the ones that he felt failed his parents. That is, at least, until Minisc defeated him and left him in Penatang Jail. The days that followed were tough, but nothing like what Minisc was enduring now.

Minisc shook his head. "Not much, honestly. I remember being at the playground behind the old EC building, and Ignis shouting at me about how you were supposed to save them. That's about it."

Don sighed. "Well, in a way he was right. I should've saved them, and I tried. I tried so hard. When we were ambushed and the battle broke out, I could see the danger coming. We were so heavily outnumbered that we never even stood a chance. The fight was a lost cause before it even started. And yet his parents, in the face of imminent death, stood strong. They sacrificed themselves to make sure that everyone else escaped. They were heroes in the truest sense of the word. Even though they had a son waiting for their return, and knowing that they'd never see him again, they still sacrificed everything to ensure our safety." Don paused, the painful memories still stirring up a harsh tightness through his chest. "But...I was the Hero of Light—the one who swore to protect everyone, no matter the cost. But when that day came, I faltered. I let overconfidence blind me, and if it hadn't been for their heroic acts, we all would've likely died with them. And what's worse is that I couldn't even face Ignis to tell him. I couldn't explain things to him because for so long, I couldn't even face it myself. I know that in those days I wasn't around very often, so you might not have noticed — and you were also pretty upset about Ignis as well — but I didn't leave my room for a week straight. I couldn't move from my bed. I was so devastated by what had happened, and I honestly struggled to keep going. I wanted to quit. I was The Hero of Light! I was the one who defeated Dusk and saved the Human and Elemental race from certain destruction! Or at least that's what everyone told me. But it was a lie. How could I possibly call myself a hero after letting my friends, the people I swore to protect, die? Not only that, they died protecting *me*. I was a fraud of a hero. Even a few days later, when the EC set up another mission to go after those criminals, I refused to go. I was too scared to face it again. That's when your mother finally talked some sense into me." Don paused briefly, glancing up at the moonlight before continuing his emotional account. "Looking back, I can't even begin to imagine the strain I put on your mother at the time. A husband who couldn't pull himself out of bed, and a child who lost his best friend from my actions. But of course, as she always had been, she remained a shining light for us both, keeping us from falling into despair for too long."

Minisc was listening intently, and Don put his arm around his shoulder.

"If she were here right now, she'd tell you exactly what she told me: 'Sometimes in life, we fall down. We have a setback. We fail. And although those moments can sting, they don't define who you are.' I know it's hard — excruciatingly hard at times. You wish that you could help everyone who needs it, but that isn't always possible. Sometimes, unforeseen circumstances arise and bad things happen. But if I've learned anything from being The Hero of Light, it's the power of hope. The power of knowing that one person can make a difference. That's what being The Hero of Light meant to me. It gave people hope for better days."

Minisc remained quiet, letting the words sink in. He never considered that his father would've ever suffered such a devastating moment in his career. Still, he harboured doubts about his own abilities.

"But what if…what if I fail again?"

"You won't."

Don stood up, knowing that his job was done. If this failed to snap Minisc out of his funk, nothing would work. Now he just needed to let his words marinate in his son's mind for the night.

Left to himself now, Minisc stared blankly at the sky and then back at the ground. Whenever he'd thought about Ignis, he'd always wondered what could've been done differently. If he'd tried just a little harder, maybe reached his hand out a little further when they were children, perhaps he could've kept Ignis from the path that he ultimately fell down. But there was no changing that anymore. The past was set in stone, and his friend was gone. Robin, on the other hand, was still within reach. But what if he failed once again? What if the small amount of Celestial Light he could use wasn't enough to stop Dominos?

In the end, it didn't matter. If he couldn't use Celestial Light, then he'd find another way. He had to. He couldn't lose another friend. Not like this.

# CHAPTER 13
## ATTENTION TO DETAIL

THE NEXT MORNING CAME AND, LIKE USUAL, MINISC headed off to the EC. Regret still followed him like a stray dog at his heels, but he refused to let it stop him.

He'd wasted enough time in bed. Now was the time to make sure that he did everything in his power to be prepared for a rematch with Dominos. He would *not* fail Robin again. Even if he couldn't use Celestial Light properly, it didn't matter. His goal was not necessarily to stop Dominos. If they managed that feat, it would be a bonus, but for Minisc, the mission only had one clear objective: to save Robin. Nothing else mattered.

He fought any lingering trepidation and headed to Mr. Howland's office. Unlike before, he knew that there would be no tests on the other side of the door, and no traps waiting to assess him. The real test was what would come of their meeting.

When he opened the door, the room was silent. Mr. Howland stood peering out through the window, hands behind his back. When he turned around, his face was unreadable, but his eyes told another story — the same story evident in Minisc's eyes. They were both fearful of what was to come.

"Hello, Sir," Minisc said quietly.

"How are you feeling?" Mr. Howland asked.

Minisc frowned and rubbed his arm. "Honestly, pretty bad. Things have been tough since…well, you know."

"I can say the same…which is why I called you here today. I believe that I owe you a full explanation of what has been going on."

Minisc looked at him with confusion, but then took a seat on the couch, and Mr. Howland joined him.

Instead of tea this time, there were a number of folders, similar to the one that he had seen on Dominos before.

"What are all these?" Minisc asked.

"They're profiles. Over the past six months, I have been doing extensive investigating on the Adenji gang and Dominos. I have been collecting information on all of his top leaders, trying to stop Dominos in his tracks." Mr. Howland flipped open a couple of the folders.

The first one Minisc looked through had a man on the page named Marco Hannifin, a fire Elementalist. Unlike Dominos, he looked weathered, with ghostly white skin and a bit more bulk to him. Something about his eyes made Minisc feel uneasy. They seemed to be always moving, always watching. Even in a still image, they were unnerving.

"This here is Dominos' right-hand man and most trusted companion, Marco. He has been part of the Adenji gang for longer than you've been alive, and he has always served as second in command. Do not let his age fool you — he is far stronger than he appears. His signature move is to summon a flaming phoenix that can act independently of himself. Essentially, he can turn the numbers of any one-on-one battle in his favour. Dominos rarely acts on his own without Marco being close by for backup, and when the two are together, they are powerful beyond measure."

The next folder displayed a younger woman closer to Minisc's age, but still a bit older. She was stunning, with long blood red hair and a devilish grin on her lips that evoked fear.

"In contrast, it appears that Dominos has added another aid to his cause. This is Kari Grant. Not much is known about her, but inside information reveals that her element is ice. She is a danger to those who fall for her charm," Mr. Howland explained.

The final folder was slightly different. Instead of just one person, the image showed a man and a woman, both of them appearing to be in their mid-thirties. Unlike the others, these two had their photos staged on the background of a criminal sizing chart. The man was skinny and small, slightly balding with hair just on his sides, and broken glasses—a complete contrast to the woman beside him. She was a hulk of a woman, looking like a professional bodybuilder. Her strength was intimidating just from the photo alone, nevermind what it would be like to meet her in person.

"I have been digging hard to find out more about these two. They're quite new to the ecosystem of the Adenji gang, and they are known as Dominos' 'Eliminators.' They're named Tufa and Lufa, and although I'm not sure of their elements since they are not registered in any directory, we do know that they are considered the most dangerous of the group."

Minisc read the note at the bottom: "Avoid at all costs. If encountered, do not engage. Seek help and attack in numbers."

"Indeed," Mr. Howland said, "I dare say that they may be more dangerous than Dominos himself."

A tense silence filled the room as visions of what was to come invaded Minisc's mind.

Glancing up at his mentor, he said, "Why have you been doing all this? What's Dominos planning?" Minisc wasn't sure if he wanted to know the answer to that. After all, if it involved Robin, it would only gut him more. But he *needed* to know.

"It is not so much what he is planning, but rather what he is trying to accomplish. Dominos is trying to save his mother from death."

"I'm afraid I don't understand."

Mr. Howland sighed thoughtfully. "It started a few years ago, when his mother became extremely ill. She was struck by a rare heart virus that would, over time, debilitate her until she could no longer survive. This loss was inevitable, but it destroyed Dominos. He was working to find a solution, though sadly there wasn't enough time. He grew desperate. And when your father took down the former leader of the Adenji gang, he saw his chance. He made promises of healing the sick and saving the dead, all to get people on his side. I don't know if he truly believes that he can do it, but I am sure that he will sacrifice everything in his way to try."

Minisc felt a wave of sadness—a more pitiful sadness than before. He understood the fear of losing a mother all too well.

"However, things became a bigger issue this past week when the EC stopped his shipment of chemicals. He needed those supplies to keep his patients alive, and now he is playing with borrowed time."

"But Sir, how do you know all this? There's no way you could've gathered this level of detail without having talked to Dominos at some point."

Mr. Howland stood up and walked back over to the window, catching Minisc by surprise.

"You're right. And although everything I have said is strictly a theory, I'm sure it is all true."

Minisc felt ill, but then recalled his battle with Dominos. "Wait—when I was facing Dominos, I used Celestial Light… and he knew about it. And he knew about you. He seemed to understand what I was trying to do." The gears in Minisc's head began to spin. He pictured the two side by side in his mind, and then gasped. "Dominos…he's your son, isn't he?"

Mr. Howland turned around, overtaken by melancholy. He silently nodded, taking a moment to gather his thoughts.

"His real name is Dominic, and the woman in my 'theory'… she is my wife. That is how I know this, and also why I know how little time she has left and how desperate Dominic is to save her—even going so far as to kidnap her from her hospital and risk immediate death. Dominic is doing everything in his power to keep my wife alive while he finds a cure for her illness, but it is too late. Even if he could, the damage to her body has become irreversible. What he is doing now is nothing short of cruel torture."

Minisc sat in shock, his mouth open, trying to utter something. Anything. But what could he say? There was *nothing* to say.

Mr. Howland filled the silence with one final thought. "If I know my son, this is why he targeted Robin…and it's also why I know he is safe. The EC currently has all of Dominic's supplies—supplies he needs to keep his so-called patients alive. Which means that in his own twisted logic, we took something of his and so he chose to take something of ours. Specifically, someone who I hold dear."

"And that's why he wanted Robin and didn't care about me…"

"I believe so. Still, we too are on borrowed time. The second that Dominic realizes he can't save his mother, Robin will be of no use to him and his life will be in danger."

"We can't let that happen!" Minisc demanded. "We have to get him out of there!"

"I know, Minisc. I know."

Tensions were high, and a knock on the door made Minisc jump. In came Adelle and Yuri, to both his and Mr. Howland's surprise. Adelle had two folders under her arm, and her face carried the same look of anguish that Minisc was brandishing.

"Sir, we've got an issue," Yuri said. "Dominos is demanding

that we surrender all the supplies we confiscated last week to the Adenji gang now, or else Robin is dead."

"Please, Sir — we need to do something fast!" Adelle begged.

She handed the folder over to Mr. Howland, who was horrified at what he saw. "Damn him…" he grumbled, snapping the folder shut. "Tell him we'll get him the chemicals, but he's not to harm another hair on Robin. If he does, the deal's off. Now if you'll excuse me, I need time to think of a plan."

Mr. Howland was ready to march for the door, but Adelle stopped him. "Wait, Sir. I think we need to talk."

He glared at her dismissively. "It can wait."

But Yuri jumped in to back her up. "Sir, you're gonna want to hear this. Believe me."

Everyone in the room was on edge. Adelle looked unsure, glancing between Mr. Howland and Minisc, but then she took a deep breath and handed Mr. Howland the other folder.

"This is a detailed sketch of the Adenji compound," she explained. "It also displays a sealed back entrance that'll bring you underground from the forest on their property. There's also a key card attached to the sketch. If we approach from the front and back, we'll leave Dominos with nowhere to run, and we'll be able to save Robin, too."

Minisc was absolutely shocked — and so was Mr. Howland. They both stared at Adelle. "How did you get your hands on these?" Mr. Howland asked her.

She hesitated again, and looked to Yuri for support. He encouraged her with a small nod.

"I…I got them…I got them because I used to be part of the Adenji gang." She glared down at her feet, trying to avoid seeing the judgement on Mr. Howland and Minisc's faces.

"It was a long time ago, and I had nowhere to turn. They brought me in and really treated me like family…at least for a little while. But that's all in the past. Please understand — Robin was the one who brought me out of those shadows. He gave me a second chance, and without him I wouldn't be here today. I'd probably be in some dusty cell rotting away with my so-called friends. I've tried to rid myself of everything having to do with the Adenji gang...but I know that this is what needs to be done. We have to save Robin at all costs."

After a brief pause, Mr. Howland looked at Adelle with genuine understanding, and perhaps even some sympathy. He took the folder and tucked it away. "I understand...and we *will* save Robin. Thank you for this—the folder and the information. I know it must have been hard to share such a secret. But, again, I do need time to think. If we are going to pull this off, we have to make sure that we have every angle covered. Give me a few hours and call in as much support as we can afford. Also, tell Dominos that he'll get his precious chemicals."

Mr. Howland's investigations into the Adenji gang, and the rescue mission for Robin, were bumped to high priority. Time was of the essence, which would make things tough, but after only a few hours, they managed to put together a team.

Though Adelle and Minisc wanted to rush in and save their friend, they both understood that such hastiness would only derail their plans. They needed to trust the EC, and, more importantly, Mr. Howland. They knew that he'd do everything in his power to make sure their mission succeeded.

Since Lily and Jules worked under Yuri, who had been working with Mr. Howland in the investigation of the Adenji gang, the two students were requested to join the mission, too. They'd be capable sets of hands if a sticky situation arose, and Mr. Howland could use all the help he could get.

The three, along with Adelle, sat in a briefing room. It looked like a university auditorium, filled with police officers and other EC members.

An eerie, intense vibe permeated the room as Mr. Howland explained the situation. He used his own notes as well as Adelle's insights to help pave a path forward.

As part of the agreement between Mr. Howland and Adelle, he didn't inform others of where he received his intel, although many questions were being asked.

All in all, the meeting took just over an hour, and in another hour they'd be heading out. Things were happening at a rapid pace, barely giving Minisc any time to process.

But he wasn't the only one stewing. Jules could feel his body becoming a little tenser, a little stiffer. Much like Minisc, he'd suffered his own failure against the Adenji gang, and doubts of his own strength began to creep in.

Lily informed him of Minisc's struggles, and when he heard the news, he wished that he could've helped. He wanted to be beside his friend and help him fight. But once again, he found himself hurt from the boat investigation, and was deemed useless.

He needed his own sign of hope—and that sign came when he looked over at Minisc. What he saw was a face of determination, a look that Jules had noticed many times from his friend in previous tough situations. When he saw that look, he knew that everything would be okay. Minisc believed, and that made Jules believe, too. He'd carry them all to success, no matter the cost—just as they all knew he was capable of doing.

Everyone in the room focused intently on each word that Mr. Howland spoke, absorbing them like sponges. It was clear that everyone shared a common goal: Bring down Dominos, and save Robin from the deranged leader. This unwavering support from both his friends and Mr. Howland brought Minisc hope that they'd succeed.

Mr. Howland finished his speech by saying, "I do not need to explain the urgency that this mission presents. But as long as everyone plays their role, we will leave the Adenji gang—and

Dominos—with nowhere to run. Once they are trapped, our number one priority is to bring Robin home safely. Getting rid of Dominos is a bonus."

Minisc noticed that Mr. Howland kept his gaze squarely on him, as if he was the only one in the room. How could Minisc possibly forget the objective? It was the one thing that continued to haunt him. He obviously wanted to put a stop to Dominos and his henchmen who were behind all this, but, as Mr. Howland said, that would only be an added bonus. What they needed, above all else, was to see Robin safe and in the hands of those they could trust.

Mr. Howland continued. "Most of all, I want to make something clear. Nobody in this room is to sacrifice themselves for any greater good. You are all to come back from this mission alive."

If Minisc had needed any further clarity as to the perils of their task, that statement made it crystal clear. They would *not* get another chance at this.

The group started to break off into their teams and then walked down the stairs to the bottom of the auditorium.

When Minisc, Lily, Jules, and Adelle hit the bottom step, Yuri waved them over from the crowd. Since Don was no longer capable of going on these heroic missions, that meant that they lacked the protection of The Hero of Light. Yuri, although he could never replace the Hero's strength, still felt that it was his obligation to provide guidance and keep the three safe. He put his hand on his brother's shoulder and said, "I know this isn't exactly your first mission with the EC, and you've been through more life-and-death battles than I can count, but as is always the case, the number-one priority for you three is returning safe." He turned to address the others as well. "This isn't the same as before. We don't have the shield of Minisc's father to back us up in a fight. This will be dangerous. That said, we have many experienced Elementalists in this room, along with law enforcement on our side. Remember — Mr. Howland is placing you on this mission because of what he knows you've gone through with Luminosa, but don't let that go to your head. It's okay to rely on the rest of the team for help. Understand?"

All four of them nodded in agreement.

"Good. Now let's go get Robin back."

# CHAPTER 14
## RETURNING HOME

FOR THE DAY OF A RAID, THE AFTERNOON WAS gorgeous. Brilliant rays of sun beamed down, a soft and refreshing breeze swirled through the air, and the streets leading to the main Adenji compound were peaceful. A typical calm before the storm, one might say.

Without time for developing an elaborate plan, they worked to keep things simple. Using the map provided by Adelle, Minisc and Mr. Howland were to head in from the forest, sneaking in to find Robin before Dominos knew what was coming.

The front team, led by Yuri and comprised of Lily, Jules, and Adelle, as well as the first wave of officers surrounded the northern gates. The goal was to have the entire building sealed off, leaving Dominos with nowhere to go. They were expecting heavy resistance if things went south, but in truth, nobody knew what would happen.

Apart from Mr. Howland's team, all EC members were deployed a half-mile from their destination to avoid any unnecessary attention. There was a long roadway that stretched down the compound, and to the east and west was nothing except for run-down, abandoned homes. If nothing else, they didn't need to worry about any excess property damage if the mission went awry.

The compound was made of four large, square walls that encased one larger square in the middle, and to the north was miles of forestry.

Each of the four outer squares that connected to the main building were shielded off by steel gates stretching nearly ten feet high. Decades ago, it had been a sales lot and dealership for old cars, but when the Adenji gang moved in they continued to revamp the hideout until it was seen as an impenetrable fortress.

However, with the use of a warrant, along with elemental force, gaining access to the compound was a more realistic prospect for the team — not that they expected things to go peacefully.

With any luck, the sneak attack would catch Dominos off guard and make rescuing Robin a far easier task for Minisc and Mr. Howland. Of course, all those involved knew that such hope was nothing more than a fallacy. Dominos would never concede defeat so easily, and certainly not on his home turf.

When executing a hostile search and seize warrant, the Elemental Council would always join with the police to carry out their plan. Although the EC is used most times as frontline protection during battles with other Elementalists, it holds no legal authority to make arrests.

That's where the police played their role. Battles with Elementalists were far too dangerous for law enforcement, so they'd provide support and make arrests as safely as they could.

Throughout the years, and thanks to improvements in technology, certain equipment had been created to help them handle Elementalists, though this was only useful after an Elementalist was detained.

The officers and a number of different Elementalists stood at the steel gates of the Adenji compound, waiting for the signal. Yuri, Jules, Lily, and Adelle were on the eastern compound gates, staring up at the structure. For a moment, Jules and Lily were overtaken by the scope of their situation—the police at the ready and all the Elementalists around. They were merely two students of EA who happened to be part of Yuri's team on apprenticeships. One could certainly argue that they were out of their league.

Also, most of the police were concerned about having kids on such a dangerous mission. However, those on the force long enough knew never to doubt Mr. Howland's logic. If he trusted that the kids would do the job of full-fledged EC member, then they'd simply have to believe that as well.

They were only minutes away from starting. Jules and Lily took a moment to lock eyes. Together, they took a deep breath and shared smiles of reassurance.

Although neither of them was necessarily tied to Robin the way that Minisc was, it didn't matter. They both knew what Robin represented and how important this mission was for Minisc. Besides, there was an innocent life on the line.

Just because they weren't fighting side by side with their best friend, they'd still always have his back. Dominos would be stopped and Robin would be saved.

The air grew thicker, and just seconds away from battle, Yuri whispered a warning to his group once again. "Remember— your safety is first and foremost. You already know what these Elementalists are capable of, so never drop your guard."

The situation was still being set up when down the middle of the street drove an unmarked freight truck. Everyone, including the Adenji gang, knew that it was being driven by the EC, but that didn't matter—just as long as it had the Adenji gang's supplies inside.

Out of the truck stepped a heavyset man in street clothes. He was only a few feet away from the compound's main doors when he tapped the side of his jacket pocket.

Much to their surprise, the gates to the compound opened, out of which walked a tall, thick woman. She said a few words to the driver and then they began walking toward the truck. Evidently, she wanted to see the supplies before they made any sort of deal.

When they cracked open the back doors of the truck, there were rows of crates, all loaded up.

It was hard to make out what was happening. The silence was unnerving, and Jules could feel his knees shaking.

But it wasn't from fear — it was something else. He glanced at the ground and noticed the pebbles by his feet jumping.

Suddenly, Adenji members came pouring through the streets like a horde of zombies. They were launching a full-scale attack on the truck. Then, at the drop of a hat, the gates to their destination swung open, and swarms of Elementalists dressed in Adenji gear came rushing out.

The group quickly turned their direction to the danger, but before they could react, a monstrous man came crashing through the side wall. His arm was covered in a thick hide that looked like tree bark, and he stood a towering seven-feet tall.

As a result of the crash, Jules and Lily flew through the air and skidded back behind Yuri.

In this moment, all hell broke loose. Pillars from the earth rose to the sky, carrying a group of Adenji Elementalists with them. Waves of ice and strikes of lightning rained down from the rooftops, and more Adenji members came flooding in through the huge hole in the wall. They were prepared, and it seemed likely that all the main fronts were facing a similar ambush.

Walls of ice began to form, attempting to cut off reinforcements, but Jules had no clue which side was creating them.

Yuri pulled Jules up by his collar, while Adelle grabbed Lily's arm.

"Follow the ice walls…they should lead us to a way inside!" Adelle ordered.

"But what about the others?" Jules frantically asked.

"They'll be fine! This is what they're paid to do!"

"Adelle's right!" Yuri added. "If there're this many Adenji members here, there must only be a few inside!"

Yuri's group, guided by the walls of ice, kept running. Since none of them were fire Elementalists, there was no option of breaking straight through. Not only that, there were still the steel barricades on the other side. But if they could find a different entrance and slip in amongst the chaos, they'd have a chance.

On the other side of the walls, they could hear titanic battles taking place, but they kept their eyes forward and refused to slow down.

Lily pointed as they rounded the corner to the back of the Adenji compound. "Look, the wall stops!"

"There should be an entrance nearby!" Adelle added. "Hurry!"

When they came to a stop, there was far less commotion, although that was because the entire area had been sealed off by ice and rock. They were standing on a giant rectangle of grass with small, stone walkways heading up each side. On the other end was what looked like some form of garage or storage area. All they needed was to rush in, and then phase one of their goal would be a success.

But it wouldn't be as simple as they hoped.

"Look out, above us!" Yuri shouted. Adelle was first to react, raising her hand to create a barrier. Sparks of electricity rained down from the sky and collided with the icy barrier as Adenji members dropped from the rooftops in front of them. As the smoke cleared, the members came into view, each one with venomous faces.

"Damn, we were so close!" Jules fumed. He raised his fists, ready to fight.

"Wait—these guys weren't in the folders that Mr. Howland gave us..." Lily noted. She'd studied the briefs in depth on their way to the mission site.

Adelle shattered her barrier and took a step forward. "You don't need any folders to know who these three are. They're the disgruntled three: Nails of the Night Katherine, Mummy the Manic, and Crazy Curtis."

On the left was a tall, skinny man with dangling limbs, his face covered in filthy bandages that matched his arms and legs. Only a single eye was visible, and a small tuft of blond hair poked out from under his wrappings. His Adenji name was Mummy.

In the middle was an athletic woman, wearing a long, black dress with a thin slit halfway up her thigh. Flowing green hair covered her left eye, and she had long, scissor-like nails at the end of her fingers. There was no mistaking her for anyone but Nails of the Night Katherine.

The third man was shorter than the other two and wore a torn and tattered suit, with a tie halfway around his neck. He had a crazed look about him, with messy black hair and a twitch that suggested he'd mentally dove off the deep end years ago. He definitely fit the bill of someone named Crazy Curtis.

"Looks like someone decided to spring our trap," Curtis laughed hysterically.

"Indeed they did!" Katherine seethed with an evil snarl. Then she locked eyes with Adelle. "And not only that, they've brought us a friend. Welcome back, Adelle—it's been a long time."

The rest of the group remained quiet, until Lily asked, "Adelle, what is she talking about?"

"So, you never told them," Katherine marvelled. "You never told them about Frosted Witch Adelle..."

Jules said, "Wait. Adelle? You…you were part of the Adenji gang?"

Adelle slowly nodded, lowering her head for a moment. "I was. And these three were my team…they were my family." She looked over at her old "family" again but then quickly snapped out of her fear. "Look, I can explain that later. We're just wasting time! We need to hurry and get inside!"

"Get inside?" Curtis mocked. "So this is what they've done to you? They broke you, moulded you, and turned you into an EC puppet. I never thought I'd see the day…"

Katherine stepped forward. "Now, now — that's enough Curtis. Is that any way to speak to an old friend? Adelle, my dear — can't you see? This is a sign. Your calling. You were meant to be with us. Return to the Adenji gang and I'm sure that all will be forgiven. Master Dominos could use your talents."

Adelle gulped, fighting her emotions by keeping her head down.

"Adelle would *never* go back to you creeps! She's with us now!" Jules shouted.

Adelle heard his words, but they didn't quite click. A secret that she'd tried to keep for so long had been outed. But, fortunately for her, the judgement she'd expected from the others never came.

"Is that so?" Katherine said, bristling. "You would actually allow a former Adenji gang member into your circle? Someone who actively fought against the EC, broke countless laws, and stretched morality to its limits? That's a woman you're willing to trust to watch over your life? You may want to reconsider." She was clearly trying to bait the group into turning on their own.

Lily confidently stood next to Jules. "Whatever Adelle did in the past, it doesn't change the fact that she's our friend. She chose to be here with us to help get back a *true* friend of hers.

And we won't let you three stop her — or us. So get out of our way, or we'll be forced to show you just what we're capable of."

The tone in Katherine's voice became darker. "This is the choice you've made? To turn your back on us after all we did for you? Have it your way then. Master Dominos is on the verge of saving this disgusting world, but if you choose to stand in his way, we'll be forced to kill you."

"Saving the world?" Adelle questioned, incredulous. "Is that what you guys think you're doing? No, what you're doing is preying on people's emotions, the same way you did with me."

"Don't listen to them, Adelle," Yuri told her. "People like this will come up with any excuse to justify their actions."

Those words irked Curtis, who began to twitch as he spoke. "How dare you question master Dominos? He is the cure to this world's sickness. Through him, we'll usher in an age where nobody will know death. An era you could've been a part of, Adelle. But instead, you chose to abandon us." He raised his hand to the sky, and flames began to dance around him, then fired off one by one.

"I've got this!" Lily rushed in front, waving her hands and sending small waves of water to envelop the flames and extinguish them.

"Looks like we might be in for a real fight this time," Jules said as wind began to swirl around his body.

"No!" Yuri shouted. "We don't have time for this. By now, Dominos is already on the move, and that puts Robin in immediate danger." He glanced to his left; the garage was within sprinting distance. They just needed to make a break for it.

"Yuri's right," Adelle said, holding her arm out to stop Jules. "Robin is our number one priority, and I'd never forgive myself if something happened to him because we were too slow. Everyone on the outside is nothing more than a distraction at this point."

She recognized the ease with which she and Lily had averted her enemies' attacks, even after being taken by surprise. They were no stronger than the last time she saw them, which she knew meant that those three — her former friends and allies — were as expendable as the rest of the minions outside, at least in Dominos' eyes. They were nothing but pawns for him.

"Perhaps Adelle is right," Lily said.

Adelle gripped her fist, eying the three intently. "I know that I'm right, and every second we doubt it is a waste of time. We need to go right now!"

Adelle swung her hand horizontally and, with a bright flash of white, a wave of ice arched at least 20 feet into the air. "Come on — we're out of here!"

Following Adelle's orders, the four began rushing for the door. Lily got in first with Jules and Yuri following, but Adelle was a step behind. She came to a skidding halt as streams of fire ripped through the ice, narrowly missing her by an inch.

Katherine cackled, "You wouldn't mind abandoning your friends again, would you? After all, it appears you're really good at it!"

Adelle reacted quickly, summoning another wall of ice in front of the garage door.

It wasn't a blind reaction, though — she had a strategy. First, her actions would allow Yuri and the others to go on without her, though she didn't know if they actually would. The other benefit to sealing off her location was that it stopped the enemy from splitting off and chasing her friends. If she could just defend against these three, then the others would be freed up to explore inside.

Adelle blocked another attack, this time one of electricity, as she put some distance between herself and the Adenjis. Three rapid flicks of her wrist later, there was so much ice around the field that there was no chance of escape for anyone.

"Clever as always, I see...blocking off the entrance for your friends," Curtis mocked. "That's something you would've done for us once upon a—" He was abruptly cut off as a shrill spike of ice flung in his direction. It missed him by a hair, but it was still a well-placed warning shot.

"You of all people should know not to take your eyes off me, Curtis," Adelle spat.

Katherine was livid. "You have some nerve coming back here. We took you under our wings when you had nowhere to go. We brought you into the Adenji family and treated you like one of our own, and this is the thanks we get in return? You should be ashamed!" She unleashed her nails like claws, and streams of water sprayed toward Adelle.

Refusing to back down, Adelle froze the water in its place, creating poles of glistening ice that shattered as they hit the dirt. Pillars of ice shot out from her body, slamming Katherine up against the newly created back wall and pinning her in place.

Adelle whipped another two pillars forward. Instantly, all three of the Adenji members were pinned along the wall like toxic pieces of art. The ice glistened off them from the bright sun above.

"I'm not as foolish as I was when I was a child," Adelle told them. "I understand now what you were doing back then. You didn't bring me in to give me a family—all you did was take a scared and lonely child and used her for your own gain. Those crimes we committed, those battles we fought…they weren't for some greater good of the world. They were for the Adenji gang's own personal gain. That's why you had no problem abandoning me when the EC came for us. Or did you forget about that part? Family doesn't mean anything to the Adenji gang—for them, it's just a means to an end. You begin to realize that when you find a real family."

With all three of her foes immobilized, now all Adelle needed to do was wait for the police to arrive and finish the job.

She pulled out her communicator and set off a buzzer so that her location would be known. Until then, she'd need to find another way into the building.

After taking a quick look around, the sounds of battle were beginning to soften. It was hard to tell at that point, but from what she could assume, the EC was winning. At least that's what she hoped.

One other thing she assumed was that her three trapped Adenji friends wouldn't be receiving backup. It was obvious that they were just pawns used to slow down the EC's progress.

She glared scornfully at the three of them. "If only you'd been caught with me, maybe your lives could have been different, too. But that would involve you actually caring. But you ditched me…you chose to work with a man like Dominos instead of looking for a brighter future. Such a waste of your lives."

Her job now done, she prepared to help elsewhere. As she began walking away, a strange, faint smell invaded the air. She spun around and noticed a burgeoning red glow from the chests of her trapped enemies.

*I knew it was too easy.*

Katherine and Mummy were trouble, but Curtis was the matchup nightmare for her — and he was about to prove it. His imprisonment gradually changed colour from pale blue to hot red, and a burst of fire exploded out toward Adelle.

Reacting quickly, she rolled out of the way, but then a pair of bandages materialized and wrapped onto her legs. She gasped, realizing that they were the bandages from Mummy, and then let out a wild scream as bolts of lightning began conducting through her body.

The shocks were violent and unrelenting, but they weren't enough to stop her. Fighting through the agony, Adelle forced her hand into a knife made of ice, and sliced through the bandages as if she was cutting tape. She dropped to the ground but had no time to rest. She leapt to her right, dodging a torrent of water that was marked for her head.

She jumped back and looked at her three opponents, each one now up and free from their icy prisons.

"This is bad," Adelle whispered to herself.

"Oh? Is that fear I hear in your voice?" Katherine balked. She'd always portrayed herself as the leader. "You think that you know our motives? You think that we're wasting our lives? That's what you said, wasn't it? You know nothing!"

Curtis twitched his head, looking like he might snap his neck at any moment. "I'll give you credit—it was brave to choose sacrificing yourself so that your new friends could move ahead. But like always, you're too soft. You should've killed us when you had the chance." Curtis opened his mouth and spat out menacing balls of fire. Adelle dodged them swiftly, but she was still outnumbered.

"Here's one of the key principles you might remember of the Adenji gang: Those who hesitate end up with a knife in their back," Katherine said ominously.

"Mummy, it's your turn!" Cutis yelled, and more bandages came flying through the air in Adelle's direction. As the tattered white cloth weaved through the air, Adelle froze the bandages and smacked them to the ground.

She then hardened her resolve, realizing that any sign of fear would lead to her death. *You can handle this. Backup isn't coming and you've got nowhere to run, but that doesn't matter now. We've all got a job to do, and this one is yours.*

Even with doubt creeping in, she kept up a facade of strength. Just like Robin would—the boy who'd taught her so much about the good in people. He'd never cower in fear at being outnumbered or over matched. He refused fear, even when staring down Dominos.

As students, there were many areas in which Adelle surpassed Robin. Talent, knowledge, and strategy, to name a few. When it came to work ethic, they were equals. But when it came to act, when a time of need presented itself, Robin was always ready. Whenever that time arrived, he ignored rules, tossed caution to the wind, and sacrificed himself, all to selflessly help those around him. But it wasn't just that—it was his ability to believe in the good of people, treating them with warmth and kindness. It was the same quality that saved her and gave her the opportunity to become more in life. She refused to waste that chance.

Stuck, Adelle saw Katherine slash directly at her face with her sharp claws. With no other option, Adelle froze her cheeks, taking the slash before sliding backwards.

"Quick thinking," Katherine taunted. "Learn that skill from the EC?"

Adelle was almost tempted to feel sorry for Katherine and the other two, as they also could've broken free from the Adenji gang. Instead, she composed herself and smugly said, "Maybe I did. You could've learned lots, too. All you had to do was abandon the hate you have for the world and opened your eyes."

"Our eyes are plenty open. This world is full of suffering, and we're working to cure it. Something the EC would never be capable of."

Instead of anger, upon hearing these words Adelle felt warmth and happiness—not for her current battle, but for her situation as a whole. It was all thanks to Robin, the boy who showed her the joys of the world. The memory in her mind was vivid, never to be forgotten. It was the day that Robin saved her from a grim fate.

As a child, Adelle didn't know her family. She was alone, lost, and left to wander the streets. She lived with her aunt up until the age of ten, but, growing frustrated with the cruelties of life, she ran away from home. That's when she was taken in by the Adenji gang. She was given a purpose, a family. People who had her back.

But the crimes they committed, the people they hurt…that always haunted her. She wanted an out.

Then everything changed. She got caught and was taken in by the EC. At that point, she conceded to wasting her life in a cell until the day she died. Society would give up on her, and so would her so-called friends.

But instead, something surprising happened. She was enrolled in EA and given a mentor, a young boy just starting out in school alongside her. He was everything she'd been taught to hate: kind, generous, and trusting. He embodied the good in society, and as those who made the decision to send Adelle to EA had hoped, Robin made a solid impression on her. Together, they pushed each other to be the best and hoped to change the world.

Adelle tightened her fist. "Being taken in by the EC was the best thing that could've happened to me. They saved me from continuing down a path that led nowhere. They showed me the good in people's hearts. And it's why I came back here. You three should know better than anyone that if you mess with someone I care about, then I'll make you pay personally."

A chilly wind filled the arena, along with another flash of white light. Before anyone could react, the yard turned into a tundra of glittering ice. On the floors, the walls, and even overhead was now a ceiling of ice. They were standing inside a literal ice cube.

"Whoa! What the hell?!?" Curtis yelled.

Adelle spread her arms wide, shouting, "Arctic Icicles!" Like a field of turrets forming from the walls, pellets of ice came raining down from every direction, repeatedly crashing into the Adenji members. No matter where they turned, more frosted rocks pounded down on them like a swarm of punishing

golf balls from the skies. The attack was relentless, fierce, and a culmination of everything Adelle had worked so hard for since starting EA.

Katherine yelled, "This is a bit much, don't you think? We can still talk about this!" She took an ice pellet to the chest and crumpled into the wall, as did Mummy. Then she yelled an order at Curtis, who was lying face down on the floor, appearing to be unconscious. "Curtis, get it together and turn up the heat!"

Just as Katherine demanded, Curtis' eyes snapped open with a psychotic glint. He raised his hand to the ceiling, and flames burst outward from his palm. He pushed himself up as more flames began to erupt from his entire upper body. It turned into a tornado. Just when Adelle had managed to flash freeze the yard into an ice rink, Curtis had turned it into a sauna.

"Guess you *have* learned a few new tricks," Adelle said, finding it hard to believe the scene before her. The shock of seeing her most powerful attack being wiped away fueled her fear. She was outmatched and out gunned.

Even so, she still had to fight. Robin would never concede, and neither would she.

"Good work, Curtis!" Katherine lauded before turning to face Adelle once again. "Face it—going to that school, making friends with those people…all it's done is turn you soft. Now I'll show you just how big of a mistake you've made. You should've come crawling back when you had the chance."

"Mistake? Return to you? You're delusional if you truly believe that. My only mistake was putting faith in the Adenji gang. You guys are monsters, led by that tyrant Dominos."

"Oh, my dear girl—you have it all wrong. Dominos is the furthest thing from a monster. You talk a lot about how the EC gave you hope…well, did you ever once care to ask why people like us joined the Adenji gang or why we brought you in?"

Adelle remained quiet.

"It's because just like you, we wanted hope. After society gave up on us, the Adenji gang gave us a second chance. I used to be an incredible actress, and I married the love of my life on the grand stage. But one day while performing my most prominent scene, a rope holding the stage light broke and it killed him. It was devastating. In my sadness, I lost everything and my life had no meaning anymore. And when I was finally ready to return to the stage, I learned just how little the world cared for my broken heart. They left me with nothing. This place though… my family—they gave me purpose again."

Curtis joined in on Katherine's sentiments. "I lost my mother and father to a helicopter accident, and after drinking myself half to death, the Adenji gave me a home. They gave me a belief again when society had quit on me. And as for Mummy, his entire family burned in a house fire. Three kids and a wife—all gone. But did society care? Not one bit. They left us all damned, but now we have purpose, we have pride, and we'll do what the Adenji has always done. We'll follow our leader to the bitter end. That's what it *really* means to be part of the Adenji gang."

With a fist engulfed in flames, Curtis went in for a screaming haymaker of a punch, ready to flatten Adelle's skull.

*Clang.* His fiery fist was met with an unexpected affront.

Adelle stood firm, despite her ears ringing. Half of her face was shielded by ice, continuously regenerating to avoid being burned by Curtis' punch. She jerked her leg, knocking Curtis off balance before jumping away. The flames graced her cheek just enough to melt the makeshift face shield. She needed a new plan.

*All right, if I can't beat them with my element, then I'll have to beat them with my brain.*

Adelle chose Mummy as her first target. With bandages conducting electricity coming her way, she moved fast, heading straight for Katherine.

"Hey, Mummy—what the hell do you think you're doing?!?

Control those bandages!" Katherine barked. She moved out of the way, preparing for her own strike, which was exactly what Adelle needed. She turned course for Curtis, who readied to spit out another wave of fire. As he did, the flames were met by Katherine's watery blast.

"Damn it," Curtis griped. "She's using our elements to protect herself!"

In a split second, Adelle slid under the water, and the bandage of electricity cut right into the flow. Sparks surged through the water and then through Katherine's body. She dropped to the ground.

With her down, Adelle was just inches away from Curtis, who failed to react in time. She encased her fist in ice and swung with vengeance, sending him crashing into the wall. He slumped down into a puddle of water, which also happened to be connected to the stream conducting electricity. The jolt knocked his body unconscious, leaving only Mummy left. Adelle smirked. She shot a blast of ice, freezing Mummy to the wall as she had before, but with Curtis now out of commission, he had no way of breaking free from his icy shackles.

All three of them were incapacitated and trapped behind sheets of ice, unable to fight back. Adelle put her hands on her knees, trying to catch her breath.

"You're right, Katherine," she said aloud, though she knew the viper couldn't hear her. "I never did ask why you three joined Adenji. Because I guess I didn't care to know. But I guess now I do understand why — all you really wanted was for someone to give you hope. In that sense, we're alike. Who knows what would've happened if Dominos had got to me first? But when I thought that society had failed me, I met someone who was able to set me straight. I hope that one day, you guys will find someone like that, too."

# CHAPTER 15
## BEWARE THE EXTERMINATOR

"ADELLE!" YURI, JULES, AND LILY YELLED IN UNISON. Jules and Lily rushed to the door, pounding on it with all their strength. But it was useless, as the coating of ice walled off any hope of reaching the outside.

"We have to help her!" Jules yelled.

"There has to be another way to get through!" Lily added.

"No," Yuri whispered. The two panicked teens spun around to stare at their leader.

"What do you mean, 'no?'" Jules barked.

Yuri could feel the worry overtaking his two subordinates. And admittedly, he was fearful as well. But when it came to missions such as this, the key factor was trust.

"Look, we're gonna succeed in this mission, but we all have a job to do. Adelle understands better than anyone the strategies of the Adenji gang and how they operate. She did what she believed was the best course of action for us to get Robin back. We have to trust her."

Though Jules and Lily appeared less than convinced, they

knew that he was right. Adelle could handle herself. Besides, for her, that fight had been personal.

The Adenji compound was rather linear in its design. All the hallways were long, but had few rooms to be checked out. Even so, the team busted open each door for good measure, ready to strike if need be. One after another though, they came up empty.

"Looks like everyone is still outside fighting," Yuri observed. "Even so, we need to be careful. We can't be sure how empty this place is."

"But there's no way that Dominos would be outside with them, right?" Jules asked. "Which means he either escaped or he's wherever Robin is."

Lily added, "Adelle's map showed a place under the compound, right? I think we need to find a way below."

They continued ripping open doors, only to find bathrooms, bedrooms, and other ordinary spaces, but no offices of any sort, and certainly no obvious sign of Robin and Dominos. In fact, much of the eastern compound was empty. The search took less than ten minutes, and it was clear that they were alone.

Yuri pointed off to the side. "Over here—we can follow this path straight to the central compound and see if anyone else made it in."

The next room they entered was a fair bit larger in comparison to the last few areas, and far more decorative. Ornate chandeliers hung high above them, and fancy couches with a glass table sat in the middle. There was no way that the Adenji could be preparing for a fight here.

"Brace yourselves—this could be a trap," Yuri commanded.

"It looks like it could be sort of office," Jules said, taking a few steps into the room, failing to notice the red laser, hovering inches off the ground. The second his foot crossed the line, a blaring alarm sounded. Lights blinded them with red, and the doors in the room slammed shut. Jules whipped around to see Lily behind him, but Yuri was on the other side of the door they'd entered from, now sealed shut.

"Yuri!" Jules and Lily cried out in a panic. Lily pounded on the door, but it was no use.

"Hold on, you two—I'll find a way in!" they could hear Yuri yelling through the steel door, his voice low and muffled.

The blaring of the alarm grew louder, and Lily could feel her heart jump into her throat.

"I can fix this! I can fix this!" Jules yelled, darting his eyes around the room.

Then Lily spotted their solution. "Jules, the other door!"

They hurried to the other side of the room, but that turned out to be their next mistake. Once they reached the center of the room, the floor below them caved in like brittle papier-mâché.

Lily closed her eyes as she plummeted, attempting to shriek. But no sound escaped her terrified lips.

Thinking quick, Jules leapt in after her.

Free falling through increasing darkness and with little time to react, he opened his eyes. He could faintly make out the silhouette of Lily sailing in front of him. Thinking rapidly, he used his wind to propel his body forward and grab Lily by the waist.

"Don't worry, Lil—I got you!" he assured her, using all the strength he could to tunnel wind below them and break their descent.

"Thank you, Jules!" she managed to say, breathless.

"I wouldn't thank me just yet!" Jules gritted his teeth, fighting the force of gravity with all his might.

"Here, let me help!" Lily freed her right arm from Jules, and a burst of water exploded from her palm. It wasn't much, but between the two of them, they managed to halt their momentum in the short time that remained before crashing into the concrete pit below.

They smacked off the ground, rolling over and becoming un-entangled.

"This Dominos isn't kidding around!" Jules said, exasperated. He rolled onto his side, faintly blinking his eyes, but what he saw caused his eyes to shoot open again. Suddenly, his limbs didn't hurt as much. He scrambled to his feet. Laying in front of him were several skeleton bones — something straight out of a horror movie. Some were broken, while others looked like they'd been gnawed at extensively.

From behind, he heard Lily say, "Uh, Jules...I don't like this place..." He turned around and realized that she too was staring at a skeleton, plastered up against the wall as if it was still being tortured.

If nothing else, at least they were out of the darkness. But when they looked above, the ceiling was just an expansive, black void.

Around the room were dozens of pot lights strung up, like torches back in the medieval days. They hung all around the circular room, giving Lily and Jules a disturbing glimpse at the hundreds of skeletons scattered all over the place. Various chains dangled menacingly from the walls. The room smelled like a fresh grave, the lingering odour of the dead tightening their stomachs.

Lily walked over to Jules and asked, "Where do you think we are?"

"Honestly, if I had to guess, I'd say we're in Dominos' personal dungeon. And from the looks of it, he's not too fond of letting people leave."

Lily tried to remain calm, despite being surrounded by skeletons. If there was one thing in life that creeped her out more than anything, skeletons would be it.

"There has to be a way out of here somewhere, right?" Jules wondered aloud.

Lily glanced into the void above. "Do you think you'd be able to fly us up?"

Jules shook his head. "Not likely. I can fly parallel quite well, but gaining height is still too much of a strain for me. And from the distance we fell, we'd never make it."

"I was afraid of that. I guess we should start looking around then. The sooner we get out of here, the better."

"Yeah, good idea. I hope Yuri is okay though." Jules said.

"I'm sure he will be," Lily tried to reassure. "He's still on the surface with all the other EC members and officers around. But the sooner we get back and join with the rest, the sooner we can find him."

They started to make their way around the room, and soon they saw a sign of hope. In the midst of the panic caused by their dungeon surroundings, they'd failed to notice it initially, but now with a clearer head, Lily pointed to a doorway blocked by steel bars. It resembled a jail cell. There was a big problem, however—they were on the wrong side of those bars.

"Guess that's our way out. All we have to do is break the bars. Shouldn't be too hard," Jules said, concentrating. He prepared to bust the door open with vicious wind shots, but then suddenly they heard thunderous stomps from down the hall. Each heavy footstep caused the skeletons to shake, until eventually a massive shadow blocked the exit.

Lily and Jules edged themselves back to a safer distance, watching as the door creaked open.

In stepped an old, short, pudgy man wearing a button-up shirt tucked into his sensible pants. In no way did he fit the Adenji mold; he looked more like a suburban father. The footsteps couldn't have been his.

And they weren't. Once he entered the room, the stomping continued. A massive woman walked in behind him, and she dwarfed the man in front of her in both height and mass. It appeared that she was dressed in a long, heavy, green dress, although in the darkness it was hard for them to know for sure. She also had much more grit in her face than he did.

The pair walked forward hand in hand, each step the woman took shaking the room and nearly bouncing the man off his feet.

"These must be more of Dominos' henchmen," Jules whispered. He held up his fists and arched his legs to brace himself.

Lily squinted her eyes, and as the two stepped into the light, she let out a small gasp.

"Jules! That's Tufa and Lufa...from the briefing, remember? They're Dominos' executioners!" Her legs flinched as she edged back even further. She already knew that they were in for a fight—that much was obvious—but to be going up against the very people who Mr. Howland so heavily advised them to avoid? She couldn't help but fear for her life.

On the other hand, Jules had already made the decision to stand his ground. He began barking orders at the exterminator couple.

"Stand down!" he commanded. "We're with the Elemental Council, and you two are gonna tell us where Dominos is keeping our friend right now!" Jules took an emboldened step forward. Like his brother, he would embrace the role of his job and do it to the best of his ability.

"It appears that Master has sent us a couple of kids to dispose of," the man said as he leered at Jules and Lily. "How tragic the world can be, the precious life of youths taken so early. We know all about that though, don't we dear?" He side-eyed his wife, and in unison, they nodded their heads. The woman did not speak.

Unsure of what to do, Lily decided to stand beside her best friend by saying, "Cut the crap. We want to know where Dominos is hiding Robin, and we're not leaving until we get him back." Her words were far less forceful than Jules', and she wasn't keen on a frontal assault by any means, but there was no way that she could leave Jules to attempt this fight on his own. She'd never abandon her friend like that.

"Ah, yes…the prisoner." Tufa once again glanced at his wife, and together they shook their heads. "I'm afraid we can't do that. We live to serve master Dominos. With him, we may yet see the smiles of our poor daughter. He will bring back everything we've ever lost in this world. It will be an age of radiant happiness. With his powers, nobody will have to face a life cut short."

"What the hell are you guys talking about?" Jules yelled.

Tufa continued speaking, ignoring Jules' outburst. "He promised to return our daughter in his new world. It would be selfish to try and stop such a noble goal. No, no, no — that will not do. Master Dominos has led you to us so that we may dispose of you. So that is what we must do. Strike, Lufa."

The burly brute of a woman grinned, revealing a disgusting smile filled with missing teeth. She shot her fist outward toward Jules like a boxer.

From a solid ten feet away, Jules braced himself for impact, unsure of what to expect. Still, there was no way that Lufa could land a hit from such a distance, even with her size and reach.

But she did manage to do just that.

A burst of light shot from her hand, blinding the room. It happened so fast that Jules didn't have time to react.

The light quickly faded, as Jules felt an invisible fist lodge into his stomach, holding its punch for a moment. Then he went flying backwards and smashed into the concrete wall, shattering part of it. Small rocks began to tumble over top of him.

Lily whipped her head back, yelling out Jules' name. She wanted to rush over, pick him up, and check that he was still alive, but she would not be given such a chance — not while the executioners were still around.

"I wouldn't focus too much energy on your friend, my dear — or else my sweet Lufa here will leave you in a similar state. Nobody escapes Master Dominos' prison."

Lily hesitated, unsure of her next move. She knew that she needed to protect herself and Jules, though that task seemed impossibly difficult. After all, one blindingly fast punch downed Jules for the count, which meant that even if she were to fight defensively, the chances of her holding out for long would be low.

But Lily's thoughts were quickly silenced as Lufa repeated the same actions as before. The air ripped apart again, and a beam of light exploded toward Lily.

Quickly, she crossed her arms and a barrier of water surrounded her body, swallowing up Lufa's punches like branches in a whirlpool. But even with her strong defense, she could feel faint residuals from the attacks ripple through the water and strike her body.

*She's so strong. Even when blocking her punches, she's able to chip away at me. And until she stops, I can't go on the offensive.*

Tufa glared at Lily, then looked back to his wife before he spoke again, this time in a more upbeat tone of voice.

"Look at this beautiful girl, Lufa — doesn't she remind you of our daughter? Even her element is the same. Oh, our dear Melissa…how was she taken so early from us? Life just isn't fair."

The expression on Lufa's silent face twisted and contorted, seemingly in pain. Agony filled her eyes, and then suddenly her attacks became more vicious.

It appeared to Lily that the angrier the woman got, the stronger she became. And her husband, wielding his words like a knife, continued cutting his wife and making her bleed by recounting the emotional toll of losing their daughter.

After a long minute, Lufa's punches finally ceased as she paused to catch her breath.

That gave Lily an opening to counter. She put her hands together and fired off a ball of water in the couple's direction. She knew that the woman's element was light and that she had the ability to attack from range, but Tufa hadn't yet done anything except talk. Was there a chance that he wasn't an Elementalist at all, and that he was therefore using his wife to do all the fighting? That theory seemed unlikely.

But as the water ball hurled toward Lufa and Tufa, Lily soon realized that her speculations were accurate.

"I won't let anyone touch my dear Lufa," the man snarled, waving his hand like a magician. A strange darkness followed as all the lights turned black. Lily heard her attack splash against the wall in the distance and then sprinkle to the ground like raindrops. The shadows faded as the lights illuminated again, but something had changed: Lufa and Tufa were missing.

Lily hopped back, her eyes feverishly darting all around to find them. But then the darkness emerged again and, like ghosts, the duo appeared once more. And then disappeared. And then reappeared.

*I guess that answers that. Tufa must be a shadow Elementalist and can cloak them into disappearing. Well, if I can't see them, then I'll just have to listen for them.* Lily remained in tune with her senses, no longer relying on her eyes but rather her ears to determine Tufa and Lufa's location.

Over the past few years—and in particular, the past few months—while in the process of helping Minisc and his father redecorate their new home, she managed to sneak in a few lessons from the Hero of Light. Of course, she kept this information from Minisc, because she was going to surprise him one day when he finally accepted her challenge. However, he refused this constantly because he could never bring himself to lay a hand on Lily. But with Jules essentially incapacitated and her life on the line against the executioners, she needed to put that training to use.

Hearing the faint shaking of nearby rocks, she spun around to her left, and there stood Tufa and Lufa. But before she could counter, she threw up a shield again as punches cut through the air toward her. These ones were even more forceful than before, colliding with the barrier and pushing her back inch by inch until she was shoved within a few feet from Jules.

"Jules, I need your help!" she cried out.

But as Lily was doing her best to keep the ferocious blows at bay, Jules continued sitting in a pile of rubble along the far wall. Every nerve and muscle in his body screamed, and his chest, arms, and legs felt constricted and paralyzed. The only way to free himself from such pain would be to rip his limbs off. He sat there, almost lifelessly, his eyes closed and his head slumped into his lap.

He could hear the clashes of battle surrounding him, but it was only dull background noise. The pain, though beginning to subside, was overtaking his senses. He could hear Lily's call, but still his body remained frozen to the ground.

Lily's mind tried to generate solutions. *This isn't working.* She needed an opening, but she wasn't going to get it while they were trapped.

There was only one option, albeit a dangerous one. Still, it was the only way. When Lufa briefly paused her attack, Lily sprung her plan into action.

She grabbed Jules by the arm and hoisted him up. "Come on—we're out of here!" She dragged Jules, limp and lethargic, as they attempted to make a dash for the exit.

"You're not going anywhere, my dear," Tufa sneered.

Lily and Jules had almost made it to the door, but then another punch flew through the air and smashed into Lily's side. She and Jules went careening into the wall.

"Jules..." Lily whispered to her friend, concerned that he might now be in even worse shape than before. They both lay dejectedly on the ground, but she refused to concede. Climbing up to one knee, she continued to plead to him. "Please, Jules...I need you to get up..."

Despite hearing Lily's words, Jules couldn't think straight. Running through his head was a muddled mess of thoughts.

*What is wrong with me? Why can't I move? Damn it, body — get up! You can't give up so easily. Not like this. Not now.*

Jules twitched his fingers, feeling the cold, rough surface of the pebbles against his legs.

*I've worked so hard. I've done everything to keep improving — working with Yuri and learning everything I could just to get to this point. To join the EC. I know I've gotten stronger.*

He tried to raise his head, but more than just rocks weighed him down.

*But it's always me that has to be saved at the end of the day. Yuri had to save me at Scotia Coliseum, and then Minisc when I chased Bex down. Even Adelle on the boat...without her I wouldn't have survived. And now Lily is standing off against the executioners of the Adenji gang, and here I am...as useless as ever. It always ends up this way, no matter what I do. All this talk about being like Yuri, about being on the same level as Minisc, pretending to be some sort of hero... it's pathetic. It's all a bunch of lies. I'm always useless whenever something counts. Always...*

Finally, Jules managed to murmur, "Leave me, Lily...I'm not worth it."

Lufa's punches started firing their way again, and Lily did what she could to block them. To protect her friend.

"Not worth it? Don't give me that, Jules! I know that you can still fight! You've never given up on me before, and you're not starting now!" Lily demanded.

The attacks paused again, and Lily dropped to the ground. She didn't have much fight of her own left, and Lufa refused to give her any kind of a decent break before beginning to pummel her again.

Unable to move himself, Jules could feel what mental strength he had left breaking, but what made it worse is that he could hear Lily doing her best to continue their fight. To protect *him*. They both knew that she was against the executioners on her own, but Jules was now convinced that she'd stand a better chance without having to carry his dead weight around.

Lily pleaded with him again. "Jules, please, I need your help! I *know* you can still fight!"

She continued to deflect and dodge Lufa as best she could, but it seemed there was no end in sight. Worse, Jules was growing increasingly unresponsive, laying there in fashion similar to the skeletons around the room.

*I know, Lily…I wanna help you…I wanna fight with you…but I just can't. I'm not strong enough. I'm not like you guys…I always just end up in the way when the chips are down.*

Jules twitched his body, trying to grab at the rocks on the ground, but still he couldn't.

*If I don't do something, Lily is going to die. We both are, and it's gonna be all my fault.*

Ever since he could speak, and most likely even before that, Jules had idolized his brother. His older sibling embodied everything that Jules aspired to be. The strength he displayed, the compassion for those in need…and yet it was so much more than that for Jules. Yuri was courageous, refusing to blink in the face of danger. Under any circumstances, he fought proudly. He fought with all he had. Even after the loss of his element, those traits never changed. He continued to believe in himself, never allowing his confidence to slip. Everyone could look to him and smile, knowing that they'd be safe from any threat that faced them.

*I just wanted to be like you, Yuri. Your courage was what I wanted most. Like Lily's courage, Minisc's courage, and everyone else…they refused to concede defeat no matter the cost, even in the darkest times. But when I get knocked down, I just wait for someone to come save me.*

He felt his body being lifted up again. It was Lily. Suddenly, they were on the move. He was running, although he couldn't feel his feet moving. They rounded a corner, and then another, busting through a door and into a strange-looking hallway. Lily slammed the door shut behind her and grabbed what she could to barricade the door. They could hear Lufa and Tufa coming, and they were running out of time.

"Lily…I'm sorry," Jules whispered. He sat against the wall. "I was useless again…I let you down."

His dejected words were met with a smack, straight across his face. His eyes opened wide, and now he was definitely wide awake. He met Lily's eyes, her tired, beaten-down eyes.

"That's enough, Jules! I don't know what's got into you these past few days, but whatever it is, it stops here. You're not useless—you never have been and you never will be. You've always been there for me and Minisc, and you're going to do it again right now. Because that's who you are!"

"No…I'll just get in the way. I'm not brave like you guys…"

Lily could see his confidence waning more and more. But they didn't have time for that—they were seconds away from another execution attempt.

"What on earth are you talking about? You're the bravest of us all! *You* were the one who convinced us to go after Don when he faced Ignis, and *you* were the one who took down Bex after what she did to Yuri. Despite everything we've faced, you've always stood by us, even when you were hurting. And I need you to find that courage and do it again. Me, Yuri, Minisc, Robin—we all *need* you right now!"

A faint flicker of life returned to Jules eyes, and the spark of fire that had always burned in his stomach began to reappear— and not because of his unwavering courage, but in spite of it. He was scared; there was no doubt about that. The force of Lufa's punch had caused him to feel more pain than most people could even imagine. But he knew that the pain paled in comparison to the regret that he'd take to his grave, knowing that he let his friend die fighting while he remained in his own head. He couldn't live like that.

Jules glanced up at his friend. "Thank you, Lily…I…I needed that."

Lily grabbed Jules by the hand and lifted him up. "You can thank me when we get out of this mess. For now, we need a plan. And we're running out of time."

At the other end of the hall, Lily's barricade caved and the door smashed open. They knew that their time was up.

Jules took Lily's arm and started running down the long, stone tunnel again.

"Now where are we going?" Lily asked, panting.

"I have no clue, but we're not sticking around here!"

The two could hear vengeful sprinting behind them, and when Jules glanced back, he saw Lufa hot on their heels. Tufa wasn't far behind.

"No way—she wasn't that fast before!" he gawked.

Lufa started firing blasts of light at Jules and Lily, sailing over their heads and crashing into the walls. The two were close to an escape, until finally a shot made contact. A blast crashed into Lily's shoulder, dropping her to the ground and into a heap. She winced, grabbing at the spot of impact on her ripped uniform.

"I'm afraid that this is the end for you, my dears," Tufa said. "It's unfortunate, but this is Master Dominos' wish. You will now be executed."

Lily looked up, seeing the horrific sight of the executioners down the hall. She tried to get to her feet, but before she could, Lufa thrust her fist forward.

"No! Not this time!" Jules yelled. He slid in front of Lily, blocking the punch with his arms crossed. The light seared his arms, and he grimaced in pain. But this time, he held strong.

"Self-sacrifice—quite a noble thing to do for a friend, but it won't stop us. Lufa, finish them off."

"I refuse to back down so easily again! Give it your best shot!" Jules yelled at the evil duo. He uncrossed his arms and with a powerful roar, he shouted, "Galaxy Tornado!"

The wind managed to trap the assailants, nearly sending the smaller-sized Tufa sailing backwards, but Lufa didn't budge. She anchored herself to the ground and began firing off balls of light.

Stuck trying to hold the two of them off with his wind, Jules had no way to protect himself. His only option was to take the hits and remain standing. Each blow sent agonizing stings all through his body, but not as bad as before. The wind was slowing down the impact.

Finally, Lufa began to tire, and Jules let out a deep roar as he pushed his wind toward her further. Using what little energy remained in his war-torn body, the wind exploded into a heavy push that finally rivalled Lufa's punches. The blows came to a stop as Lufa's arms fell to her side and her face turned crimson red.

Tufa smirked from the sidelines. "You two are brave, choosing to fight instead of run...but your stunt was nothing more than just a slow pause before your inevitable death. Lufa, finish them!"

"That's what you think!"

From behind him, Jules could feel Lily's presence, even if he couldn't turn to see her. But it was clear that she'd caught onto his plan.

Lily stepped up beside Jules, and seeing her advancing caused Tufa's eyes to widen. Not because she was alive, but because of the glowing, blue water spinning around her body. It wrapped around her, making her appear as a water goddess, until it came together into a massive ball. It was a special move she'd worked on with Don, just for situations like this. It harnessed all the strength of her element, but it would be just the thing to take Lufa and Tufa out for good.

Due to her struggles in gathering such strength so quickly, using it in a battle seemed dicey. But with Jules sacrificing himself to buy her time, she was now ready to unleash her attack.

"Take this! Oceanic eruption!" Lily whipped her hands down, sending the ball of water, which nearly took up the entire corridor, rushing into Lufa and Tufa.

"Lufa, block it!" Tufa ordered.

The powerful woman jabbed her hands out and tried to shield herself from the impact with a wall of light, but the momentum of the attack was too strong to be resisted.

"Jules, end this now!" Lily yelled.

"You got it! Say goodnight, Executioners!" Jules raised his hands again, unleashing all the wind he could muster through the tunnel. It gripped the ball of water and effortlessly shoved it past Lufa's shield, ending with an incredible eruption.

Blinding rays of light lit up the corridor, followed by layers of smoke and mist. Jules and Lily raised their arms to shield themselves from the light, but the ripples tossed them through the air. They landed, exhausted but exhilarated, into a heap.

Lily got up first. She turned her attention toward the nefarious pair, and then exhaled when she saw them. The Adenji executioners lay crumpled on the ground, unconscious. The battle was over.

Now that she had a minute to stop and allow the tolls of battle to sink in, Lily bent over with her hands on her knees.

Her body spasmed like a small, venomous creature was crawling through her skin, and her muscles were cramped. She'd sunk all of her strength into one final attack to take down Lufa and Tufa. Luckily the plan had worked, but only thanks to Jules.

Lily gingerly walked over to her friend, holding her injured left arm close against her body. She knelt down on one knee, staring at Jules with admiration. He had small drops of blood on his arms, and his chest was rising and falling rapidly as he stared up at the rock ceiling above them.

"We did it, right? We won?" Jules said, wincing and breathing heavily as he spoke.

"Yes...yes, we won," Lily said, almost completely out of breath herself. "And it was all thanks to you! You were incredible!"

Jules managed a smile. It was a weak one and all he could muster, but his confidence had returned. He didn't always come up short when the chips were down after all.

Lily stuck her hand out to pull him up, but when he tried to move, he struggled.

"Everything hurts..." he groaned.

"I know, but we still need to find a way back to Yuri. Do you think you can walk?"

Jules ran his fingers along the bumpy ground. He could feel the harsh coldness of the floor, stained with his blood. But it also meant that he was still alive. Using the same courage he'd showed when taking the executioners down, he took Lily's hand and weakly hoisted himself up.

"Yeah, I'll be fine eventually. I can manage. Let's find a way out of here and get back to Yuri. He's gonna kill me for this..."

Lily stumbled over to where Lufa and Tufa lay defeated. There was a strange glow emanating from Tufa's belt, looking like some sort of key card. She unbuckled the small chain from his waist, holding her breath as she did, still fearful that they'd wake up and finish her off. But no—the hideous pair were truly done. And now with a key in hand, they just needed to find a door.

"If there's a key, then there must be a way out of here," Jules said. Lily agreed.

As she began to follow her friend, she looked back toward

the disgraced husband and wife and frowned slightly. "I feel sort of bad for them, you know? All that talk about losing their daughter, and Dominos weaponizing such pain and using it to his advantage…I can't even imagine."

Jules became a bit somber as well. "What do you think they meant when they said that Dominos would be able to return their daughter to his new world? You don't think he was talking about actually reviving the dead, do you?"

Lily looked back from the defeated duo to Jules, still frowning with melancholy. "I don't know. But what I do know is that the past can't be changed. The pain of losing someone can never be fixed, no matter how hard Dominos might try. All we can do is help support each other through the dark times and focus on the present. If we live our lives full of lingering regrets for those we've lost, we'll never be able to move forward. Day by day, we'd be allowing the darkness to consume our minds until there's nothing left. And clearly, that's what's happened to Dominos."

Jules agreed with Lily—after all, what she'd said was in accordance with Yuri's teachings. Living in the past and being saddled with regrets would never create a better future.

"All right," he nodded. "Let's get moving."

# CHAPTER 16
## NEVER LOSE HOPE

ROBIN'S EYES FLUTTERED OPEN. THE ROOM WAS DARK, his body limp. He tried to force his eyes to adjust to his surroundings, but with such sparse light, the effort was futile.

"Where am I?"

He moved his arms and heard a strange jingle, chains rattling. He glanced down to see that his assumptions were correct. Metal chains, nailed into the concrete wall behind him, were strapped to his arms and legs. It was like he was trapped in a dungeon.

"'Bout time you came to. I've been waiting almost an entire day. For a second, I thought I might have to hook you up to one of these machines to keep you alive."

The voice was familiar, mocking, sinister.

Dominos.

The lights around the room flickered on, and Robin realized that he wasn't in an actual dungeon, but it was eerily similar to one. It was, in fact, a dull and sparse hospital room. On the other side of the area was an empty bed, on which there were various machines, looking primed and ready to function. At first, Robin thought that he was about to be experimented on, but something told him that wasn't the case. He continued to squirm his way loose, to no avail.

Then he spotted Dominos, seated in a chair in the middle of the room. He was bald and thin, wearing everyday street clothes. This was the same man who'd hunted him down in the first place, and it was a face he wouldn't soon forget.

"Oh no you don't—you're not going anywhere there, Junior. Not until you see what I've got for you."

Dominos stood up from his chair, pulling a photo from his jacket and tossing it on the ground in front of Robin. The picture was of a young boy stationed in a hospital bed, his hair only a shade lighter than Robins. His eyes were closed like he was at peace, but the machines that were hooked up around him suggested quite a different story.

"You recognize this kid?" Dominos asked. "You should. See, I did a little research on you. How could I not? After all, you're that old man's pride and joy. And what a shock it was for me to learn of your little brother and his lingering illness…"

"You monster!" Robin yelled. "Don't you dare bring Edin into this! Whatever your plans are, he has nothing to do with it!"

"Now, now—what happened to that unwavering positive aura you were trotting around with before? I thought that's what made you so special. Or at least that's what I remember the old man telling me once."

Dominos walked up to Robin, taunting him like a caged animal. "You know, we actually share something in common. Your little brother and my mother—they both share the same heart-destroying virus. An incurable plague that slowly whittles down their will to live until they have nothing left. Doctors say that there's no cure…but I disagree."

Dominos picked up a few vials from beside the empty bed,

shaking them about. His face was becoming more delirious as he talked.

"You see, I know better. I know that we can make a cure. We can save all these people...Edin, my mother, and so many more...but we need more time. Time that they don't have."

Robin regained his composure. "What are you talking about?"

"Let me spell it out for you: I've been working on a way to preserve these dying bodies, attempting to keep them in a stasis to buy time until a cure could be made. I was close, too. But when the EC snuck onto our ships and took my supplies, what they were really doing was allowing for all of these people, just like your brother, to die. And of course, the EC is too high and mighty to dare and try anything such as putting bodies into a stasis, so I know that they'll never make proper use of my work. I need those chemicals. Edin needs those chemicals. That's why I need you."

Robin couldn't believe what he was hearing, but he was rapt by every word. Dominos approached him even closer.

"Any minute now, the EC will be showing up on this doorstep to take me down—and to take you back. And when they do, Edin will be handed his death sentence, just like all the rest. There'll be no getting him back. But if you tell the EC to call off their attack right now, and hand me over all the supplies I need, then you have my word: I will find a way to save your brother."

Robin had listened to what Dominos was saying very intently. He stared down at the picture of his little brother. Even in Edin's sleep, the two looked so very much alike.

The day when Robin had learned of his brother's doomed fate, it tore him up inside. It destroyed their entire family. Such an innocent young boy, given only years to live.

His mind was paralyzed and his heart was pained. Everything he did, the work he put in, the relentlessly positive attitude—all of it was to make his brother smile. It was his whole reason for the path he chose.

Robin hung his head, tears beginning to drop to the floor. "No," he whispered. "I won't do that. What you're doing is wrong. I know it's impossible, but sometimes we have to accept our losses. We've known for a long time that this was Edin's fate. And I wish I could change it. More than anything, I do — but what you're doing…it's just causing more pain to everyone involved. I love my brother, and this isn't what he would want. What he would want is for me to stop you, just like The Hero of Light would." Robin raised his head, trembling as he fought back his emotions.

In contrast, Dominos' reaction was one of pure fury.

"I get it. He's brainwashed you, too. You have a chance to save a life that's so precious to you, and you're going to let your own stupid morality get in the way? Well, Junior — that was the wrong answer. I'll be getting those supplies back regardless. I *will* achieve my goals. And when I do, I'll make sure to leave both you and your brother to a slow and painful death."

But as Dominos headed for the door, he felt the ceiling shake above him, and small chunks of debris began tumbling down.

The door flew open, and two people stepped into the room. One was a withered older man with ghostly pale skin, and the other a striking woman with a glare that was cold as ice. Marco and Kari, Dominos' top two aids.

"Master, the EC is attacking," Marco said. "We must begin moving immediately."

"I'm done here anyway. Leave the boy." Dominos followed his two subordinates out and slammed the door shut.

The room fell dark again, and Robin could hear the commotion from up above. He needed to act. He needed to be the hero his brother had inspired him to be. He needed to stop Dominos.

Like a wild animal, Robin shook the chains with all his might, and soon he could feel them coming loose. But it wasn't because of his strength — it was thanks to the thunderous clamour above, loosening the pins holding him captive. With each faint crack in the wall and each moment the pins popped out further, Robin's body weight dropped. With a clink, the chains finally fell off and, thinking quickly, he used the nails to break his cuffs free.

*You better watch out, Dominos. This time you're not getting away.*

He left the room that he'd been shackled in and started down the long hallway. The path ahead was straight and narrow, with not a single turn or corner in sight. The only way was forward.

Robin could feel his heart pumping. A full-on sprint would have been more ideal, but he needed to be on the lookout for traps, especially not knowing where he was.

After a minute or so of walking, he heard footsteps. He picked up his pace, knowing that he had to catch Dominos.

But his sprint gradually slowed as three figures came into view in front of him.

Dominos came to a stop, steadily turned around, and crossed his arms. "Look, Junior — I was nice enough to let you live, but you're starting to get on my nerves. Just go running back to that old man, would you? Leave me be. I've got bigger fish to fry."

Marco and Kari raised their fists, but Dominos showed no signs of fighting.

Robin raised his as well. "Not a chance. I already told you that this is wrong, Dominos, and I won't let you take it any further. And while we're at it, you and everyone else with the Adenji gang are under arrest for the torture you've put so many through."

Dominos rubbed his temples in frustration. "Why does nobody ever see what I'm trying to accomplish…?"

"If you just give up now, maybe we can still find a cure in time. Wouldn't that still be worth it?" Robin was almost pleading now. "You have a chance to do the right thing, Dominos. You need to take it."

But Robin knew that it would ultimately be hopeless. He recognized that face, that terror in the man's eyes. It was a dangerous look that he was far too familiar with.

"You're nothing but a fool," Dominos muttered, placing his hand on the stone wall beside him. Two soaring pillars shot out of the wall, aiming to crush Robin between them.

Dominos stared at his pillars, but Robin had vanished. *This kid's faster than he looks.*

The pillars returned into the walls, and then suddenly there stood Robin, a few feet back. He was breathing hard, but refused to take his eyes off Dominos. He could still feel the stabbing pain in his ankle, though; his previous injuries clearly remained an issue.

"I told you, Dominos—I'm not letting you continue this."

"I've had enough! Kari, Marco—deal with him." Dominos gave a mocking salute to Robin, before turning to leave. "Adios, Junior—and say hi to the old man for me."

As he departed, a stone wall rose from the ground and sealed his exit, leaving Robin alone with the fiend's aids.

Marco cracked his knuckles while Kari licked her pale lips. "This place will be your grave," she told Robin with an icy glare.

Kari stood by the wall where Dominos had just been and placed her palm against it. In a flash, the temperature plummeted and their surroundings were coated in ice. That was bad enough, but then Kari began creating jagged spikes of icicles and pillars that sprouted out from every angle.

"I've already seen this trick! It won't fool me again!" Robin wiggled his way through the attacks, gliding across the icy bedrock toward his opponent.

He cocked a glowing, golden fist and slammed it into Kari, who raised her forearm in an attempt to block it. Then he jammed a ball of light into her stomach, and it exploded with a blinding bang.

Before Marco could react, Robin fired a blast of light toward him, exploding like a flare and blinding the fire Elementalist. Robin made a diving dash at Marco, refusing to let him attack. He landed a gut punch that sent Marco flying into the wall and crumpling to the ground.

Robin knew his own strength, so he could easily assume that his attacks were nothing more than pillow hits to his opponents. However, there was no chance of chasing down Dominos as long as they were still fighting. He'd have to take them out swiftly.

"That was a big mistake, kid," Kari seethed under her breath, placing her hands on the floor.

Robin came to a skidding halt as pillars of ice began to form in front of him.

*This is bad. As long as we're sealed in like this, I can't keep avoiding her attacks. And if Marco unleashes those flames, they'll both have me pinned.*

Feeling stuck, Robin heard another incoming attack. He spun around to see layers of ice sprinting toward him. He squished his body tight, attempting to dodge the deadlier ones while smashing the thinner ones. Soon, the entire hall was laced with sharp icicles sticking out from every inch like a porcupine's hide. They were even sprouting outward like branches on a tree. It was never ending.

Luckily Robin managed to dodge most of the attacks, but when Marco got to his feet, trouble was on the horizon. He raised his hands, crossing them into the shape of a bird. The flames in his palms slowly formed into a phoenix, flying high to the ceiling. It began soaring through the room, breathing fire and leaving Robin with no place to run.

There was, however, one benefit from the flames. It weakened the ice, giving Robin a chance to return blasts of light and clear out as many icicles as he could. But even so, things were turning into a battle of endurance—something that he lacked at the moment.

*This is insane. If I focus on the icicles, Marco's flames will burn me to a crisp. But if I take my eyes off Kari, I'll be skewered. And they're so quick that I can barely keep up.*

Unless backup arrived, which he had no reason to expect, he was on his own. But he refused to concede. He'd made a promise to his brother, and he would win—no matter the cost.

Acting quickly, Robin shot a ball of light into the air, colliding with the stream of fire from Marco's phoenix. Simultaneously, he slid along the ice, dodging the overhead icicles falling in his path. Each with a glassy bang, the tops of each icicle were shaved off before clinking to the ground and shattering like crystal. Robin hurried to his feet again, and then he saw his opening. Kari needed to catch her breath. The icicles were slowing down.

Marco got to his feet and scurried beside an exhausted Kari. The two were glaring through a finely crafted mini landscape of spikes and pillars and saw Robin on the other side. The EA grad stood proud, confidently assured.

Robin had been fighting admirably. He was holding his own against poor odds, but every second he wasted on Marco and Kari, the further Dominos fled.

"I'll admit it—you're not half bad, kid," Marco confessed. "The Adenji gang could always use a talent like yours. But since you're so hellbent on being a thorn in Master Dominos' side, playtime is over!" Marco's menacing tone was indicative of his powers. He cast his hand forward, and a wave of fire leveled the entire battlefield. The ice evaporated in a literal flash, while Robin crossed his arms and created a barrier of light to protect himself.

"As long as you stand against Master Dominos, you won't make it out of here alive!" Kari added, speaking just as fiercely as her partner.

Robin clenched his fist. "I don't care. I took an oath as Mr. Howland's student to do all I could to protect this world. I made a promise to my brother that I'd never let people like you hurt others. And those are two promises that I refuse to break!"

Robin remained resolute. Yes, he lacked an exit strategy, but so did Marco and Kari; they were locked in battle together, which meant that all he needed to do was win. Or die.

Marco yelled out to Robin, "You're so unbelievably naive! Dominos will be the one to fix this world. He'll heal the sick, and he'll cure the incurable. Imagine a planet where people can escape death. It would be the perfect world."

"Perfect for who?" Robin shouted in return. "The people you test on? The families you put through this torture? All you're doing is trying to play God. And I won't let you do it anymore!"

Marco raised his hands to the sky, releasing another phoenix. It roared majestically as flickers of fire flew off its tail.

"Face it—you're outnumbered, kid! You don't have a hope in hell," Marco roared.

Beside him, Kari twisted her foot into the ground. Just like before, pillars of ice shot from the floor and toward Robin. But this time they were slower, with less spikes protruding from them. The woman was becoming taxed. He could see it.

"I don't care what my odds are...I'll still win!" Robin thrust out his left arm, and five precise blasts exploded from his fingers, leaving a path of destruction in their wake.

The balls of light closed in, shaving off the tops of the icicles and clearing the field for Robin to move freely.

"Marco, block it!" Kari ordered. The second-in-command of the Adenji gang did as he was told, stretching his hands out and preparing to counter with flames. But as he prepared to unleash the fiery burst, a silhouette appeared through the final ball of light.

"You might be strong, but make no mistake—when it comes to heart, you'll never beat me!" Robin shot out from the light, thrusting his fist into Marco's gut. It sent the man flying backward as Robin skidded to a halt.

The blinding light from Robin's attack forced Kari to shield her eyes. "Kid, you just don't know when to give up!" she shouted.

"Give up? To monsters like you? Never!" Robin grabbed the woman's arm and spun her around, firing a blast of light into her back. Then, with bullet-like speed, he shot back at Marco, who scrambled to his feet in defense. A jumble of thoughts ran rapidly through Robin's head:

*I've got no choice — I can't hold back for even a second. If I do, I'll never make it to Dominos. My best strategy right now is an all-out assault while they're tired. This is everything I've trained for…everything Mr. Howland has taught me. Everything that Edin wanted me to be. I can win this. And I will win this.*

Robin continued springing back and forth, doing his best to take elements out of the fight altogether. He could tell by just a glance that the two of them were only average in combat, and that their true strength was in the environment and their elements within it.

Brilliantly, he decided to use his own element as merely a distraction. The balls of light would never be fast enough to strike on their own, but they'd be blinding enough for him to gain an upper hand. He could also use the rays to shield himself from a surprise attack as he went for his frontal assault.

"Can't you see?!? Master Dominos is doing this world a favour!" Marco shouted vehemently.

Robin roared in anger, continuing his relentless attack with an uppercut that could shatter a jaw.

All the while, his mind continued to race, drawing up every memory, every experience, and every lesson he'd ever learned:

*Read their movements. Stay focused. And don't give them a second to react. As long as you keep bringing the fight to them, numbers don't matter.*

A beam of light rocketed outward from Robin's hand and sent Kari crashing through the spikes, cutting her arms and legs.

Both Macro and Kari now lay crumpled on the ground, while Robin stood only a few feet away, prepared for round two. But he needed to catch his breath. The desire to stop Dominos spurred his strength to new heights, but keeping such a level of speed and tenacity for so long had wreaked havoc on his body. His knuckles were bleeding, his clothes ripped, and his face covered in dirt and grime. Not that it mattered, though—he could rest later, when Dominos was defeated. And not a moment sooner.

"Had enough?" Robin hollered at them through shallow breaths.

Marco rose to one knee, his arms dripping in blood, while Kari remained on the ground. She showed no signs of movement.

"Youth...so cocky, but also so negligent. That's the thing that'll cost you your life," Marco said, his face turning into a demonic smirk.

Robin opened his mouth to react, but suddenly he felt a chill run through his left leg. The cool sensation then turned into a searing, burning pain. The same pain began surging through his right arm. Before he knew it, he was gasping and sputtering a mouthful of blood.

"Shouldn't have taken your eyes off me," Kari snarled, pushing herself off the floor. Her hand had an icy wind swirling around it.

A faint streak of ice bent around Robin, and then three thin but extremely excruciating icicles pierced his arms and legs. They stabbed into him like knives, leaving him strung up like a puppet.

"You were a worthy opponent, kid...but now it's over." Marco and Kari both stretched their hands out, building the final ounces of power they still had.

Meanwhile, Robin hung his head low, his hair hiding the agonizing pain on his face. Blood slowly dripped out of his arm

and thigh where the small spikes were digging deep into his flesh. It was the exact same way that Dominos had got him the first time — and the reason he was stuck in this position now.

"I told you that I wouldn't lose…" he growled under his breath.

A fire still burned deep in his stomach. Perhaps his life was being drained by the second, but his will to fight was only growing stronger. This fight was far from over.

With his free hand, he ripped the jagged spike from his arm, tossing it to the ground. Then he tore the one out of his thigh and threw that one aside, too.

"Let me make something clear to you guys: I set out to stop Dominos…and I'm not going to quit until I do. This is one fight that you *won't* win."

A jolt of pain raced through his thigh like a scorching burn, but he bit his lip, attempting to numb the pain. He recalled the memory of his past injuries. He'd always survived. He knew that these wounds were intense, but he also knew that he could handle it. At least for a while.

Marco gawked in astonishment, stunned at how tenacious Robin was.

*This boy…how does he keep fighting? Such an extreme amount of pain from the wounds…how can he tolerate it? It's madness! Would he actually sacrifice his own life just to keep us from curing the world?*

Marco and Kari were summoning up their final reserves of power in hopes of putting Robin down for good, just as the EA grad was preparing his final gambit. Holding out his uninjured arm, Robin summoned up what remained of his element.

"Light of justice!" he roared. Like a shotgun, a beam of light exploded, colliding with Kari and Marco's fruitless attacks.

The earth shook, the walls struggling to contain the power that had been unleashed.

Then the room fell silent.

On the floor, Robin could feel the harsh ice on his face, the coolness of it touching his nose. The rest of his body was numb. His arms twitched with a relentless throb, but it was like all the nerves in his body were so far past their limits that they'd broken. He tilted his head, glaring over at his fallen opponents. Thankfully, he wasn't the only one to suffer the shock waves of his attack. He could faintly make out the bodies of Kari and Marco, unconscious on the floor. He'd won the battle.

But with Dominos' whereabouts unknown, perhaps he'd lost the war.

# CHAPTER 17
## TREACHEROUS PATH AHEAD

THE REVVING OF HELICOPTER BLADES WERE deafening. Minisc could barely hear himself think up there careening through the skies, which did nothing to help his nerves. They were still a little way off from the Adenji compound, giving everyone else on the ground time to get into position. As for Minisc and Mr. Howland, they'd be dropping down in and amongst the commotion caused by the raid. They'd swoop in, grab Robin, and use the key card provided by Adelle to escape through the forest before Dominos even knew he was gone.

Minisc looked out through the long side window, but they were still up quite high, and certainly too far away to see anything of note.

"I don't get it," Minisc said, sitting across from Mr. Howland on one of the two black benches that ran parallel to each other.

"Don't get what?"

"Dominos' endgame. Let's say that we made a fair trade, Dominos gets his chemicals, and we get Robin back. What then? It would only buy him a little more time, right? So unless he magically found a cure for your wife's heart virus, he'll need more supplies to come in. And now everyone at the EC will be looking for them. And he won't have Robin as a bargaining chip next time. Even if he wins, he's going to lose in the end."

Up to this point, Mr. Howland had been sitting in silence and deep in thought, but Minisc's questions prompted him to speak.

"It's hard to say for sure. What I do know is that my son is cunning. That is how he seized control of the Adenji gang in the first place. He has been preying on those who have lost someone near to them, exploiting their despair, and telling them that he can cure their loved ones of sickness. But I think deep down, he knows that he can't. He knows that he is going to fail, which is why he is doing this. As much as he wants to save his mother, he also wants to punish me for not being a better father, so if he is going to lose, he wants to bring me down with him. And he will do that by way of Robin, which makes it all the more important that we hurry."

Minisc still struggled to fathom the concept of Dominos being Mr. Howland's son. But at this point, it didn't matter. What Dominos was doing and the pain he was causing had to be stopped.

"Remember, Minisc—Dominic is not your burden to bear. Our goal is to rescue Robin. The rest will play out how it will play out."

"Understood."

There was no going back now. The countdown was on. Soon, the Adenji compound came into the helicopter's view.

That's when Minisc's nerves really began to go into overdrive. He took a deep breath and looked to Mr. Howland for comfort, who provided none. The man's face remained somber, maybe even regretful.

Then they heard a small explosion. Minisc leapt up from his seat as his heart jumped into his throat. They turned their attention to the window. Below them was the start of an all-out war. Adenji members were rushing from the north, east, and west compounds. Minisc was instantly struck with the fear of what could befall Lily, Jules, and the others. But he knew that he had to believe. They all had their jobs to do, and his was getting Robin back.

Stunned by the chaos, Minisc was pulled out of his shock by Mr. Howland.

"Get ready. We won't get a second chance at this."

Minisc nodded.

With their parachutes loaded, they were finally ready to jump. They'd hit the back door of the Adenji compound and despite the craziness taking place all around them, they'd gain easy access inside and find Robin. From there, they'd take the underground corridors until they reached the escape hatch in the forest. Then they'd head south, until they were within what the EC considered a safe zone.

Mr. Howland pried the helicopter door open, and the wind pressure nearly knocked Minisc backward. But he held firm and took another deep breath. Who would've thought that jumping out of a helicopter would be the least of his worries for the day? But that was nothing more than an afterthought. For now, his mind was focused solely on the mission ahead.

The helicopter came to a stop, hovering amongst the clouds. Mr. Howland nodded and then waved his hand for the boy to jump. Minisc followed his command, springing out of the aircraft and into the skies, followed by his teacher.

The two darted down like missiles. Minisc tried to shield his eyes from the potency of the wind, but they were freefalling so quick that moving his body was tough. Luckily, it didn't feel too much different than battling Jules, which meant that he could at least withstand the force.

They could see the entire Adenji compound below and the

state of what it currently looked like. Clouds of smoke, walls of ice and rock, and bright flashing lights, all of which signified how intense the battles were.

"Pull your chute!" Mr. Howland ordered.

The words almost missed Minisc entirely, as he was so caught up in the views beneath him, but when he heard the sounds of his partner's chute flapping fiercely in the air, he instinctually did the same. He felt his body jerk upward, and then his momentum gradually slowed as he descended.

Step one complete. Minisc landed in the massive open field between the towering forest and the south end of the Adenji compound. He glanced over at the large, two-story building. There was nobody around, just as they'd planned on, but that didn't mean that getting in would be simple. Any windows on the second floor were blocked by some sort of vine-like web, probably from an Elementalist. And the chances of the back door being left wide open seemed unlikely.

But luckily, they caught a break. Thanks to the Adenji member that Lily had apprehended a few days ago, they had a passcode. Just as that disgraced member had feared upon his arrest, he'd cracked under the pressure.

Minisc started clicking a series of buttons and ripping off the straps of his chute before following alongside Mr. Howland, who was already moving. Now freed, they bolted for the Adenji complex.

Just like at the front compound, there was a large, sealed-off garage entrance. Mr. Howland punched in the code, and they heard a jingle confirming their access.

"Looks like that Adenji member was telling the truth. Good. Let's go." Mr. Howland slid the door open and they piled into the garage, not wasting any time with admiring the surroundings.

"This way!" Mr. Howland rushed over to a staircase on the

far end of the room, skipping every other step as he hurriedly ascended. Minisc followed closely behind, keeping his eyes
peeled for any ambushes. But it appeared that the Adenji gang
already had their hands full.

They started barging doors open and saw various living quarters, but all the rooms were empty.

Finally, Minisc found something at the back. "Mr. Howland!
Come look at this!"

The EC elder statesman ditched the room he'd been peering
into and rushed to the end of the hall. When they entered the
room, he nodded, "Good work. This must be what Adelle was
talking about. Let's go."

The two hurried down a long, winding spiral staircase until
they found themselves deep underground. They came to a sudden stop.

"This place…it looks like they just ripped an entire floor
straight from a hospital," Minisc whispered.

"Knowing my son, he might've. But that's not our priority.
We need to check every room that we can and find Robin. He
must be down here somewhere — I'm sure of it."

Minisc and Mr. Howland started opening doors, frantic. But
when they saw what was on the other side of them, they were
stunned.

"Are these…?" Minisc gasped.

"Yes, the people important to the Adenji gang…all those that
Dominic claims he can save. Loved ones desperately holding
on."

"They don't look like they're being saved…" Minisc said. The
body right in front of him was of a deathly-coloured man tan-
gled in wires.

"Because they're not. It's all just a lie." Mr. Howland turned
away, and began his search again.

Normally, they would've been calling out, praying for Robin to give them a sign of life, but that was too risky. They still couldn't confirm if they were even alone.

They eventually found the hospital room that confirmed Mr. Howland's worst fears. He stared at the bed through the open door, looking like he'd seen a ghost. His generally calm composure cracked, if only slightly, and his face began to twist in pain.

Minisc stared at the woman in the bed. She was frail and decaying from the cruelty of time, with tubes and wires running in and out of her. The monitor on the wall indicated a pulse, but she was clearly just barely clinging to life.

"That's her, isn't it?" Minisc whispered.

Mr. Howland silently nodded and turned his back to the woman. "We need to go…this has to stop," he quietly said before walking away.

Minisc couldn't fathom the pain that was in his mentor's heart at that moment. He wanted to say something, to do something. He wanted to save the woman, just like Dominos had done. But Mr. Howland was right—there was no saving her. From what he could tell, Dominos was only prolonging her death.

The pair continued their search through the spooky hallways, until they saw two bodies up ahead on the ground. They were surrounded by remnants of a massive battle, with cracks in the walls, shattered ice, small flickers of flames, and more signs of mayhem.

Minisc and Mr. Howland rushed up to the scene, but came to a sudden stop when they recognized the bodies.

"That's…that's Kari and Marco, isn't it?" Minisc asked.

"It certainly is…which means that Robin must have orchestrated his own escape. Come on—he can't have gone far."

On the run again, at the end of the next hallway they spotted a door that was slightly ajar. Peering in, they noticed a boy collapsed next to the wall. He was dripping with blood, his head facing flat into the ground.

"Robin!" they both called out. Stunned, the two rushed toward the boy, getting to their knees to check on him.

Mr. Howland grabbed Robin and embraced him. "You're alive…" It might've been the first true sign of affection the man had ever given a member of his team.

Robin's eyes slowly fluttered open, and he let out a raspy cough. Trying to push himself up, he said, "Mr. Howland… Minisc…you guys came…" He managed a faint smile, weak but elated.

"Of course we came! Friends don't leave friends behind, right?" Minisc said, beaming at the sight of his friend. Just moments ago, Robin's fate had been unknown. And now here he was. A little worse for wear, but alive and conscious.

"Right," Robin smiled.

Mr. Howland nodded. "We need to hurry. The hatch to the forest should be close by. Once we get there, we can make our escape. Minisc, take Robin's arm."

Mr. Howland and Minisc each took one of Robin's arms and slung them over their shoulders. They helped carry him forward, moving as fast as the injured boy was able.

"They really got me good, didn't they?" Robin said, trying to bring a small bit of levity to the situation.

"I'd say that you did a number on them, too," Mr. Howland said. "We saw the state you left those two in. You did well, Robin."

"Thank you, Sir."

Shortly after, they reached another sloped staircase that led them to the metal hatch they'd been searching for.

"We made it," Minisc said, feeling prematurely triumphant. "I just hope that the others are doing okay."

"Stay focused. We're not in the clear just yet," Mr. Howland reminded him. He went into the hatch first after popping it open with a quick swipe of Adelle's key card.

What they were hoping to be greeted with was sunshine and fresh air, but no such pleasure was to be found just yet. The forest smelled rancid, and the light was struggling to pierce through the large branches overhead.

"Where do we go from here?" Robin asked.

"South," Mr. Howland advised, and the three began walking again.

As they set off on their way, Minisc soon became caught up with thoughts of the forest's path. Something felt strange. He had his own forested backyard once, and this one felt quite different. The paths were clear and flat. When he used to walk through the forest near his old house, it had branches, leaves, dirt, and all sorts of other things that made traversing the grounds quite tricky. Not to mention wildlife. Here, there was none of those things.

"Something doesn't feel right here," Minisc said, his eyes darting around cautiously.

"What do you mean?" Robin asked.

"Minisc is correct. Brace yourselves," Mr. Howland warned.

They trudged ahead for another minute or so, but soon something odd piqued the attention of Minisc's ears. He stopped. "Do you guys hear that?"

"I don't hear anything," Robin said.

"Come on, boys," Howland instructed. "We need to keep moving."

An uneasy feeling of calm hung above them throughout the forest. No sounds of Adenji members coming their way, no voices talking—just the eerie feeling that they were being watched. They kept their chatter to a minimum; they couldn't let anything give away their position.

The three rounded another section of the forest and ended up on a four-way path, pausing to reassess the situation.

But then Minisc heard the strange sound again, like something sprouting up from the ground. And it was moving quickly.

This time he wasn't alone in his suspicions. Mr. Howland furrowed his brow, then turned around and yelled, "Boys, move!" Minisc, with Robin draped around his arm, stumbled to the left, while Mr. Howland moved toward his right.

Suddenly the ground started shaking. Huge pillars shot up from the earth and formed a wall, sealing off Howland on one side, and Robin and Minisc on the other. But the pillars didn't just form a single wall—the trees around them were now connected by strange, earthy branches, creating a labyrinth of sorts.

"Sir, are you okay?!?" Robin yelled from the other side of the wall. They waited for a reply, but the vines were so thickly entangled that no sound could be heard from the other side.

Beside him, Minisc lay in a heap on the ground, but he sprung to his feet quickly enough. He groaned, staring up at the mass of intersecting branches that caged him in. *That was close. It's a good thing that Celestial Light increases my hearing...*

He looked at Robin and lamented, "Well, this is bad. Something tells me that Dominos knows we're in here...and he's not pleased about it. Come on—we need to find Mr. Howland and get out of here."

"Yeah, but I'm sure there has to be another way through," Robin coughed, still slightly weak.

"Right. Are you able to walk?"

"I'm fine. This stuff is just a scratch, really." Robin took a shaky step forward before his legs nearly folded to the ground. Minisc reacted quickly, propping him up and feeling Robin's full weight on his shoulder.

"Hey, take it easy. I can't carry you out of this place if you're dead, you know," Minisc snickered, attempting to laugh off his fear and bring some ease to the ordeal.

But despite them returning to the hollowed-out forest pathway, the lingering pit in his stomach remained. Mr. Howland was now cut off from them, and it had him worried. Especially knowing that Dominos was out there somewhere.

# CHAPTER 18
## THE BITTER PAST

THROUGH THE VINED CORRIDORS, MR. HOWLAND marched. He understood the cause of their new predicament. It was obvious. Dominos knew that he lost, and now he was doing what he could to bounce back from his defeat.

And yet, despite being separated from Minisc and Robin, Mr. Howland knew that they'd be safe. For one, they could definitely handle themselves, even with Robin's injuries. But more importantly, because he knew his son. And his target was no longer the boys.

He stopped suddenly, small flakes of debris falling all around him. The ground began to shake again, just as it had when the vined labyrinth first formed.

*He must be cutting off different paths to make sure that I come directly to him. If he can carry out such tricks and still plan to fight, then he's grown even stronger than I'd feared.*

Guided by the forest's path, Mr. Howland traveled until he reached a round, barren part of the forest. Almost everything around him had been obliterated, creating somewhat of a giant, empty arena. Was it by design? Surly Dominos wouldn't waste time crafting this circular space when he knew that he needed to escape. But no, Mr. Howland decided. This was exactly what Dominos wanted. And his father would be forced to oblige.

Alone, standing in the middle with his arms crossed, was the man that Mr. Howland was now hesitant to call "son." With a demented look in his eyes and the nervous tick of a killer, he'd been waiting for him.

Mr. Howland came to a stop at the far end of the vast space. "It's time that you put a stop to this, Dominic." He took a step forward, cautiously observing his surroundings and plotting out a plan. "This is what you wanted, isn't it? For me to find you. For me to find my son…"

"'Son?'" Dominos spat. "Don't you *dare* try that with me! We both know why we're here. And I refuse to let you stand in my way!"

"I know that, Dominic. But what you have done to my apprentice and the lies you have fed your new followers…" Mr. Howland sighed. "I was not sure at first, but after everything I have seen, I now know. You are messing with forces far beyond your control, and I will not let you continue. I am putting a stop to this right now."

"Is that so? Well then tell me something, old man — you think it was wise coming here alone? You didn't care to bring your little EC army to back you up?"

"This does not concern them."

Mr. Howland whipped his hand out horizontally, and three bolts of lightning zipped from his fingers through the air in a rapid flash. Each one struck Dominos, and he dropped to one knee, grimacing.

"Cheap shot, old man…whatever happened to fighting with honour?"

"And I thought that I taught you to never drop your guard, Dominic…"

Dominos winced at the name. He dug his fingers into the soil before looking up at the man he once considered a father.

"You have some nerve to call me that! My name is Dominos now," he seethed through short, violently heaving breaths. He then got to his feet, his body hunched over.

"You would actually toss away the name that your mother and I gave you? Are you so truly beyond reach that even using your own name is now a disgrace? How far you have fallen…" Mr. Howland could see the agitation in his son's eyes as he continued to prod him. Although Robin and Minisc were admirable fighters, Mr. Howland was the only one who understood exactly how to frustrate his son.

"Don't you *dare* talk to me about her! You're the one who left her for dead. From the second she became ill, you did nothing! You didn't even try to save her! But not me. I promised that I'd find a way to cure her, to wipe out the disease that continues to infect this world. And it's all within reach. I've run all the necessary tests. I can keep her and everyone else alive until I've discovered a cure. Don't you understand? I'm on the verge of stopping death! I can keep everyone in this wretched, unforgiving world from going through the pain that I did! How could you even think of stopping me from saving this world?!?"

In an instant, vines began forming along the ground and chasing Mr. Howland. But the veteran Elementalist moved with fluidity through the obstacles, even in his old age. It was almost as if he was levitating as he shifted left and right, avoiding being snatched up with simplicity.

"You actually believe that I did nothing? You don't think that I tried to find a cure for your mother?" Mr. Howland shouted. "You think that any of this has been easy for me? To see the woman I loved—the woman I created a family with—ripped away from me by some act of fate? You are a bigger fool than I thought! The loss of her eats away at me every day. But what you do not seem to understand is that what's done is done! We cannot keep living in the past, praying for her to return."

Dominos was still armed with that devilish look in his eyes — cocky, even — as Mr. Howland continued to confront him.

"I know that it was you who took her body from the hospital. It was you who took all of those bodies — but I never imagined that it would lead to this."

He then adopted a slightly softer tone, a painful sense of guilt washing over him.

"Look, Dominic. I know it has been hard, but sometimes death comes for those we love. They are taken from us far too early, and although it feels wretched and painful and we hate it with every fiber in our body, there is nothing that can bring them back. All we can do is rely on those we love to pick up the pieces and pull us through as we grieve. The day her of diagnosis, I know that a part of you died. It did for me as well, but what you are doing now…can't you see that all you are doing is exploiting everyone for your own personal prayers? All so that you can try and achieve the impossible! It's wrong, and I know that we taught you better than that."

"Taught me?" Dominos laughed in his face. "You didn't teach me anything! You were never even there for me! Too absorbed in that stupid technique of yours. And who cares if I gave hope to a few people? At least I helped them go on living. But none of that matters. I know that we'll find the cure, and then nobody will have to suffer the way that I did. Tell me — how is a world without suffering not worth the price of a few cracked eggs? I'd say the end more than justifies the means!"

"Because I know you, Dominic. You will never stop at just one. You will crack as many eggs as you have to, and you don't care what pain you cause while you do it. Yes, perhaps one day you might be able to cure some sadness, but you will be creating far more of it in the process."

Sparks suddenly began flying off Mr. Howland's body and toward Dominos, but it was merely a distraction. While he moved, trails of lightning started intersecting with the various spikes that Dominos continued to create. Soon, an entire barrier of electricity was circulating back and forth, and Dominos was now trapped in a web of electricity.

Dominos tried to move, but with every step he took a bolt of lightning shot outward from the spikes and zapped him. They were of minimal strength—certainly not enough to put him down in his heightened state of rage—but it would at least restrict his movement.

"It's time to accept what has happened. You know that what you are doing is wrong, Dominic, and that is why you left. You knew that I—but, more importantly, your mother—would never approve of your course of action. If you were really set on bringing your mother back, you would have stayed with me and worked, using all the EC's resources and equipment that were available to you. But instead you chose to take the route of violence and manipulation. You took advantage of a gang of criminals who found themselves leaderless, and you played them for fools. You riled them up with fake promises to buy their loyalty. You used the same pain that you have carried all these years and wielded it as a weapon. All so that you could attempt this sociopathic idea. This is never what your mother would have wanted for you."

Mr. Howland charged his electricity further, dropping Dominos to the ground. As long as he was pinned and being constantly bombarded, the use of his earth element was no longer a threat to Mr. Howland.

"What do you know?" Dominos shouted up at his father. "Your words can't fool me! I've seen the care you showed for those two boys...I know that you're even trying to teach that damn child your stupid technique! And when you thought that he was going to die, you dove in after him without hesitation! You never showed that sort of concern or compassion to your own family...not even once!"

Mr. Howland peered over his son, who was now on his hands and knees, ready to snap.

"You're right, Dominic...I failed you. I was so wrapped up in my work that I never paid enough attention to my family. And as your father, I should have been there for you when your mother was struck with her illness. If I had done my part, perhaps I could have helped you down a different path. But I couldn't. Selfishly, I was so devastated myself that I couldn't even begin to comfort my son. I was absorbed in my own pain, and I never stopped to see the toll that life was having on you. I understand now that I am as much responsible for this path as you are. Perhaps that's why I hold those boys dear. Because I want to guide them the way I failed to guide you. But what I do for them will never change the past...and I realize that. And now it's time you learn to accept your loss as well."

Dominos let out an agonizing, defeated cry, before slamming his fist on the ground.

"No, it can't end like this! I won't let it! I'm so close! I refuse to let you of all people rip her away from me!"

"You must face it, son—you cannot beat me. I can conduct electricity through anything you throw at me, and without your element at your disposal, you simply do not stand a chance."

The vast, circular, forested space then fell silent, albeit with small drops of sweat and sparks of electricity filling the air. Mr. Howland lowered his head, fighting back his own emotions.

Out of nowhere, he felt a gut-wrenching punch into his stomach. It sent him sailing back, skidding along the rough grass and dirt.

"I thought that you said never to let your guard down, old man," Dominos sneered, pushing himself up off the ground. The shocks were still impacting his body and causing his muscles to relentlessly twitch, but his rage enabled him to ignore the pain.

"I told you—I'll cure this sick society. But right now, I'll be making sure that you're not around to see it."

Mr. Howland grabbed at his stomach, turning his head upward toward his son, urging his body to stand. But his lungs lacked the air, and his body the strength. Also, the amount of energy used to create such powerful electrical barriers had taken a massive toll on his stamina. He let out a rough cough, and right away he knew that his ribs were broken.

He noticed that Dominos' entire left arm was covered in a rough casing that resembled tree bark, which explained the effectiveness of his punch. But this was the least of Howland's concerns. The look in Dominos' eyes and the hatred on his face made it very clear that he wouldn't hesitate to kill—even his own father. Mr. Howland's "son" no longer existed. He'd been replaced by an absolute monster.

Howland sighed in defeat. As Dominos marched toward him, his heart felt as though it was breaking.

*Robin…I'm sorry…and to you as well, Minisc. I did this to ensure your safety above all else, and I sincerely hope that you will not hold that against me. I know that you have both learned this…but sometimes, we simply cannot save the ones we want to. And to you, my son…I am so sorry. I could not handle my own grief at the time, so how could I handle taking on the grief of my son? I turned inward when really we should have dealt with our loss as a family…the way anyone should deal with loss — by relying on others.*

***

***

Unaware of the battles taking place inside the forest, Lily and Jules continued limping through the tunnels below the Adenji compound, searching for any sign of hope. Eventually, they came across a door at the end of a hallway, and using the key that Lily had picked off of Tufa's body, behind it they found a staircase leading to the surface.

When they reached the top of the stairs, Lily sighed. "We made it. Never thought I'd be so happy to see the Adenji compound again."

"Yeah, and I've seen enough skeletons for a lifetime," Jules agreed.

Lily took a quick look around, wondering where they were. Unfortunately, most of the compound appeared similar, and now they were in a garage just like the one they'd first entered. However, based on where they walked, they figured that they must be somewhere near the southern end of the building.

The clashing elements sounded distant, which also made them believe that things were beginning to wrap up. Or at least that's what they hoped.

They left the garage and stepped out into the large grassy field that stretched between the compound and the forest. From memory, this was where they expected Minisc, Robin, and Mr. Howland to be.

The two debated their next move, when suddenly from the left, they heard a horde of troops rushing in their general direction.

"Shhh!" Lily whispered, holding her finger to her lips. She and Jules slipped back into the garage and sidled up against the wall.

The steps became louder and louder until Lily and Jules gauged the group size to be at minimum five or six people.

Jules glanced over to Lily and whispered, "You don't think it's more Adenji, do you?"

"I don't know, but we need to be ready."

The steps grew closer and closer, until they blew past the kids and into the center of the garage.

Once Lily and Jules got a decent look at the white and red uniforms, as well as the small group of police officers, they called out, "Yuri!" They both beamed as he turned around and locked eyes with theirs.

"Jules! Lily! Oh, thank God you two are okay." Completely forgetting his mission and where they currently were situated, Yuri rushed over and wrapped his arms around both of them. Then he took a step back, a look of utter shock on his face. "What happened to you guys? We need to get you medical attention right away!"

Jules, who had a fair share of blood on his clothes, was in particular cause for concern. Yuri started to instinctively examine his arms, lifting them up and carefully moving them as he checked for any lingering damage.

"Yuri, I'm fine—I promise," Jules said, trying to wiggle his arms out of his brother's grip.

Lily, noting Yuri's sustained look of horror, added some context to the injuries. "When we fell into Dominos' trap, it turns out that it was his cell for the executioners, but we managed to defeat them and run away."

"Wait, you two went up against the executioners? And you *lived*?" Yuri asked in disbelief. "Why didn't you run?"

"Believe me, we tried! But we can talk about that later. Have Minisc and Mr. Howland found Robin yet?"

After a short examination and multiple reassurances from Jules and Lily about their conditions, Yuri turned his attention to the forest.

"We've lost all contact with Mr. Howland's team, so it's fair to assume that they got themselves trapped in the forest by Dominos. Makes sense, because we haven't found him either." Then

Yuri turned to the officers and said, "Get everyone who's free and have them surround the perimeter. If Dominos and Mr. Howland are still in there, then we have a chance. I'll go with Jules and Lily and see if we can find anyone else who may have gone inside. Remember, stay vigilant. I have a feeling that the worst is yet to come."

Everyone nodded in agreement, and they took off to tend to their respective duties. What lay beyond the shadowy veil of the forest front couldn't be guessed, but one unlucky group would be heading straight for the battlefield that everyone was hoping wouldn't materialize.

Along their route, the three could feel tension thick in the air. The remains of the vined walls were unlike anything they'd ever seen, and they spelled trouble if Mr. Howland's team remained trapped.

Jules grabbed at the vines, giving them a yank. "This is definitely not normal. Do you think that Dominos could've done this?"

"If I had to guess, yes," Yuri replied.

"Maybe using the forest as our main plan of escape was a bad idea…" Lily fretted.

"I'm not sure that any of us could've imagined that Dominos had this kind of power bottled away. To control the entire forest with vines…it's baffling," Yuri said.

In the faint distance, they could hear crashing sounds and thunderous bangs, followed by booming tremors. They could only imagine what might be happening, and pray that everyone involved would be okay.

But then, not too far off, heavy breathing alerted them to someone's presence nearby. Yuri held his hands out and whispered, "Stand back, you two."

Slowly emerging from the lingering shadows of the forest and stepping into the dull sunlight, Lily detected a familiar face.

"You guys!" Lily cried out with elation. "It's Minisc!"

"Are you sure?" Jules asked cautiously. "Who's slumped over his shoulder then?"

They could see Minisc struggling to drag the weight of someone's limp body, their face staring lifelessly at the ground.

"He's got Robin with him!" Yuri said as he gained focus. "He's in rough shape, too." The three ran over to help.

Minisc lifted his head upon hearing someone approaching, fearing that it was an Adenji. But once he saw Jules' full-faced grin and Lily's beautiful but worried smile, he breathed deeply with relief.

"Minisc! Robin!" Jules called out. They rushed over, and Robin slowly raised his head with a weak smile.

"Are you two okay?" Lily asked, then gasped as she spotted the puncture wounds on Robin's body. "What happened? We need to get those wounds looked at right now!"

Jules took Robin's other arm, relieving Minisc of some of the weight so that he could explain.

"Robin managed to break free before we'd even arrived," Minisc reported, clearly distraught. "But when we hit the forest, Mr. Howland was separated from us. I'm sure he's going after Dominos right now. Can you guys take Robin to get attention? I need to go back and help Mr. Howland before it's too late." The growing distress in his voice was clear as day.

Before they could levy any sort of a plan or agreement, Minisc lifted Robin's other arm off his shoulder and announced, "I'll see you at the meeting spot when I find Mr. Howland. Thanks, guys," before bolting back into the shadows of the forest again.

Yuri, Jules, and Lily all wanted to yell out to him, to bring him back so that they could regroup together, but none of them were in any condition to fight. Also, although Mr. Howland was strong, he was fighting on borrowed time, and facing Dominos alone would accelerate that clock rapidly. They'd just have to trust in their friend, as they always had.

Left with decisions to be made, Yuri said, "Okay, change of plans. I'll hurry back and get the other EC members to send help into the forest as backup. It shouldn't be any more than a few minutes for me. Hopefully Minisc can hold out that long. You guys take Robin to get aid, and then prepare everyone to hurry and reach the meeting spot. We can still cut Dominos off if we hurry."

They agreed, and Yuri began to retrace his steps as quickly as he could.

Lily grabbed Robin's other arm and tried to hoist him up, but he waved her off. Then he put his hand on the rough bark of a tree and leaned into it, propping himself up. "Jules, you can let go, too. I can still walk."

"Are you sure?"

"Yeah, I'm fine. It's nothing, really." The cold bark briefly numbed his pain, but when he took a cautious step forward, the agonizing pain shooting up his leg and into his stomach quickly returned. He smiled defiantly, trying his best to ignore the pain, then slowly turned around before taking a hobbled step in Minisc's direction.

"Whoa, Robin—what do you think you're doing? The path out of the forest is the other way," Lily pointed out.

"We can't wait for the others. Minisc and Mr. Howland need my help right now. I won't let Dominos get away with what he's doing."

"Robin, you can't!" Jules argued. "You need to get those injuries looked at. And besides, you'd be a sitting duck in your condition."

"These things?" Robin said, looking himself up and down. "They aren't as bad as they look. And I'm not leaving those two behind." He was lying through his teeth, but nothing would stop him from pushing forward. He'd made a promise to his brother never to concede. And no matter what it took, he needed to keep it. No other result was acceptable.

Jules didn't know what to say. Admittedly, his own injuries were almost as bad, and yet he wanted to help Minisc as well. On the other hand, Yuri had given him strict orders, and although he'd never been good at obeying commands, he knew this time that Yuri was right.

Stuck, he looked over at Lily, who was often the voice of reason in such scenarios.

"I think we should go," she said in a whisper. "You know how Minisc is — he's gonna need all the help he can get. He needs us."

Jules looked at Lily, and then to Robin. He was outnumbered, but still he refused to ditch his friends. Instead, he turned on his heels and said, "You know that Yuri is gonna kill us for this, right?"

"It's fine — I'll take the hit on this one," Robin coughed, stepping away from the tree and onto two steady feet. "Now, come on — we need to hurry."

# CHAPTER 19
## TIME FOR A HERO

*JUST HOLD ON A LITTLE LONGER, MR. HOWLAND. I'LL be there soon.*

As Minisc followed along his path, he was becoming frustrated. All the different vines made it impossible to know where he was supposed to go.

*This is ridiculous. I need a straight path through if I'm gonna make it to Mr. Howland.*

Two parts exasperated and one part scared, an urge suddenly came over him.

All week, he'd been instructed to maintain 8% power when using Celestial Light, but that wasn't going to cut it. The vines were thick, and he needed more strength to clear a path forward.

Minisc closed his eyes, and a surge of power flooded through his veins. *Focus. Clear your head. You can do this. Just pretend it's a faucet, and let the power flow through you a little more.*

Minisc opened his eyes, still taking deep breaths and trying to keep his power under control. It surged through his body, rapidly begging to be unleashed to its full potential, but he fought the urge to lose his focus. If he failed, he'd be rendered useless for the rest of the mission. There was no way that he'd let that happen.

Once Minisc calmed down, he said to himself, "I did it—Celestial Light, 12%. This should be enough."

He held his hands out and the sparks danced off his fingers into a Lum Bomb. Normally, it would never break through the layers upon layers of thick jungle, but he trusted the increased strength that was powering him. With one blast, he exploded a massive hole into the vines, plenty big enough to walk through. "Now we're in business. Hold on, Mr. Howland…I'm on my way."

Minisc lit up the forest as he raced through at blazing speed. The amplified power of Celestial Light made him feel as light as a thin cotton sheet, blowing carelessly in the wind.

Still, even while moving, he worked to maintain his concentration. He knew that if he were to lose focus or break his concentration for even a second, he'd surely be left for dead along with his mentor.

He raced past the original hatch that led below the Adenji compound, certain that he was getting closer to the circular, expansive space from earlier. From there, he followed the path straight ahead until he saw even more of an opening. But he heard no sounds of battle. Was it all over? And if it was, who won? Both questions would be soon answered after hearing Dominos' voice.

"I told you, old man!" Dominos hollered out. "Nothing is going to stop me—least of all you."

"Well then, what about *me*?" Minisc said, standing at the far end of the entrance to the arena-like space.

He radiated confidence, and the energy bursting from him was palpable, even if it was just an outward facade. His mind was on frantic overdrive and his body was trembling. Not just from the increased power of Celestial Light, but from the exhilaration of having a second chance.

He saw Mr. Howland crumpled on the ground, Dominos looming over him.

Dominos averted his attention from his seemingly defeated father and glared at Minisc, then back to Mr. Howland.

"This is your idea of a trump card, old man? The kid you're trying to teach that stupid technique to? Fine by me! I'll wipe you both from existence, and the world can forget that Celestial Light ever existed in the first place! How's that, old man? The very thing you tossed your family away for, turned into nothing but a myth!"

"That's enough, Dominos! You're not hurting anyone else!" Minisc looked into Dominos' eyes, but rather than the frustration he showed during their first fight, his face was now filled with sheer malice. The tone in his voice was different as well. The man, in his desperate attempt to keep his ambitions alive, was slowly descending into madness.

"Minisc…" Mr. Howland coughed. "I told you to leave…with Robin…" Minisc saw that he was sputtering up blood as he spoke.

Under normal circumstances, Mr. Howland would never play second fiddle to a teen who wasn't even officially part of the EC, but seeing the concentration and determination in Minisc's eyes and the radiating aura of his technique, he could tell that Minisc had gone above even his limit. And he was showing great control.

Howland was torn on how to react. To let Minisc take total control of the situation would be an unfair burden to the boy. But on the other hand, he was supposed to be Minisc's new mentor at the request of his former protégé. This, in some sense, meant that this was a test for Minisc, to see how he'd handle being the pillar of hope when he was called upon. He knew that Minisc had once put his life on the line and failed, so how would he rebound?

Or perhaps that was all just a way for him to justify his own defeat. He was no help fighting against his son anymore. And they both knew it.

"I left Robin with Yuri and the others. They're taking him to get help. There's no need to worry now. He'll be just fine."

Seeing his chance, Dominos lunged at Minisc and shouted, "I'd worry about yourself first, kid!" He used the same thick, bark-covered arm he'd created against his father to swing at Minisc.

Minisc focuses intently. *Concentrate. Keep your power at 12%, and don't lose control. Watch for the vines, and don't drop your guard for a second.*

He hopped to his left, kicking off one of the trees and readying a strike for Dominos.

But Dominos dropped to the ground, and Minisc sailed right over top of him.

Before Minisc knew what was happening, waves of thorny vines were coming at him from all directions. He needed to think quickly. With no chance to block through the air, he fired a blast of light into the ground, creating an explosion to destroy the closer vines. It also launched himself high toward the ceiling. He kicked off the top branches of the thick forest trees, shooting down like a rocket and firing a massive Lum Bomb. It cut through the smoke, dispersing it from the battlefield.

But to Minisc's surprise, even his strength wasn't enough to hit Dominos.

Minisc landed on one of the thin stakes and peered down toward Dominos. The tyrant was resisting the blast, doing all he could to hold the ball of light in place.

Minisc prepared to strike again, but before he could act,

Dominos let out a ferocious roar. The ball of light started to sail back toward Minisc. He dropped down onto his stomach, and the repelled attack flew past his head, high through the trees.

The massive energy blast exploded, creating a violent earthquake. The layers of rock, branches, and other debris from the ceiling began to crumble and eventually dropped entirely, creating a wide hole about twenty feet in diameter. The explosion not only blew Minisc off his perch, sending him falling into a pile of rubble, but also tossed a limp Mr. Howland backwards.

Minisc struggled to get to his feet. Using Celestial Light was amping up his pain, and he could feel the searing rips in his muscles. He opened his eyes, trying to push himself up.

He heard Dominos say, "Why does everyone keep getting in my way? You naïve, stupid, child! Can't you see that I'm making this world better? I can rid it of sadness! I can cure humanity of death!"

"At what cost, Dominos?" Minisc asked, finally getting to his feet. He decided to try a different tactic: rationale and logic. "Look, I get it. I understand the pain you're going through. I've dealt with it myself. We've all lost someone special in our lives. That's part of living. It hurts, and the pain is inescapable. It makes us want to crawl into the darkest hole we can find and never come out. But if you refuse to accept it, and if you keep living in the past, trying to fix what's already been done, then you'll never be able to move forward."

Minisc gripped his fists tight, blood trickling down his fingers. He was trying to reach Dominos on a personal level. He knew the feeling all too well of losing a loved one so early. "Listen to me, Dominos: Sometimes you have to accept reality for what it is. There'll always be times when things don't work out. Where you feel lost, alone, or even like a failure. But when those times come, you need to rely on not only yourself, but on others around you, too. Allow them to bring you out of this despair you're living in. Give us that chance, Dominos. Let us help you." Minisc extended his hand, despite he and Dominos being dozens of feet apart.

Even Mr. Howland stared at Minisc with admiration, knowing that the boy was right. But there was no room in Dominos' heart for such emotion.

"Rely on others...and what if the only person you could rely on was taken from you, stolen away by a fluke sickness? And what if the ones who should've been around for you are the same people who abandoned you, leaving you to rot in this hopeless hell? What then?" Dominos glared past Minisc, looking at his father with scorn and fury.

Guilt shrouded Mr. Howland, staring downward and aware of the cold, harsh truth. Dominos was right.

Dominos clenched his teeth, and the bark-like casing on his right arm started replicating itself on his left. Next, two thick vines formed from his back, suddenly supplying him with four arms to attack with. "You think it's as easy as just talking about it?!? You have no clue! Nobody understands what I've been feeling, this pain I've endured! Nobody!"

Minisc could sense a plan brewing as Dominos plunged deeper into despair. There was no coming back, and the only way to put an end to such madness would be by stopping the monster entirely.

Dominos tilted his head in Mr. Howland's direction, ready to strike.

Minisc followed his eyes, but that proved to be nothing more than a trap. He winced as he felt a vine wrap around his bicep, squeezing it tightly. Another grabbed his leg, sweeping him off the ground. Before he could react, Dominos slammed him into the wall of trees.

Minisc rolled over and onto his face. He gritted his teeth as the fiery pain ripped from his arm through his chest and to the rest of his body. Although painful, the damage done wasn't nearly as lethal as it could've been. Clearly, Dominos was losing strength, or else he would have already buried the boy six feet under. This weak surprise attack was nothing more than a distraction for Dominos to make his escape.

"Someone so naive could never understand the world I'm trying to build…the peace that I could accomplish."

Minisc cringed, seeing another pair of vines rapidly weaving in his direction. But this time he caught them, yelling, "It's not peace if you're going to make others suffer along the way!"

But as he did, Dominos began to rise up on a nearby mound of rocks, leering over Minisc and Howland like a god.

Just when it looked as though Dominos would escape, Minisc heard voices — voices he'd assumed were long gone.

"Minisc! Minisc, we're here…"

Minisc and Dominos turned to look at the hole in the wall. There stood Lily, Jules, and Robin, each one seemingly on the verge of collapsing.

Jules yelled, "It's over, Dominos! Just surrender now and we can end this peacefully!"

They all knew that he was bluffing, but with little else in the way of threats, he hoped to plant a seed of doubt in Dominos. Besides, there was strength in numbers.

Instead, Dominos' eye twitched and his face became scrunched. "It's not over until I say it's over! It's not over until I cure humanity!" He punched part of his pillar, chipping off half a handful of small boulders and sending them hurling toward the group.

Lily and Jules both stepped up, using their wind and water to halt the rocks before sending them crashing to the other side of the room and out of harm's way.

Minisc turned to his friends and started giving orders. "Lily, Jules, get everyone to the meeting point quickly. We can still win this!"

Finally, the second chance he'd longed for had arrived. There was still a chance to end all of this. To save Robin and defeat Dominos. To prove that he was capable.

"Dominos!" Minisc shouted. "This ends here!"

"Listen to me carefully, kid: I'm about to make this place your grave!" Dominos gripped his fists tighter, and suddenly vines came whipping out of the forest from every direction.

"I won't let anyone stop me—least of all some child trying to play hero!"

The vines snared everyone on the ground, dangling them around like ragdolls. Dominos' body was seemingly becoming more solid and stronger as well.

"Minisc, help!" Lily cried out.

The others also started shouting and trying to break free, but with no energy left, they failed.

"You want to know what *real* loss is, kid? Watch as I kill everyone who's precious to you. Remember, you brought this on yourself!" With a diabolical laugh, Dominos started tossing his captives around.

"No…I won't let you!" Minisc yelled. Desperation overtook him, taking away every rational thought. The energy coursed through him, filling his body with a raging fire. His arms and legs began to glow and shine as gusts of wind surrounded him.

"I won't let you hurt anyone else!" Minisc shot forward furiously, and the ensuing ripples cleared the battlefield of all debris below him.

"When will you get it through your head, kid? I'm doing this for the greater good!" Dominos roared.

His sanity was all but gone, and his words became more frantic and enraged.

The ground around them was vibrating and shifting. The trees in the forest were being ripped from their roots, crashing to the ground as Dominos harnessed more power. The forest had become a warzone, and Dominos had created a monster — a twisted, mangled, swirling, and whirling monstrous mess of fallen trees. And hanging proudly at the top of it was Dominos himself, strung up and wrapped from head to toe in vines.

With the trees around them uprooted, sunlight beamed brightly overhead. Minisc raised his fists, his body glowing like the sun. His power radiated outward, and he knew that this was it. There was no reason to hold back or preserve himself. The energy enveloped Minisc like a warm blanket. It granted him sanctity of peace, the likes of which he'd never felt before.

Now positively enraged, Dominos ripped up the pathways with waves of spikes, heading straight for Minisc. Now that he was hanging in the air from the vines and guarded by his impenetrable defenses, he was plenty safe from Minisc and still free to attack.

Minisc leapt backwards, avoiding the spikes as they fired toward him. He continued to do so until the threat stopped, but he and Dominos were too far apart to land any sort of a hit.

He could see his friends suspended mid-air, dangling. He needed to protect them.

The shooting spikes ceased, but only because the structure that Dominos was commanding suddenly became his power outlet. Tentacle-like vines jetted out from the base of the roots, big enough to crush a house. He dropped one of the tentacles down like an anvil, and it left a crater in the earth.

Minisc dodged again, but he was running out of places to go. The expansive space they were in was nothing more than one long war zone, and he couldn't risk veering too far off course, nor chance other places being demolished in Dominos' path of destruction.

When Minisc landed again, the second tentacle came dropping like a missile, ready to crush him. There was nowhere for him to dodge it, and he threw up his arms to protect himself, scared. He managed to block the vine, holding it off with all his strength. It was attempting to drive him into his grave.

Minisc closed his eyes. *No, I refuse to lose like this. I won't fail this time!* Sparkling gold rays shone from his palms as beams of light shot through the sky, slicing the tentacle off in one clean cut.

He felt a burning sensation shoot up his arm, and then it began coursing through the rest of his body as well.

Minisc flew back through the air and skidded down the forest, ripping up the path as he landed.

When he opened his eyes, he could see thousands of tiny rocks and bits of dirt raining down like snow. He was breathing hard, but as he looked down at his arms, he saw the golden veins running along his body. They were gleaming, and his body felt hot, almost as if he was closing in on the sun.

He'd felt this sensation before, and it wasn't a good sign. *I let myself panic! I lost control of Celestial Light!*

A few seconds passed, and then the pain hit him. Agony flooded through him, like daggers digging into his body. His muscles were being carved out from the inside. He dropped to his knees and doubled over. *No, please…not now. I was so close. I need to get my power back under control.*

He winced, looking up at Dominos who was quite far away by this point. The devilish fiend appeared to be nothing more than an ant on top of his mountain.

Minisc saw no other option, so he came up with a dangerous plan: a full-frontal assault.

*It's only a matter of time until my body gives out. If I've already unleashed my full power, I'll just have to use it and end this as quickly as I can. Please…please just let my strength last long enough to do this.*

Minisc gripped his fists, allowing the full extent of his power to explode. There was no use in holding back now. He focused on every tiny aspect of his body. *Let the energy course through me.*

*Let it consume me and flow freely. Man, I hope this works…Celestial Light, 100%!!!*

The power around him erupted like a beam cutting through the sky. Then the ground began shaking, and he felt a strange calm overtaking him. It was like an out-of-body experience. His mind was clear, but he couldn't feel anything. He felt nothing at all.

He turned to look back at the tree-like monster that Dominos had created. He saw the arms coming for him once again, but this time there were at least six of them, ready to strike.

Suddenly, Minisc disappeared into the air. The vines smashed down on the road, one after another, until Minisc reappeared, standing on the tip of the final one. Even he was shocked by the ease of his movements; it was like he was gliding through the air. There was no resistance to his reaction time. His speed at full power was faster than even Dominos could detect.

Just as he'd planned, Minisc jumped up high, and Dominos began sending a barrage of vines his way.

"I will crush you!!!" Dominos roared.

But Minisc was moving far too quickly for the tyrant to attack. Through speed, power, grace, and courage, he zipped through Dominos' advances. He could feel a supreme confidence growing within him. If only for a second, the adrenaline of his fight counteracted the grueling pain he was currently putting his body through. He could do this. He *would* do this.

Radiating heroism, he landed in front of his rage-filled opponent. "Face it, Dominos — this is one fight you're going to lose."

"I haven't lost anything! I was meant to cure this world, and a child like *you* could never understand that!"

"You're wrong — you aren't curing anything!"

Minisc prepared to finish the job. Everyone had done their jobs needed to reach this point, but now it was time for Minisc to step in and reign triumphant. Just as the Hero of Light would.

He held his hands out parallel to the ground, and a beam of light exploded from his palm with extreme force. This pillar of light attack, amplified by Celestial Light's full power, engulfed the spikes before shattering them into millions of tiny pebbles.

The recoil almost blew not only Dominos away, but also everyone he was clutching within his vines.

"Hang on, guys—it's about to get bumpy!"

Minisc jumped high in the sky, blocking out the rays of the sun as he cast his shadow over a petulant Dominos.

"I swear, kid—you will know my pain! I'll kill you if it's the last thing I do!" Dominos spat. He glared up at Minisc, standing in his way and using the technique he despised.

"I made a promise, Dominos—a promise to always help people in need, and that's exactly what I'm going to do." Minisc began his descent, readying his fist for the final blow. There was only one move that would be effective enough to end this monster.

From the depths of his being, Minisc roared, "Solar Impact!" His fist began to shine with the golden light of a god.

Dominos shielded his body with layer upon layer of vines, hoping to block Minisc's final attack. But it was no use.

Minisc's golden fist collided with the barriers, as the light beaming from him stretched to engulf Dominos and the structure he'd created.

The air exploded with a massive boom, and the shockwaves of the blast threw Minisc and everyone else high into the air.

Down below, Dominos lay decrepit and defeated, while the ruins of his creation fell around him like confetti. He was unconscious and, like anyone else who'd ever endured the power of Solar Impact, clinging to life.

Minisc had finally won the battle. He'd rescued Robin, and he'd proved that he could use Celestial Light. And, most importantly, he'd shown that he was capable of protecting the world the way his father could.

But this victory led to another problem.

Minisc, Lily, Jules, Robin, and Mr. Howland had been tossed hundreds of feet into the air, and now they were rapidly descending back to earth. They could see over the vast remains of the obliterated forest and the compound in the distance, along with the barren street that lay in ruin. This time, however, there were no platforms to land on, nothing to slow their fall, and Dominos would certainly not be creating a structure for them.

"Hold on tight, guys — this might be a rough landing," Robin said. He was still smiling though, which magically put the others at ease.

"Jules, you need to do something!" Lily cried out, grabbing onto Minisc as the two soared downward.

"I can't! I don't have enough strength to break our fall!" Jules replied, slightly panicked.

Minisc looked down over the street, trying to come up with a plan. He'd come too far to have it end like this.

At first, he tried to maneuver his body so that Lily would take less of the brunt when they hit. If he couldn't stop the fall, then at least he could still protect her.

Then he considered trying to use blasts of light to slow his descent, but there was nothing left in his body. He couldn't attack even if he wanted to.

Fearing the worst and running out of time, he heard voices calling out from below.

"Minisc! Lily! Jules!"

Below them and running down the empty street were the others. Specifically, Yuri and Adelle, who were trying to pinpoint where the group would likely fall.

Other EC members began creating updrafts of wind. The vortexes rose high and with ferocity, catching Minisc and the rest of the group. But it wasn't enough. The counterforce slowed their descent, but their momentum would still leave them flat as pancakes when they hit the dirt.

"It won't slow them down enough!" Adelle gasped. Quickly, she thought of a new plan. She waved her hands and formed a massive rectangle of ice, like a skating rink. The walls began to rise up over eight feet.

"All water Elementalists, fill the pool with as much water as you can, and it'll break their fall," Adelle ordered.

A group of men and women climbed the icy wall, with help from earth Elementalists lifting them up. Adelle also made an icy ladder of sorts. With all the energy left in the group's collective body, they held out their hands, the water pouring from them like waterfalls until the pool was ready to spill over.

Minisc glanced down, his eyes growing wide from the sight of his old nemesis: deep water. There was no longer the fear of falling, but of his likely death from drowning. He knew that when he plummeted into the giant swimming pool, he'd never survive.

He shared a petrified look with Lily. She squeezed him tight and said, "Don't worry—this time I've got you. Just close your eyes."

As much as Minisc trembled at the idea, none of it actually mattered. Before he could verbalize any of those thoughts, he came crashing into the pool like a cannonball. Geysers of water shot up, splashing into the sky like fireworks.

Minisc began flailing around like an angry fish, holding his breath as best he could as he sank deeper. Unlike when he fell off the cliff, this time he was fully aware of what was happening.

He felt Lily grab his hand, and she started to kick her way up to the surface, dragging Minisc with her. How she mustered the strength with what little energy she had left Minisc wasn't sure, but somewhere deep down, she found a way.

After being pulled out of the pool, Minisc rolled over on the broken gravel that remained from the road. He coughed up water, groaning and sputtering. His golden aura was gone, and his eyes were closed as his body tensed up.

"I hate water…" he moaned.

"Minisc, are you okay?" Jules and Lily both asked, trying to help him sit up.

"I've seen better days…" Minisc groaned again, refusing to move. He could hear a clamour of commotion and people rushing down the street, as well as ambulances and police cars, but all he cared to ask was, "Is it finally over?"

"Yes. It's all over." Lily said.

"You did it, Minisc—you stopped Dominos!" Jules smiled.

Through the use of Celestial Light, and with a little help from his friends, Minisc finally put a stop to Dominos' plans. And although those plans had been rooted in a desire to bring back his mother, given the cost at stake, Minisc knew that what he did was right. He'd refused to let anyone else be a sacrificial lamb for the twisted man's desires. Their fight with the Adenji gang was finally over.

# CHAPTER 20
## A BRIGHTER FUTURE

AFTER A LONG WEEK AND A TOUGH BATTLE, MINISC and his friends could finally rest. Although Brooklyn was still out in the world, and with that came the looming threat of Luminosa, none of it mattered for the time being. They just wanted to take a second and not worry about the future, choosing instead to live in the present. There'd be a time and a place to explore the depths of what awaited them over the horizon, but for now, it was time to enjoy the brief peace they'd fought so hard for.

With the mission successfully completed, Dominos was taken into custody, ready to spend the rest of his days under the watchful eye of the Penatang jail. Most of the Adenji members who'd been conquered on the way to Dominos were also taken away, though they'd be sent to low-level jails depending on their transgressions.

Everyone else involved in the mission were taken to the hospital for examination. For the likes of Robin, Minisc, Jules, and

Mr. Howland, they'd be spending a couple more hours, if not days, than most in recovery from their injuries. Not that they minded much. In the end, all the sacrifice had been worth it.

Unfortunately, there was a sad reality to their win. The people that Dominos had been keeping alive were also taken to the hospital. They'd be treated with the respect that they deserved, but there was no changing the inevitable outcome of their fates.

Minisc sat up in his hospital bed, his father sitting in the chair beside him. He had a number of bandages around his arms from where Dominos had skewered him, but other than small wounds, the rest of the damage to his body was minimal.

But those were only side details. He was far more interested in the transformation that his body had undergone during his fight. He examined his arms up and down, holding them out for his father to see.

"I've never felt anything like it! My entire body was on fire, but at the same time, I felt nothing. All my energy was coursing through my body, and before I knew it, I was moving faster than I'd ever imagined possible. And my element—everything was so effortless! It was incredible. Is that really what it feels like to use Celestial Light at 100%?"

"I'd say that's accurate. I just can't believe that you were able to hold out long enough using that much power. The leap from 12% to 100% in a flash was incredibly dangerous. Frankly, you're very lucky to have survived it."

Minisc leaned back, dropping his hands to his sides and staring up at the white-tiled ceiling, "Well, I mean, it's not like it didn't come with consequences. It still feels like my muscles have a mind of their own, and even getting out of bed for a few minutes a day is a killer. It's one hundred times worse than the first time you and I tried training," Minisc smiled.

"True. But I guess it's safe to say that you definitely have the ability to master Celestial Light. Now it's about getting your body used to such a heightened state. Mr. Howland did tell you to stick to 8% for a reason, and this is why. He didn't want you to wreck your body the way that I did," Don laughed.

He could recall all the times that his mentor had scolded him for going overboard on a mission. Of course, that was how he'd become so accustomed to using his power at its limit for long stretches, but the consequences indeed led to the situation they were in. Now he was no more than an average Elementalist, ready to hang up his heroics for good.

"But still, I'm proud of you," Don told his son. "What you did was nothing short of a miracle—not just for you, but for Robin as well. You refused to give up on him, and in the end, you kept your word."

Minisc smiled softly. "It's really thanks to you...and Lily... and everyone who helped me through it. In the end, I just knew that I wouldn't be able to live with myself if I shied away from what I knew was right. I guess I just needed you guys to help me see it for myself."

Then Minisc's face grew quizzical. "Do you know how Robin's doing? Or Lily and Jules, for that matter?"

"There's no need to worry. Everyone is doing just fine. They'll need some time to recover, but it's nothing that you guys won't bounce back from."

"Good, I'm glad."

"You could use some more rest yourself, though. You should go back to bed for a bit."

Minisc nodded, a small yawn escaping his lips. Even that amount of effort hurt, so he dropped his head onto the pillow, and very soon he slipped into a deep sleep.

***

After a full day's rest to recharge his body, Minisc finally mustered up the strength to leave his bed. He was far from healed, and his knees nearly buckled when he took his first steps for the day, but that wouldn't stop him from doing what he had to do. He wanted to see Mr. Howland. He needed to speak with him.

Luckily, the EC headquarters were nearby. Thanks to Lily and Jules, who helped ensure that he didn't collapse along the way, he managed to make the trip.

"Do you want us to come with you to speak with him?" Lily asked.

Minisc shook his head. "No, I think I might be better off alone for this. It won't take long."

He started gingerly limping down the same hall that had usually caused his anxiety levels to skyrocket. He reached for the door, but then stopped short. Debates on whether there was a trap on the other side raged in his mind, but common sense told him that the paranoia was unjust. This wouldn't be like his first encounter.

He cracked the door open and peeked inside. Mr. Howland was sitting on the couch with a pot of tea, sipping from his cup.

"Hello, Sir..."

Still a little on edge, Minisc stepped further into the office, shifting his eyes around and taking note of any oddities.

"You can relax—I have no tests prepared for you. I think that you have more than proven yourself after the events of the last week." Mr. Howland wore an unusually somber smile as he took another sip of tea. "I want to thank you, Minisc. Truly. You showed the same strength and conviction to help people that your father displayed for all those years. You also managed to activate Celestial Light while using your full power, and you showed just how incredible your resolve is. Without you, Dominic would have continued to prey upon the wounded, building up his forces until he was unstoppable. So thank you for stopping him. For saving my life, Robin's, and the lives of many others."

There was a moment of awkwardness when Minisc looked at Mr. Howland. After all, they were talking about the man's son—his own flesh and blood.

Minisc tilted his head downward. "Thank you, Sir…but…I still wish I could've talked some sense into him. I really wanted to show him that what he was doing was wrong, and that we could've helped. Once I realized the reasons for his actions, it made fighting him even more difficult."

"Raise your head, Minisc. You have nothing to regret. What my son was trying to accomplish was no more than a manifestation of my own guilt, nothing else. He had to be stopped before he caused any more pain."

Mr. Howland's voice softened as he continued. "I told you about my wife before…how she became ill with a rare heart virus. Her death was inevitable. What I failed to mention was that neither myself nor my son were in any position to handle it. My wife was the glue of our family, and without the time to process what was to come, we fell apart. I became so wrapped up in my regrets as a husband, at not spending enough time with the woman I loved, that I became blinded to my son's pain. It was my own selfishness that drove Dominic into his path of desperation. While I dwelled in my own pain, I ignored him, and that caused me to overlook the man he was becoming. If I hadn't shut out the world, maybe I could have helped Dominic see the error of his ways. But just like anyone who's lost a loved one, oftentimes they are willing to surrender all moralities if they believe that it can give them one last chance to see that person."

Minisc frowned. "I understand. But I do have one question, if you don't mind?"

"Yes?"

"Do…do you actually think he could've done it? Could he have kept those patients in stasis long enough to actually find a cure and save them?"

Mr. Howland shook his head and sighed. "No, no I don't. At best, he would have just prolonged the inevitable. Even in a deep coma state, my wife's body was withering away. All of those people were. That's why he was so desperate to act. He could see it, too — he was only stalling fate. Which, for him, never would have been enough. He would have only kept pushing further, risking whatever or whomever he needed in order to achieve his goal. Even if that's a tough truth to accept."

Minisc nodded. Finally knowing Dominos' story — well, Dominic's story — made him feel sympathetic in a strange way. Not for the horrible crimes the Adenji leader committed and the pain he'd caused, but knowing the sting of losing a loved one resonated with Minisc strongly — especially the desire to bring them back.

"I can sort of see where Dominos was coming from…" Minisc paused, his words catching in his throat for a moment. Even years later, he struggled to explain the emotions that followed his personal story. "I lost my mother when I was young, to a heart virus…"

"Yes," Mr. Howland said quietly. "I remember your mother well. She really was one of a kind. It's unfortunate that she and my wife both fell victim to the same virus."

"So in a way, I get it. If I thought even for a second that there would've been a way to save my mother…to see her again…I would've done whatever it took. Especially when you see no other option because you're all alone."

"Indeed. But where I failed, your father was the true hero. I remember those days vividly. He did everything he could to be with you, to show you how you were not alone, and how much you were still loved. He battled grief with his family, whereas Dominic and I did not. We faced grief as individuals. And in the end, that tore us even further apart."

Minisc hung on that thought for a moment. Those days were

a vague recollection of memories, and over the years it had been hard to pinpoint exact moments. However, the more he thought about it, he did recall spending more time with his father than usual during that time.

Maybe even more than they'd spent together when Minisc started training. Something that was a rarity in those days.

A warmth filled his heart. He realized the hurt that his father must've endured, and yet he still put his son first and made sure that he would heal.

Minisc smiled. "Everyone goes through loss. It's inevitable. But no matter how wretched the pain is and how far it drags us down, we need to be able to rely on others to support and protect us. I know that without my father or Lily and Jules, I never would've made it to where I am. I would've never been able to accept my mother's death, let alone find the strength to save Robin. Without them, I'd be just like Dominos."

"You show a lot more wisdom than most, Minisc. And, unfortunately, I realized such a lesson far too late in my life. But all of that is in the past now. It's time to look toward a brighter future. You, Robin, Adelle, Lily, and Jules…what you've accomplished…well, you all have shown me something special. You have the world in your hands, and I know that you will face it proudly, challenges and all."

# PREVIEW
## ELEMENTS FREEZING HEARTS

"An opportunity like the Hero of Light retiring…"

"Indeed. The EC and the police do what they can to quell everyday threats, but do not let what you see on the surface fool you. There is an underworld to this city, filled with those who have felt disenfranchised, forgotten, or outright abandoned by those who walk freely. And now that we lack the blanket of protection known as the Hero of Light…well, you can see the direction the city is going in. Criminals are ready to revolt and bring the underbelly of this city into the limelight once again."

Coro gave a quizzical look. "Once again? You mean like when Dusk first rose to prominence?"

"Precisely. Let me ask you: As someone born after those days, how much do you know about the history of Elementalists in this city? Or around the world, for that matter?"

Coro shook his head. "Honestly, not much. I spent most of my childhood in a laboratory with my father, and history wasn't really something he talked about."

"Right. Well, the history of this city is not something I would say most people your age knows about. But there is a reason for that. It can be difficult for less mature students to wrap their heads around."

Coro could hear pain in his partner's voice, something not heard before.

"I know it was bad…but was it really that awful?" Coro asked.

# AFTERWORD

Holy (insert bad words of choice here), this was difficult to write. I must have started nearly from scratch four times, including writing the story I finally chose to go with in a feverish span of four days. It's hard to explain; I wanted to push the depths of this book's message while still keeping it light at times, yet filled with what I believe makes the Elements series…well, the Elements series. But everything I did just didn't seem right. The ideas were fine, but they didn't quite get across what I believe about people who are prone to dealing with loss and tragedy. I hope that I managed to present that in a way that was also interesting.

The second factor that made this so tough was for how personal things felt. For those who skipped over the dedication, this book is and always will be dedicated to my Aunt Lynne. She passed away days before I released my first Elements book, and she never got the chance to read it. I try not to dwell on it too much, but it will always be a regret of mine.

I started the first draft of this book shortly after her passing, and I knew that the story would revolve around someone trying to save the people they loved, and also how they would deal with loss. As for how that would come about, I really had no idea. In the end, I'm proud of how things unfolded with the series. I wanted to quit so many times and just stop writing, but I didn't. My Aunt never would have wanted that. She wouldn't have accepted it.

All of that said, I'll finish with this, like always:

Thank you to StalkingP for her continued commitment to this series, even as her art continues to blossom.

Thanks also to Rob Peace for his care and dedicated focus with the editing process.

Thank you to my family and friends for not being the kind of people to tell me to "just give up…nobody reads these books, anyway — who cares?" I appreciate your support immensely.

And last, but most certainly not least, thanks to Aunt Lynne, for everything you've done for our family and for me personally. Life has never been the same without you. We all love you.

9 781777 473471